LOVE'S FIRST

'Will this do?' asked an unfamiliar voice.

She turned quickly to see the gentleman standing at the door with a lap robe of fine sable in his hands. It was the first time she had looked at him directly, and now, despite the agitation of the moment, she found herself staring at one who was the physical ideal she had dreamed of since schoolgirl days. He was tall, with fine broad shoulders and a lean face marked by a nose as patrician as any Caesar's.

It was not her way to stand tongue-tied and gaping, certainly not in the presence of a gentleman of the first rank. She blinked, seeking to recover herself, but before she could reply to his offer, his light grey eyes had moved . . .

Sweet Passions

DEBORAH CHESTER

SPHERE BOOKS LIMITED
London and Sydney

First published in Great Britain by
Sphere Books Ltd 1985
30–32 Gray's Inn Road, London WC1X 8JL
Copyright © 1983 by Deborah Chester

Set in Times New Roman

Printed and bound in Great Britain by
Collins, Glasgow

To Lacey Belle,
with love . . .

Chapter One

Swaying along in the coach as it jolted over the frozen, snow-blurred road, Anna Templeton folded her cold, gloved hands together and gazed out the window in an effort to conceal her rising qualms. There was nothing, she thought, quite so daunting to one's self-confidence as becoming betrothed. Despite the rapturous matrimonial opinions of other young ladies of her acquaintance, Anna could not bring herself to fly into alt. Perhaps, however, she would be less nervous when she was at last introduced to Mr Molineux. And it was not far now to Farrowsleigh.

'Well, Anna, my dear,' said her father, laying aside the little volume he had been perusing to peer at her over his spectacles. 'We are nearly there. Nearly to Farrowsleigh.' He sighed in the greatest satisfaction. 'Wealth and happiness, my dear. One may not call them a lofty achievement, but twenty thousand pounds is a comfortable sum, eh?'

'Comfortable?' She turned her troubled gaze from the window. 'Extremely generous is a better term. I find it too overwhelming of Grandmama—'

'Nevertheless,' he broke in hastily, casting a swift glance at Mr Murvey as though to be sure the solicitor did not misconstrue her words, 'it is all arranged, Anna. All arranged.' He removed his spectacles and put them away in a pocket before giving one of his faint coughs. 'I must say it takes a great deal of worry from my mind, Mr Murvey, to know Anna's future is assured.'

Mr Murvey smiled at Anna. 'Of course, sir. The matter of dowries is the concern of many a parent. Young ladies may be delightful creatures, but they are expensive as well.'

'Indeed, sir?' Mr Templeton permitted himself a dry smile. 'I have always said a daughter is greatly to be preferred over a son.'

Mr Murvey's grayed, rather heavy brows came up. 'Good heavens! What a startling opinion.'

'But practical, sir, most practical.' Mr Templeton raised a forefinger. 'Can you imagine me buying colors in some tomfool regi ment on my two hundred pounds a year? Or else there would be tailoring bills and gaming debts and the muslin company—' He cleared his throat. 'Anna, however, has never drained my meager resources.' He beamed proudly at her while she sent a deprecating glance the solicitor's way. 'Only think of it! Twenty thousand pounds. I confess I never thought Lady Riddell would become a forgiving woman in her dotage.'

'Grandmama is terribly kind,' said Anna in considerable haste, treading on her parent's toe. 'This is all so sudden, Mr Murvey. I hardly know if I am on my head or my heels. And Mr Molineux . . . can he truly desire to wed me?' She colored and was obliged to drop her eyes from the solicitor's gentle gaze. 'After all, we have never met.'

Mr Murvey patted her hand. 'You need not fear you will fail to provoke his admiration, Miss Templeton. As for her ladyship's change of heart, why, she is greatly advanced in years and cannot expect to enjoy many more, as much as we might all wish for her to. She desires her affairs of business to be settled. And as her only granddaughter, you cannot very well be ignored. I must say she is most pleased with your willingness to marry your cousin as she desires.'

Anna inclined her head demurely. 'Thank you, Mr Murvey. You are patient with my tremors, but I have been so used to viewing Grandmama in a less than favorable light, it feels most peculiar to be grateful to her now.'

'You will grow used to her by and by,' said Mr Murvey with a smile. 'She is really most excited about your arrival and means to do her best to like you.'

'And me?' asked Mr Templeton with some impishness as he opened his book once more. 'I daresay she doesn't want to see *me*.'

'Her ladyship is . . . resigned to your presence, sir,' said Mr Murvey with care. 'After all, you did take her youngest daughter to Gretna Green four-and-twenty years ago, but let us quit the subject. Lady Riddell is determined to overlook past quarrels, which is much to her credit.'

'Oh, of course,' agreed Mr Templeton, turning a page.

'Mr Murvey,' said Anna with some constraint. 'Please, would you tell me about my Cousin Molineux?'

'Ah, a natural curiosity,' he said, happy to converse with her.

2

'He is a most estimable gentleman, willing to undertake any number of commissions for Lady Riddell. He keeps a house in London for the season and spends the rest of the year at Farrowsleigh or at the homes of his many friends. He is, I believe, very well liked by all who know him. Certainly his intellect is good. He is university educated—'

'Which one?' asked Mr Templeton, abruptly glancing up.

'I am not sure,' said Mr Murvey, appearing rather taken aback by this sudden show of interest. 'Cambridge, I think, but—'

'Ah,' said Mr Templeton with a shrug and delved into his book again.

Anna laughed. 'Pray, do not regard him, sir! Papa's interests are extremely blue.'

'Yes, I see. Of course.' Mr Murvey took out his watch from the waistcoat pocket which stretched snugly across his middle and checked the time. 'We should be there in time for tea, providing the snow holds back yet a little longer.' He rubbed his hands together briskly. 'Mrs West serves an excellent tea. I always look forward to it. Her cakes are truly delightful.'

'Then I hope we arrive in time to sample them,' murmured Anna. It seemed her father's distraction on the subject of Mr Molineux was to prove lasting. Rather vexed, she longed to prompt the solicitor back to their discussion, but modesty held her silent. She did not wish to appear too bold or inquisitive. Still, the meager amount of information she had gained was sufficient to please her. From all accounts, her betrothed was a gentleman of quiet and orderly pursuits, knowledgeable and popular, without being fond of the wilder elements of present-day society. Anna herself was not a shy person, or one inclined to blushes and stammers, but neither was she prone to seeking out attention.

In looks she was most agreeable, possessing classical features, level brows, and dark gray eyes flecked with amber. Her brown hair was deplorably straight, refusing to lend itself to fashionable ringlets, but of an attractive burnished shade. She wore it coiled beneath her poke bonnet and never permitted a straying lock to escape. Indeed, her entire person was neat as wax despite the rigors of a lengthy journey in a hired chaise-and-four. She was dressed in a traveling costume of blue twill with a matching spencer and a woolen shawl pinned at her bosom with her late mother's

3

sapphire brooch. Although she was not one to think excessively about her appearance, her height, which was Junoesque, discouraged her considerably. Still, that sort of worry could not matter now. She was soon to be betrothed, and she hoped with all her heart that her cousin was not short.

These speculations were abruptly cut off by an unexpected slowing of the coach.

'It must be snowing,' said Mr Murvey, his fingers entwined in his watch chain. 'Bother. Now we shall be late for tea.'

But he was mistaken in blaming the weather. Looking out, Anna was dismayed to see a private chaise half in the ditch, canted at a severe angle, and with one of the horses down in a frightful tangle of harness. More to her startlement, however, was the sight of a man, swathed in a voluminous drab coat with numerous capes at the shoulder, holding a smoking pistol in his hand as he bent over a boy lying either unconscious or dead in the road.

'Great heavens above!' exclaimed Mr Murvey, his eyes starting as their own carriage drew to a halt upon this scene. 'It's Rotham and Lord St. Byre! Whatever can have happened?' He reached past Anna to thrust open the door – letting in a blast of wintry air – and jumped out to run to the boy's side.

Anna and her parent exchanged glances.

'St. Byre, did he say? St. Byre?' Mr Templeton blinked and put away his book. 'Is that not the name of one of your cousins, Anna? I believe it must be. The name seems quite clear to my memory.'

'We must see what we can do to help,' said Anna, tying the strings of her bonnet more tightly. 'Whoever he may be, he cannot be left to lie out in this deadful cold.'

She climbed out, rather awkwardly because no one had bothered about letting down the steps, and was obliged to clutch at her bonnet to save it from the wind's vicious pluck. Gasping from the cold, she bent her head and hurried to Mr Murvey's side, taking small heed now of the gentleman with the pistol since it seemed he was not the villain.

'Thank God he is not dead,' Mr Murvey was saying. 'Ah, Miss Templeton! You know what to do? Splendid. Such a relief.' He moved back from the boy's side as he spoke, making room for her to kneel there.

She took the handkerchief with which he had been awkwardly

4

attempting to staunch the flow of blood at the boy's temple, and began to work more expertly. 'A doctor must see to this,' she said, frowning. 'What on earth happened?'

'Highwaymen, Miss Templeton,' said Mr Murvey with an anxious glance at the gentleman, who was now directing his coachman's attempt to free the injured horse from its broken traces. 'A bad business. Most shocking. And not above five miles from Farrowsleigh! The magistrates must be informed at once.'

'This young man had better be taken up off the ground before he catches his death,' said Anna. 'If you and that gentleman, or perhaps Papa, could lift him into our carriage, then I can see about binding his head properly.'

Mr Templeton lent his assistance and together he and the elderly solicitor laid the boy – who looked to be about sixteen –upon the seat of the job-chaise. He stirred slightly and groaned at their handling. Anna made a pad of her father's handkerchief and used St. Byre's own neckcloth – deploring the starch in it which made it clumsy to work with – to tie up his head.

'There,' she said, eyeing her work critically. 'I wish he would stop bleeding. And if we have something with which to keep him warm—'

'Will this do?' asked an unfamiliar voice.

She turned quickly to see the gentleman standing at the door with a lap robe of fine sable in his hands. It was the first time she had looked at him directly, and now despite the agitation of the moment she found herself staring at one who was the physical ideal she had dreamed of since schoolgirl days. He was tall, with fine broad shoulders and a lean face marked by a nose quite as patrician as any Caesar's.

It was not her way to stand tongue-tied and gaping, certainly not in the presence of a gentleman of the first rank. She blinked, seeking to recover herself, but before she could reply to his offer, his light gray eyes had moved past her to St. Byre.

'Poor Neddie,' he said in a drawl of London stamp. 'Sink me, but I was certain he'd cut his stick. He took a ball before I could loose off a cursed shot. Devlish fellows, these highwaymen. My best wheeler is gone lame, damme, so he has. It quite puts me out of temper.' Shaking back the lace at his wrist, he helped himself to a fastidious pinch of snuff.

Speechless at such affectation, Anna took the lap robe and spread it over the boy. She frowned. Little wonder he had been shot, with only a mincing townbeau to protect him.

'Did you say, Murvey, that this young man is St. Byre?' asked Mr Templeton.

The solicitor cleared his throat. 'Yes. Dear me, I am all amiss with my introductions. Forgive me. Your grace,' he said with an awkward little bow to the lazy-eyed gentleman, 'may I present Mr Templeton and Miss Templeton . . . of Farrowsleigh.'

A gleam of interest shone in the gentleman's eyes before he hooded them. ' 'Pon my soul,' he said, raising an ornate quizzing glass to study Anna, who colored in some anger, 'so this is Lady Riddell's granddaughter. An honor indeed.' He flourished a bow. 'And I, dear ma'am and sir, am Rotham. A neighbor, in fact.' His simpering expression clouded, and he glanced at St. Byre again. 'You had better drive on at once. We shall clear up the amenities later.' He stepped back, one gloved hand grasping the door to shut it.

Anna's manners compelled her to lean forward. 'But we cannot leave you here, stranded with your conveyance in the ditch, sir!'

'Tut, ma'am,' he said airily, giving her a smile empty of all save charm. 'I've three horses to untangle. My coachman has gone ahead on the leader to fetch the local quack for you, so you need not linger here. Stap me, the boy needs looking after, not I.'

He slammed shut the door and commanded their postilions to take the chaise on.

Anna sat down, carefully positioning St. Byre's head upon her lap. 'Poor boy. How pale he looks.'

'He was to have come on the stage,' said Mr Murvey, likewise sending an anxious glance at the boy. 'From Eton for the holidays, of course. It would seem, however, that his grace was bringing him instead. The duke lives very near. In fact, his land marches with Farrowsleigh.' Mr Murvey shook his head. 'Highwaymen in Linwick. It passes all things. On one of the great turnpike roads, one may expect lurkers and that sort of thing at every turn, but here, in this county! What is the world coming to?'

'It hardly seems surprising, however, that they would choose to set upon his grace,' said Mr Templeton dryly. 'Did you notice, Anna? He travels in a private chaise, with a crest emblazoned on the panels in the most ill-advised advertisement of "Here, come and pluck me," and not even a single outrider for protection. It is not to be wondered at. Those who are careless are frequently gulled.'

'Yes, indeed,' said Mr Murvey with a sigh. 'I am so sorry, Miss Templeton. You will be arriving with confusion to meet you instead of the warm welcome you merit, and with bloodstains upon your dress as well. I am so very sorry.'

She found a smile for the solicitor as she sought to cradle her young cousin's head from the worst of the chaise's jolting. 'You need not feel obliged to apologize, sir. I am merely thankful we do not carry worse news than a graze from a pistol ball.'

Mr Murvey looked stricken. 'Yes. Good heavens! He is, after all, the heir.'

'To Riddell?' asked Mr Templeton sharply.

'Why, yes. Lord Byre's father was the earl's younger brother, but he, unfortunately, broke his neck three years ago in a hunting accident. It was a sad day indeed. A very sad day. But I am sure his lordship will grow up to be a worthy successor of the line.'

'Lord Riddell has never married?' asked Anna and received a rather shocked look.

'Dear me, no, Miss Templeton.' Mr Murvey blinked. 'The earl is quite mad. Marriage was always out of the question.'

'Mad!' Anna realized she was staring and hastily sought to school her expression. 'Papa, did you know?'

'Hmm?' asked her parent, reabsorbed in his book.

Anna abandoned him with exasperation. 'Mr Murvey, you cannot surely mean—'

'Oh, yes, I fear it is quite confirmed. But unlike the king, there is no hope of recovery.' Mr Murvey shook his head. 'Such a pity. He fell down the stairs as a boy and was never the same again. Such a blow to Lady Riddell.'

'Yes,' said Anna, conscious of relief. He had not been born insane, thank God. She need not fear for any strains of madness in her children. 'Where is he—'

'Oh, at Farrowsleigh. You need not look alarmed, please, Miss Templeton. He is not the least bit dangerous and lives in a wing to himself with his own servants to care for him.'

Anna smiled, rather ashamed. 'You must think me heartless, Mr Murvey.'

'Not at all. It is a natural shock, of course. Ah, here is the drive at last.'

Since she had her back to the horses, Anna was not able to view the long approach to the house save indirectly. Certainly in the spring the flowering trees and ornamental shrubs must make the drive most pleasant, but now she was more conscious of how cold and miserable and hungry she was, growing cramped from the effort of making her cousin comfortable. They drew up at the wide steps at last and she had a confused impression of a vast, towering edifice of stone standing rather grimly against a pewter sky of threatening snow. The footmen came out in smart crimson livery, only to fall into confusion over the injured viscount. He was carried inside, and an austere butler greeted Anna and her father with half his attention until he had been assured a doctor had indeed been sent for.

'Very good,' he said, bowing, and seemed relieved when a short bustling woman in a black, high-throated dress and white, starched apron appeared.

'I've seen his lordship put to bed, Mr Dobbs. What a to-do it all is. Thank goodness his man came ahead by the mail coach and is here to do for him. Have you sent for the doctor?'

Dobbs told her this had been done and gave away to Mr Murvey, who introduced her as Mrs West, the housekeeper.

She curtsied with a warm smile upon her face. 'It's time you came to Farrowsleigh, Miss Anna. I was about to see tea served, but perhaps it had better wait until the doctor comes. Her ladyship will be that frantic, she couldn't eat a bite. And goodness! You've blood all over your dress. We must fix that right away.'

Gratefully Anna allowed herself to be led through a hall of Renaissance proportions, hung with awesome tapestries that muffled the echo of her steps, and up a massive staircase of black oak, so wide six people could walk abreast.

'Thank goodness this is not to be my permanent home,' she said, half-laughing as she followed Mrs West along a corridor of bedchambers in what was called the Ladies' Wing. 'I should spend all my time seeking not to be lost.'

Mrs West paused to send her a look of dismay. 'Oh, I hope you are joking, Miss Anna. Mr Oliver loves this house more than anyone. I'm sure he wouldn't like to hear you tease about it.' Then as Anna gazed at her, surprised indeed by a reproof from a servant, Mrs West ducked her head and opened a door at the very end of the passage. 'These will be your rooms. I hope they are satisfactory.'

'Yes, I am sure they will be—' Breaking off in mid-sentence, Anna stopped and simply stared, unable to believe that a sitting room of such magnificence had been assigned to her. It was done in the daintiest French style, with gilded delicate chairs covered in white damask and small fringed rugs scattered about the parquet floor. In one corner stood a charming escritoire, supplied with ink and elegant hot-pressed paper, and before the window was a harp, its graceful lines commanding the room. Anna was enchanted. She had expected a great deal of comfort in her new surroundings, certainly, but nothing as fine as this. It quite overwhelmed her.

Smiling, Mrs West opened another door, and Anna walked slowly into a bedchamber beyond the furthest fancies of her dreams. In contrast to the gold satin walls of the sitting room, here the walls were paneled in rich cherry wood with an inlaid star of ebony on either side of the fireplace. The mantelpiece was marble, supported by graceful caryatids, and held a gold clock as well as a vase of white hothouse roses whose fragrance filled the air. But despite all these details, it was the bed which held Anna's attention. It stood on a dais, its four posters reaching up impossibly high to the canopy, where a gilded cupid winked mischievously down at her, the bed hangings of rich blue velvet spilling from his chubby hands.

Anna shook her head, quite dazzled by such an edifice. 'It is far too magnificent for me, Mrs West.'

'No, Miss Anna,' said the housekeeper, delighted by this reaction of awe. 'Nothing is too good for Mr Oliver's bride. Just you slip out of that dress and climb into bed to stay warm until one of the maids gets you something unpacked and pressed.'

'That's far too much bother,' said Anna at once. 'A damp cloth will sponge out the stains and—' The frank horror in Mrs West's expression caused Anna to break off with a chagrined smile. 'Yes, of course you are quite right. I cannot go down to tea in my travel dirt.'

'No, indeed, Miss Anna,' said the housekeeper firmly, taking Anna's dress over one capable arm. 'No, indeed.'

An hour later Anna descended the gloomy stairs, dressed becomingly in a walking dress of lavender crêpe with long, tight-fitting sleeves that puffed at the shoulder. Her brown hair was braided simply about her shapely head, revealing the fine turn of her long neck, and she had the satisfaction of knowing that she looked her best. But even so, she felt herself to have been stripped bare of the final shreds of her self-confidence and forced herself downstairs with quaking knees and a desperate hold on her composure. Mrs West obviously doted on Mr Oliver Molineux and had been at such pains to see that Anna should dazzle him at this first meeting, Anna felt all her equanimity to have been destroyed. She was certain she would blush beet-red the moment he looked at her.

A liveried footman was waiting at the drawing room doors. He opened these for her and announced her in such impressive tones she nearly fled, but enter she did – only to stop in some astonishment at finding the vast apartment empty save for a tall gentleman staring into the fire with his back to her. Were they to be tête-à-tête at the first instant?

Then the gentleman turned, lifting his brows before making a profound bow. Anna gave a little sigh and went forward.

'Your grace,' she said, giving Rotham a curtsy while her eyes took in the mud upon his boots, the faint creases in his buff pantaloons, and a black powder stain upon the fine lace at one wrist as though one of his pistols had misfired. Without his hat and caped driving coat, he looked much more slender than she had first supposed. His hair was pale gold in color, finely textured and arranged in a Brutus. His face, rather heavily scored about the mouth, was pinched blue with cold.

'I am pleased to see you no longer stranded upon the road,' she said, hardly knowing how she should go on in a private conversation with a gentleman of two-minutes' acquaintance. 'The day is so unpleasant.'

'Gad, so 'tis.' He smiled briefly and took his glass down from the mantelpiece to swallow its contents in a swift gulp. 'That's better. Do you care for brandy, Miss . . . er . . . Dear me, I have forgotten you.'

'I am Anna Templeton,' she said, unable not to unbend just a bit beneath his careless charm, however much she might dislike his mannerisms. 'And, no, I do not desire any brandy.'

'I suspected not,' he told her with more of a smile. 'But it's all Dobbs brought me. I just came in for the chance at a fire. Don't mean to stay, of course. I hope you will excuse my dirt.'

'Certainly,' she said, sitting down. 'How could I fault you on something so trifling?'

Lazily he raised his quizzing glass, and at once she dropped her eyes. 'Do I dismay you, Miss Templeton?'

'Dismay?' She looked up with an amusement that could not quite be checked, then dropped her eyes once more. 'Hardly, sir.'

'Gad,' he murmured. 'The lady professes no interest at all. You have lost your touch, Rotham. Perhaps the cure at Bath was too thorough.'

She had to meet his eyes then, and said with some constraint, 'I am betrothed, your grace.'

'Ah? And so quellingly spoken. I stand snubbed.'

Anger tightened her lips, but his silvery eyes were hooded, and she could not read mockery in the rest of his face. She made a slight gesture. 'Mr Molineux and I have yet to meet. Forgive me if I am not all that is gracious. My composure is rather thin just now.'

'Is it?' Abruptly he sat down across from her, putting his emptied brandy glass on a table by his elbow. 'Then I must refrain from teasing you. So you've not yet met Oliver Molineux. But how can you be engaged to him? Was it done by proxy? Did he write you a letter?' Rotham's lips twitched. 'It is just the sort of *practical* approach he would take.'

'No, no,' she said, shaking her head to repress the smile he had nearly won from her. 'It is . . . well, it is all arranged. Grandmama wishes it,' she added lamely.

'Damme, I suppose she does. Well, well!' Rotham lounged back in his chair, his tapering fingers toying with the handle of his quizzing glass. 'I have known Mollie for several years. Shall I tell you all about him?'

She had to laugh. 'How abominable you are, sir! No, I thank you. I prefer to form my own opinions.'

'Wisely spoken.' He sighed. 'I should probably lie. It is one of my little habits. Miss Templeton, you have the most quizzical expression upon your face. Have you taken me in dislike? Gad's life, how can I have displeased you?'

'I was wondering,' she said, taking care to betray no more

amusement lest he be encouraged to yet greater lengths of audacity, 'if you really are a duke. I have never met one before, but it seems to me that—'

'—a duke should act with more dignity?' he broke in lightly and affected a frown. 'My dear Miss Templeton, how dull you would have me be! Or would you rather I wax arrogant and quell you with a glare? Then we would have simpers and silences for conversation. Of course you may prefer a stolid discussion on the weather, but I never regard the weather except to bet on it. Do you—'

This prattle was interrupted by the opening of the doors and the entrance of Anna's father, Mr Murvey, and a third gentleman of perhaps two-and-thirty whom Anna instinctively knew to be Oliver Molineux.

Rotham dropped his remarks to go forward at once. 'Mollie, old fellow!' he said, grasping the hand Molineux extended rather stiffly to him. 'How is the boy?'

'Gibbon says he will have the headache for a day or two, but no lasting harm will come of this newest scrape you've led him into.' Molineux, a compactly built man with dark hair and eyes and an exceedingly forceful chin, frowned as Rotham's brows flew up. 'Yes, do not look so innocent! You may adopt that gudgeonish pose with everyone else, but I know what you are. Why did you not leave young Edwin to take the stage with his valet as he was supposed to? Then he would have been here hours ago and unharmed.'

Anna saw Rotham's jaw tighten, but his expression betrayed no anger at this forthright speech, nor did his mild tone alter as he sighed and said imploringly, 'But you know, Mollie, surely you *must* know what an intolerable bore it is to be ambushed without the company of one's friends. There I should have been, without anyone to protect save my own paltry person.'

Molineux made no attempt to keep annoyance from his gaze. 'If you were so set on protecting Edwin, I wonder how he took the ball instead of you, sir!'

'Mr Molineux!' cried the solicitor, holding out placating hands.

Dobbs entered at that moment with the tea tray, and whatever Rotham might have answered was left unsaid. He raised his quizzing glass at the delectable offerings being uncovered on the tray, smiled slightly, and made his bows.

'I'd best be off. Thank you, Mollie, for the cognac. I'm right as a trivet once again. Gentlemen. My very dear ma'am.' He cocked his pale head at an angle and sauntered out in the wake of Dobbs as complacently as though he had not just been all but directly blamed for the day's mishap.

'Jackanapes,' said Molineux explosively as soon as he was gone. 'Carpet-knight. How dare he meddle!'

'Now, now, sir,' said Mr Murvey, looking anxiously from beneath his beetling brows. 'You must not be so hard upon his grace. One must deplore his flippant manner, of course, but I believe he means well.'

'He is a cloth-head. A popinjay. A town Tulip,' snapped Molineux, clenching a fist. 'I don't like his influence over the boy. Well, Murvey, you know what he is. Next we shall have Edwin aping him, and that I won't stand for.'

'No, that would not do,' said Mr Murvey and gently took Molineux's arm. 'Sir, I beg . . . Miss Templeton is—'

'Oh, yes.' Molineux glanced round at her at last as though noticing for the first time that she was in the room.

She stood quietly, not quite wishing to meet his gaze fully lest he think her bold, and waited for a smile or even a softening of the frown in his dark eyes. But instead he eyed her a moment without expression before inclining his dark head curtly.

'Your servant, ma'am. I trust you have been made comfortable?'

'Yes,' she said, flustered by this coolness. 'I am so—'

'Good. Mrs West will see to your needs.' Molineux turned back to the solicitor. 'Now, Murvey, about those papers you brought last month for the countess to sign. I think we should discuss them.'

Mr Murvey looked longingly at the laden tea tray but was borne away.

'Well!' said Anna as soon as the door shut behind them. She sent a fulminating glance her parent's way. 'An innkeeper would have been more glad to see us. Is he so cocksure of my compliance that he feels he need scarcely be civil? Because if so—'

'Now, now, Anna,' said her father, lifting a hand. 'You are distressing yourself to no purpose. Let us sit down to this excellent little repast and drink our tea.' As if to underscore his words, he gave his faint but persistent cough and looked up at her.

She could not withstand the appeal and sat down, although her eyes remained troubled. 'But, Papa—'

'Nonsense. He has a most orderly mind. I have spoken with him and find no fault. You must not grow conceited, Anna, like one of those little London pusses who must be constantly danced attendance on. This is a marriage of convenience, and die-away airs suit neither you nor the situation.' He began spreading butter upon a scone. 'Let us be practical.'

'Yes, Papa,' she said, pouring out the tea. But she was not satisfied, and no amount of practicality could change that.

Chapter Two

Not till the doctor left did Lady Edwin Farrow come tottering downstairs to the drawing room.

'My dear child,' she said in failing accents, stretching forth both pale, pretty hands in a flutter of draperies as she floated forth to embrace Anna. 'So you are the one! How pretty you are. So slender, so sweetly complexioned.' A faint frown creased her brow. 'So . . . *tall*. Gracious, I must sit down.' She sank down into a graceful arrangement upon the sofa and sighed. 'Truly, I thought palpitations were certain to come upon me, such a fright as Neddie gave me, lying all still and bloodied like that.' She shuddered, turning so pale it looked as though she might indeed swoon. But she recovered and smiled as Anna offered to pour her a cup of tea. 'What a dear creature you are. I am persuaded I adore you already.'

Her gentle chatter flowed on, consisting of vague, uneventful remarks and compliments requiring few replies in return. Every movement was performed with languid grace as though to match her slow, melodious tones. She was not old, being still in her thirties and beautifully preserved. Possessed of a dainty, rounded figure, she must indeed have been a diamond of the first water in her early youth, for not only were her soft ringlets burnished gold but her large, long-lashed eyes were of that shade of blue men drown in.

'*Poor* Neddie,' she said again, sighing when the topic of London gossip was exhausted to her own satisfaction. 'I suppose I should be sitting at his bedside as steadfastly as a *martyr*, but then he is asleep, for the doctor gave him a powder, and it could not possibly comfort him for me to be there when he would not know it.' She smiled seraphically. 'Some more tea, if you please, Anna. How capably you pour! I never fail to dip my fringe into the sugar bowl.' She laughed as a brook might gurgle to itself, then grew pensive again. 'I am very grateful to Victor. He never fails me, and surely I must have had some presentiment of danger to my child when I wrote to Victor, asking him to take Neddie up in his carriage. He is so good to have done so. Most men are impatient with young boys, but not Victor.' She smiled, arching a brow. 'He is so very peculiar one cannot help but dote on him.'

'Do you refer to the Duke of Rotham, ma'am?' asked Anna and received a look of surprise.

'Who else? There is only *one* Victor. Is he not charming?'

Anna exchanged a glance with her bored parent. 'He is . . . most unusual.'

'Pooh! You are too careful with your compliments,' said her ladyship, laughing in a way that made Anna feel suddenly gauche. 'He is enchanting, truly the most wicked creature, who never does as he ought. The Prince Regent quite dotes on his advice, and no hostess feels her evening complete without his attendance.'

'Then he is a paragon,' said Anna, casting for a suitable remark.

'*Paragon*?' Lady Edwin opened her blue eyes very wide. 'With *his* reputation? Hardly. Oh, he is simply wicked, my dear Anna. Walter,' she called, jolting Mr Templeton from his doze, and giving him one of her angelic smiles when he frowned rather severely at her. 'Pray, don't be stuffy. You must warn your daughter, sir, to make better judgments of character. We do not want her head turned by the triflings of a duke.'

Anna's brows drew together at this playful speech, but her parent merely snorted:

'I should prefer, ma'am,' said Anna stiffly, 'to speak of Cousin Molineux.'

'Oliver?' Her amusement fading, Lady Edwin shrugged and began to pluck at her handkerchief. 'He is your paragon, my dear. I prefer to speak of people's faults, and he has none, although he has been unbearably cross since Neddie was given the viscountcy last year.'

When Anna said nothing further, Lady Edwin eyed her from beneath curling lashes and said in some satisfaction, 'Now whatever can I have said to send you into the boughs? No, you need not deny that you are cutting a stiff lip, for I can see that you are. It's very justifiable in you, I am sure, for were I in your place I should be perfectly *daunted* at the prospect of living here.'

'Living here?' said Anna in astonishment. 'But what—'

'Did you not know?' Lady Edwin helped herself to cake with an elegant turn of her wrist. 'Oliver has decided to make himself steward of the estate when Neddie becomes Riddell. And I doubt Neddie shall want to spend above a fortnight a year here so deep in the country, so you'll be free to consider it your home.' She glanced around at the vast chamber, causing Anna to look involuntarily too at the crimson-hung walls, Chinese screens, and amorously painted ceiling. 'You may become quite a hostess here at Linwick where even the shabby-genteel are puffed up by rubbing shoulders with both an earl and a duke.' She paused to smile at Anna, who began to take her measure and murmured:

'Coming it too strong, Aunt Beatrice. I think you wish to make me alarmed by the prospect of so much consequence.'

She spoke lightly and thus was startled to note the flash of annoyance in her aunt's eyes. Good heavens, was that truly her aunt's intention, to dismay her? But why? There could be no occasion for competition between a lady well forward in the ranks of society and a tutor's daughter.

'I do admire young ladies of spirit,' said Lady Edwin, her voice softer than ever. 'You take one up so sharply, Anna. Indeed, you remind me of the countess. Heavens, but I used to be quite terrified of her. Her merest glance could set me in a quake, but she is very old now and no longer as fierce as she was.' Lady Edwin twisted the rings on her fingers. 'You look to be a very sensible and well brought-up chit, however, and I'm sure the countess has made a wise choice in you for Oliver . . . providing he should decide to declare himself.'

Mr Templeton set down his cup with rather a bang, but Lady Edwin was rising with exquisite grace. She floated over to kiss Anna's set cheek. 'That prosaical expression in your eyes is just what Oliver needs. He does set such store by quiet manners and sensible thoughts. No doubt you think me as much a widgeon as he does, chattering on in my little way. But I must not linger with you, for all it is your first afternoon with us. Neddie may be wanting me now. I really must look in on him just to be sure no one can say I have not done my maternal duty.'

'Not declare himself indeed,' said Mr Templeton when she had gone. He thrust his hands under his coattail and executed a hasty turn around the room. 'Now that, Anna,' he said, shaking a finger at her, 'is precisely the sort of bubble-headed woman I will not abide. She has not a feather of intellect—'

'Oh, Papa, really!' Anna forgot her annoyance and began to laugh. 'You have your expressions confused.'

'Well, it doesn't signify. She is a ninny and what's more, she set herself to undermine you. All I can say is that I hope you have better sense in your noddle than to allow it.' A cough escaped him, despite his fierce attempt to suppress it, and winded, he sat down heavily. 'Bah!'

'There,' said Anna, her eyes twinkling. 'You have excited yourself to no good purpose. I promise you it will take more than half an hour's work to cast me into the blue-devils. But I do confess, she is admirable in her style of execution.'

'Hmpf,' snorted Mr Templeton, searching his pockets for his spectacles. 'An envious tabby, that's all she is.'

'No, Papa, you *mustn't!*' Anna choked on her laughter. 'Aunt Beatrice is lovely. You cannot be so heartless as to call her such a thing.'

'Shall call her what I like,' said Mr Templeton, frowning. 'You may be sure that she cannot read Catullus in the original.'

Anna glanced away, her lips quivering. 'No,' she said in an unsteady voice, 'I am sure she cannot.'

This having satisfied her parent, Anna rang for the tea tray to be cleared away. Then as he pulled out a slim volume from his pocket, she wandered over to one of the French windows which looked out over a terrace leading prettily down to a long reflecting pool. In the growing dusk its water lay still and black, oddly unfrozen. Anna's amusement dimmed to thoughtfulness and she turned to gaze at the back of her parent's bowed head. Dear independent Papa, he would be shocked to learn how desperately he was depending upon her now. For he could no longer earn his living; the cough in his chest had seen to that. She did not mean to repine overlong on what her aunt had said, but truly it was hard to shake off the faint chill those words had instilled in her. *If he offers for you . . .* And if he did not? Well, for her sake she would not greatly care, but for Papa's . . . well, she must inherit that money, if only to see him provided with a comfortable income in a salubrious climate. England, with its damp days and its fog, was no place for him.

That evening Anna came downstairs to dinner alone, her father having decided to rest from the rigors of their long journey. Murvey was at once all concern, but Oliver Molineux, who had been standing by the fire with one elbow resting upon the mantelpiece, came up to her with a well-executed, if curt, bow.

'Rest, undoubtedly, is the wisest course for him to follow,' he said in his forthright way. His brown eyes regarded her levelly. 'The sooner he regains his strength the sooner he will be able to enjoy a tour of the estate.'

She raised her brows at this and said with cool civility to match his, 'No doubt, sir, but I fear my father is not excessively fond of outdoor pursuits.'

Molineux curled a corner of his mouth. 'Bookish, is he?'

'He is a noted scholar,' she said rather more proudly than she had intended.

Molineux's smile became complete, and it had the trick of softening the rather set lines of his countenance. He was dressed with plain elegance in a coat of blue superfine with cream-colored breeches, yellow waistcoat, and a modest cravat. He inclined his dark head to her. 'I did not mean to dispute it, Cousin Anna. But it is my own view that an educated man need not withdraw from the world as a consequence of his learning.'

'Well-spoken, sir,' she acknowledged, noticing how Lady Edwin watched them. Anna's cheeks heated slightly and she fell silent.

'Grandmama will not come down this evening,' he said, glancing at the clock ticking softly on the mantelpiece. 'We always wait until half past the hour in case she should desire to join us. But tonight it seems she does not.' He smiled and seemed in better humor. 'Do you ride, Cousin?'

She nodded, curbing her disappointment over the countess' absence. 'But I have not done so in an age. I fear I should prove clumsy from lack of practice.'

'Then I shall take care in choosing a mount for you,' he said gravely, apparently not noticing she had spoken half in jest.

'But—'

The double doors swung open, and Dobbs advanced a step into the room. 'Dinner is served, my lady.'

'Good!' said Lady Edwin, closing the book of fashion plates she had been absently perusing, and rose to her feet. She was a vision in pink satin worn frilled and puffed at the sleeves, which were miniature in gay defiance of the chilly drafts pervading the house. Her shawl slid from one arm, and she stopped to stand in pretty helplessness until Mr Murvey hastened to rescue her from her difficulty. 'Thank you, Mr Murvey,' she said, taking his arm with a smile that made him puff out his chest. 'Do lead me in to dinner. I am quite famished. Is that not dreadfully unfashionable of me?'

His attempt at a gallant answer was lost to Anna, for Molineux had proffered his arm to her. Gently she laid her fingers upon it, and they all followed Dobbs to the dining room, where Anna's eyes widened at the incongruous settings of four places upon a table that could seat twenty more without a squeeze. The sideboard was of noble proportions to match, and fairly groaned beneath the covered dishes already being arranged upon it.

'It is a pleasant room, do you not think, Cousin?' said Molineux.

Anna, dragging her fascinated gaze away from a monstrous silver epergne rising tier upon tier from the center of the table to a vainglorious height, allowed him to seat her. 'Most handsome,' she said.

He smiled. 'Actually we do it injustice, for it is no more than the breakfast parlor, but there is so seldom an occasion to use the state dining hall.'

'Indeed,' she murmured and was obliged to make a business of unfolding her napkin in order to conceal her opinion of his pomposity.

'You must not let the size of the house overwhelm you,' he went on as the first course – turbot in a proud sauce – was brought forth. 'Naturally you will lose your way at first, but I have no doubt of your ability soon to learn to feel at home here.'

'Yes,' she said placidly. 'I am clever at adapting to my surroundings.' But as soon as she spoke she could have bitten her tongue in exasperation. What did it matter if he patronized her?

But he seemed not to take her remark amiss. 'You have admirable composure, Cousin. Murvey has spoken of your assistance to Edwin this afternoon. Most females swoon at the sight of injury. But even blood upon your dress did not overset you.'

So he had noticed her more closely than she thought at their first meeting! Anna unbent. 'You are kind, sir.'

He smiled, a glint in his dark eyes as he raised his glass in private salute to her. 'I believe in acknowledging facts.'

Rather warmed by this show of attention, Anna went to bed that night encouraged. She slept soundly and awoke refreshed, taking delight in the luxury of breaking her fast in bed with rolls and steaming chocolate. A young abigail by the name of Betty had been assigned to her personal service, and this lass – looking neat as a pin in her plain dress and starched cap and apron – bustled about, stirring up the fire and clearing away the few articles Anna had left neatly folded upon a chair.

Presently a footman came with a message from Molineux, asking if she would care to ride with him. Anna accepted and half an hour later descended the stairs, crop and gloves in hand, with the train of her shabby habit caught over one arm. Molineux was waiting for her.

He bowed in his grave manner as she smiled a greeting. 'Good morning, Cousin. I trust you slept well?'

She replied as civility dictated, and walked outside with him. There, however, she stopped abruptly upon the broad steps, her gray eyes fixed incredulously upon the two animals a groom held in the drive. Irritation spurred her into lifting a hand in repudiation.

'*No*,' she said firmly, stung further by the exchange of amused glances between the stableboy and one of the footmen. 'Good God, Cousin Oliver, I am not a flat, to be mounted on that . . . that *creature*.'

'Matilda is an extremely dependable mare,' he said, unperturbed by her refusal as he adjusted the angle of his beaver to a nicety. 'Not showy in looks, of course, but of an excellent disposition.' His dark eyes regarded Anna steadily. 'You did say you were an inexperienced rider.'

'No, I said I was out of practice.' Anna stared again at the cream-colored cob, as round as she was short, and covered in a fuzzy profusion of winter hair. Her jaw looked hard, her eye cold, and her fetlocks short, promising a stubborn disposition and a rough gait.

Molineux shrugged, moving on down the steps to take the reins of a neatish bay hack. 'Well, it doesn't signify. She is the only mount in the stables suitable for a lady.' He paused, frowning a little. 'Of course, if she truly does not suit, I daresay I can scour the county for—'

'I should not dream of putting you to such trouble,' she said rather tightly and steeled herself as she went down the steps to the

21

mare, who tried to nip her first thing. 'Let us see her paces.'

The groom gave her his hand and boosted her into the cold saddle, while the stableboy held hard to Matilda's bridle to keep her from sidling off before Anna was finished arranging her skirts and gathering her reins.

'Ready, Cousin?' asked Molineux pleasantly.

Her lips tightened, and she gave a curt nod, wheeling her stubby mount to follow his. They cut through a corner of the deer park at a merciless trot, Anna feeling as jounced as a sack of potatoes in an ox cart, and broke into a canter across the open meadow beyond. It seemed by now inevitable that Matilda's canter should be no more pleasurable than the rest of her gaits. She persisted in crossing her leads, no matter what Anna did to straighten her up, and by the time Molineux pulled to a halt atop a short hill within a copse of beeches, Anna felt herself wrenched to pieces.

Had he made some remark regarding her mount very likely she would have bitten off his nose, but instead he gazed out across the vista before them.

'All this,' he said, making a sweeping gesture with his whip, 'is Farrowsleigh.'

The house stood on fairly level ground, a deep park of noble oaks before it, and three hills circling it to the rear bordered the formal gardens protectively. The hilltops were fringed white with old snow lingering on from the last storm, but the gentle slopes were green in defiance of winter. Gaunt old hedges, rattling in the frost, ran along into the distance, where they joined to a stone wall.

'Cheveley Hall,' he answered in response to her question. The lines in his face hardened, and he rested a clenched fist upon the pommel of his saddle. 'Rotham's land. If you look closely through those trees yonder,' he pointed, 'you can see the dome.'

She did see it, though not with much clarity. 'You have no liking for his grace.'

'Do you think I should?' he said rather hotly.

Her eyes widened; she shook her head. 'I know nothing about him. And indeed, sir, if you dislike the man it is no business of mine.'

His horse shifted nervously and was harshly curbed. 'Dislike him?' he said after a moment with a mirthless laugh. 'My dear ma'am, he is my enemy. Do not trust him.'

22

Her brows came up. 'There could be no occasion where I should need to trust or distrust him. Let us speak of something else, if you prefer.'

'Forgive me,' he said, unbending then with a smile. 'You are thinking me fierce, and really, I am a mild man at heart. I simply protect what is mine.' He glanced at her swiftly from beneath drawn brows, and she saw a flash of muted anger still lingering in their depths.

She turned her gaze away. It was not a subject she would broach again.

'You are growing cold. We must not linger just because I never tire of this view. Come,' he said, spurring his horse on, and she beat her reluctant mount soundly on the rump to make her follow.

Molineux showed her the tenants' lane, rather stern as he criticized the condition of what were hardly better than hovels. 'It is all neglect,' he said harshly beneath his breath, while shivering, ragged children stared at them riding by. 'They could make a better effort, and God knows, some of them do. But there is no excuse for squalor.' His nostrils flared as Anna made herself nod and smile a greeting in return to the shy curtsy given her by a shriveled old woman in a black shawl.

'Perhaps,' she said slowly, her eyes troubled. 'Perhaps they require an example to follow—'

'The earl, you mean?' Molineux snorted, tightening the reins as his horse shied from a baby playing in the mire. A woman ran out and snatched it up, scolding it, while her eyes begged Molineux's pardon. He tossed her a shilling, casually, but his eyes were not casual, nor was his tone as he continued, 'God, if only they had an earl to respect. The bailiff is competent, but nothing beyond. I instruct him when I can, but the countess brooks little interference. *She* does not see this, or the fences which need mending, or the desperate need for instruction in modern principles of agriculture. Farrowsleigh needs a master, Cousin, and it does not have one.'

'And when St. Byre is earl?'

He laughed, with a bitterness that shocked her. 'Oh, I think nothing will change. Edwin, you see, cares not a groat for responsibility. He is shamefully spoiled, having been let run wild by Beatrice, who is nothing if not a peagoose. Worse, he is puffed with his own consequence, and chafes at my attempts to school him in his future duties. He is no more suited to be an earl than is Percy, God help him.'

'But Neddie will surely mature,' she said, wishing Molineux would not sound so hard.

He looked at her almost in a mocking way. 'His character is formed. And it is far from admirable. Just remember, you've not yet met him properly. Don't let yesterday's accident make you like him out of sympathy.'

Frowning, she meant to protest this, but Molineux had spurred his horse into a canter and there was nothing to do but grit her teeth and thump along after him. He took her back to the house, then gave her a smile of unexpected approval.

'You have been most patient, Cousin, to follow me about this morning, braving the cold without complaint. I have enjoyed your company.'

Before she could reply to this speech, he wheeled his mount and was off again, leaving her to dismount with a groom's assistance and make her way alone into the house. She did so with a faint line between her brows. Surely he did not mean to be thoughtless, but she could not shake off the conviction that, betrothed or not, she mattered not a rush to him and probably never would. She sighed, pausing in the hall to pull off her gloves. Well, it was not to be repined over. A marriage of convenience was merely that, a civil contract, and not something fancyings could alter. Not that she had experienced the least rush of romantic fervor for her cousin, but still, she thought – she *hoped* – she could grow to like him a little did he ever unbend from that odious stiffness.

'Dobbs,' she said, catching up the train of her habit over one arm. 'Is Lord St. Byre feeling more the thing? I should like to visit his sickroom. Will you inquire if he would receive me?'

The butler bowed. 'The Duke of Rotham has just come on the same matter, Miss Anna. He is waiting in the library—'

'Is he?' Anna's brows drew together. 'Alone?' At Dobbs's nod, she gave a small exclamation and put her crop and gloves into his hands. 'His grace must have the worst notion of our hospitality if he is kept kicking his heels like a gardener's boy.' She unpinned her hat and folded up the veil neatly. 'I shall go and talk to him. Will you please have Betty send down the book lying on my dressing table? Thank you.'

She walked away, a bit uncertain of which door opened on to the book room, but after only one wrong turn, she found it and entered a chamber of noble dimensions, lined with shelves of calf-bound volumes – some locked away behind glass – and with an upper gallery running along the full perimeter of the room. Anna came to an involuntary halt, her hand flying to her mouth as she stared. A choke of laughter escaped her, then the sight of Rotham's lean figure rising from a deep chair of mahogany leather caused her to suppress her mirth and go forward hastily.

'My very dear Miss Templeton.' Rotham made her a bow, his hand flourishing gracefully from multiple folds of Mechlin lace. He was attired *par elegance* in a swallow-tailed coat of brown serge, with broad lapels and a tall collar. A cravat of the daunting Mathematical style held his chin so high between towering shirt points he had to bow slightly at the waist merely to meet her eye. Certainly he could not move his sleek head more than an inch to either side. His waistcoat of kerseymere sported no fobs to draw the attention, but then, it did not need to, and today his pantaloons were unwrinkled perfection worn inside Hessians of blinding gloss. His brow was up and his expression faintly quizzical as he said, 'Tell me, am I such an out-and-outer to your eyes that you must fall into whoops upon the moment you see me? Damme, ma'am, but you shall swell my head.'

Her eyes flashed a bit, but she chose to be honest in her reply. 'I was not laughing at you, sir. How conceited of you to think so.'

'No?' He feigned disappointment, then brightened as he took her arm in the most natural way to lead her nearer to the fire. 'Then what a delightful habit you have formed, always to make so blithe an entry.'

'Pray stop teasing,' she said, half laughing in exasperation as she held out her numb fingers to the warmth of the blaze. 'If you must know, I was laughing at myself for calling this a book room when I had no idea of its magnificence. No appellation less than *library* will do here.' She smiled wryly. 'As a matter of fact, the entire house is continually showing me how paltry indeed are my own notions of grandeur. Did you know we could seat forty for dinner?' Her eyes twinkled. 'I doubt there are that many notables in the entire county.'

His own pale gray eyes gleamed with appreciation of her point, but he said airily, 'Tut. If the table was filled in Elizabeth's day when this edifice was built, I daresay it can be filled again.' He leaned his shoulders against the mantelpiece, taking no heed of how close his coattails dangled near the fire, and struck a pose. 'Why, the eleventh earl – your grandfather, you know – was used to inviting the king to sup. He and my father used to compete in outdoing each other for the royal entertainment.' Rotham yawned delicately and pulled out a cambric handkerchief. 'I daresay such dinners will be held here again, when the thirteenth earl comes about. How is Neddie by the way?' he asked abruptly, his gray eyes flicking to her face and away again before she could meet them.

She shrugged. 'I have no idea. I hope to see him this morning, if he is feeling better.' She smiled. 'We have yet to meet, you know.'

'Then I must introduce you,' he said at once. With more audacity than she liked, he put up his glass and studied her until her cheeks burned. 'I am marvelously clever at introductions.'

'No doubt,' she said tartly.

'You scoff. Yes, I profess, you do scoff.' He sighed and moved away from the fire. 'Why did you come in here to talk to me, Miss Templeton?'

Her slight vexation yielded to puzzlement at the force of his question. 'Naturally I would do so. Anyone owes a guest that small civility, although, perhaps, I have not been under this roof long enough to take such things upon myself.'

'You, my child, are the only one in this house who would acknowledge that small civility – as you call it – much less act upon it.' He smiled at her with more than just a quirk of the lips. 'For my part, I am prodigiously grateful not to be left kicking my heels alone in this drafty barracks of a room. I do so hate the solitude of my own company.'

Her brows drew together. 'But why?'

He blinked. 'Why do I detest solitude?'

'No, no. Why do you say no one of my family would bother to greet you?'

'My dear,' he said kindly. 'If I may daresay it, I know these people rather better than you do. Trust my opinion, I beg.'

'I am *not* your dear.'

His brows came up. 'A random choice of words, I assure you. Despite your uncommon handsomeness of face and figure, I

26

entertain no designs upon you.' He shook his head in mock horror. 'It would not be condoned.'

'I should think not,' she began rather stormily, then caught a muted twinkle in his eye and subsided. 'Odious, Banbury man. You are hoaxing me, and so thoroughly I should blush for being so taken in.'

Whatever reply he might have made was stopped by the discreet entrance of a footman.

'James!' said the duke warmly. 'How are you?'

The footman bowed, looking quite gratified. 'Very well, I thank your grace. His lordship desires very much to see you.' He came forward to Anna and handed her a slim volume.

Rotham aimed his quizzing glass at it. 'Do you bring books *into* the library, Miss Templeton? What an extraordinary young woman you are. Ah, a Scott novel! Splendid stuff. Do you mean to read it?'

She shook her head, smiling as they walked out through the door James held for them. 'I have read it so often I know the lines by heart. I thought perhaps my cousin might enjoy it.'

'Perhaps,' he said a bit coolly. 'Well! Up the stairs we go. Gothic, aren't they? I always feel a bit blind in this house, groping through the gloom.' He loosed a foolish laugh and sprang lightly over the last two steps to the landing.

It was necessary to pass through a long gallery set with numerous tall windows. Gilded statues of draped women bearing branches of candles stood in all four corners, and a crystal chandelier hung from the painted ceiling.

'This looks like a ballroom,' said Anna, imagining just how easily the carpets could be rolled up and the chairs moved against the walls.

'But it isn't one, alas. I say!' Rotham's quizzing glass came up and he beckoned with a lazy crook of the finger. 'You must see this, really you must. 'Pon rep, a fine rendering, is it not?'

Anna gazed up at the portrait of a haughty woman, dressed in a ball gown of another era. Her hair was powdered, and she stood by a chair with a domino flung over it as though she were just pausing on her way out. A mask of rose silk dangled from her slim fingers.

'You look something like her. Damme, yes!' The duke swung his quizzing glass from the painted face to Anna's. Disliking yet another scrutiny, she was about to rebuke him when he snapped his fingers. 'Now, now, ma'am! No need to poker up. This is your grandmother just after her marriage.' He smiled as Anna's eyes widened and flew back to the portrait. 'Has she not preserved well? Of course the rumor is she's eighty, and one must make allowances for the ravages of time, but—'

'I have yet to meet her,' said Anna, looking down in some discomfiture.

He was silent a moment as though in surprise, then he said, 'But you came by her invitation?'

'Oh, yes!' Anna's eyes lifted to his and saw they were smiling, although his expression was serious enough. Her gaze lowered again with some shyness. 'I have no doubts she will receive me, although it must be very difficult for her to do so. She hates my father, you see.'

'Gossip!' He brightened. 'What fun! Tell me this old tale, that I may tease her with it.'

Anna stiffened. 'Certainly not.'

'Fie. Must I bribe the servants?' he asked with a wink at the waiting James, who took care to look impassive. 'But this is what I wished you to notice,' he continued before Anna could give him a set-down. Affecting a cough, he flourished his quizzing glass at the countess' fine bosom. 'In the, ahem, curt manner of the French . . . Regard the necklace!'

Anna frowned. 'Very fine. But—'

'Very fine? *Very fine*?' His brows lifted in mock indignation as he placed a hand upon his heart. 'Gad, the understatement of that! My dear child,' he said worriedly, 'pray, look again. Note the size of those diamonds.'

'The painter let his brush exaggerate.'

'Not at all, I assure you,' he said, laughing. 'Those are the Riddell diamonds.'

'What an impressive title,' she said, still puzzled. 'I have never before heard of them.'

'Haven't you?' His hooded eyes glinted. 'Then you had better learn of them. Gad's life, there isn't a member of your family who isn't mad to have them. They are worth a king's ransom. Priceless! The finest diamonds in Europe. And,' he added, laying a finger against his nose, 'they are Lady Riddell's, to dispose of as she chooses.'

Startled, Anna stared at him. 'But surely they are entailed with—'

Smiling, he shook his head.

She looked again at the magnificent necklace and grew thoughtful. 'But why, sir, do you feel obliged to inform me of these matters?'

'Oh . . . ' He waved an airy hand. 'Because, I daresay, I doubt if anyone else will care to tell you. Are you not new competition?'

'You make it too vulgar.'

His smile was slight and just a trifle cold. 'Yes, I am one of those deplorable people who never wrap things up in clean linen. Well, we all have our family skeletons and if mine should hang from the ridgepole instead of being lodged discreetly in an attic closet, I see no reason why others' should not be. Come,' he said, tucking her hand inside his arm. 'Let us find Neddie.'

Chapter Three

They found the Viscount St. Byre sitting up in bed, clad in a plain dressing gown over his nightshirt, and looking little worse the wear for his adventure save for a rakish bandage upon his head. It was easy to see he had inherited his fine looks from his mother. His guinea-gold hair inclined to curl just a bit at the temples; his classical, almost perfect features, and his intensely blue eyes were all hers. He was even graceful with the same fluidity of movement despite his being at an age proscribed as awkward. A spaniel lay on the bed, and he was pulling fondly at its ear when Rotham preceded Anna inside.

'Victor! How splendid of you to—' Abruptly he broke off his greeting, his eager smile falling into a sullen expression of suspicion as he saw Anna. 'And who are you?' he demanded in a sharp tone that set her aback. 'One of Mama's toadies sent to cosset me. Go away!' His eyes blazed at her as he gestured fiercely. 'Go away and take that dashed old book with you! I won't be read to like some baby, do you hear?'

'Perfectly,' she began rather coolly, but Rotham was going forward to Neddie's bedside with a look of reproof.

'Edwin, dear boy, do take a damper. You can have no occasion whatsoever to fly into a miff at Miss Templeton, who is, you young cawker, your cousin as well as the one who saved you from bleeding to death while I stood about in a dither over how I should tend you without soiling my lace.'

Neddie had the grace to look chagrined. For a moment he seemed at a loss for what he should say while dull crimson spread across his cheeks, then at last he forced himself to meet her gaze. 'I'm most sorry. You were kind to help me.'

'That's better, young juggins,' said Rotham, routing the spaniel. He sat down on the bed, crossing his arms over his chest, and waved Anna to the chair. 'One of your mama's toadies, indeed. If I were you, Miss Templeton, I'd put a flea in his ear.'

She relented. 'If I did, we would never be able to bury the

hatchet. Shall we start again, Cousin Edwin?'

'Jupiter, don't call me *that*,' he exclaimed in revulsion. 'I'm just Neddie.'

'As you like,' she said, smiling, and laid the book on the bedside table.

At once his look of suspicion returned, marring the fineness of his countenance. 'But you *have* come to read to me, haven't you? Or . . . or else bathe my temples in Hungary water!'

'Heavens, *no!*' she said, laughing, but carefully avoided the duke's quizzical eye. 'If I'd known I was likely to set everyone on their ear simply by holding a book in my hand, I assure you I would have eschewed doing so at once. No, Neddie, I have not come to minister to you in any way, for I don't mollycoddle people and never have.'

'Well, at least that's something,' said Neddie in relief. 'If you knew how Mama is, you'd think me right to be suspicious.'

'I have met her, and . . . but we are boring his grace,' she said as Rotham politely hid a yawn.

'Not at all,' he said without making the least push to sound convincing. 'I am so glad you ride, Miss Templeton.'

'Yes, you do, don't you?' said Neddie eagerly, noticing now her attire. 'Famous, for I like nothing better than to hunt. Do you hunt, Anna?'

'Infrequently,' she said. Her eyes twinkled, although she fought to keep her lips from quivering. 'But not, you may be sure, on that wretched animal presented for my use this morning.'

'Wretched animal?' Neddie frowned. 'There's isn't a single bit of flesh in the stables that ain't prime.'

'Really?' she replied with equal indignation. 'And what of the creature with a girth like a cheese barrel and a jaw of iron?'

He blinked with puzzlement for a moment, then comprehension dawned. 'Good God!' he crowed, falling back on his pillows with a great whoop that brought a hasty look-in from his valet. 'Matilda!'

Rotham frowned at the servant. 'Go away, Beavins. I haven't strangled your master.'

The valet vanished, and Neddie sobered at once to rest a shy hand atop Rotham's clenched one. '*Don't*, Victor, please,' he said in an undertone of concern. Then the amusement returned to his young face and he began laughing again. 'Only think of it. Matilda!

31

Lord, Anna, who put you on that old horror? Victor, you didn't, surely.'

Rotham had recovered the momentary lapse of sangfroid and raised his brows. 'I? What an uncharitable accusation. I haven't the governing of your stables.'

'It was Cousin Molineux, I'm afraid,' said Anna. 'I told him I was out of practice, and he took me rather too literally.'

Rotham laughed, but Neddie said impulsively, 'It is just the prosy thing he *would* do. I'll wager he took you to see the tenants' lane and probably even a . . . a sheep pen. Lord, what a flat! It's plain as a pikestaff you want a sweet-goer who'll sail over fences in clipping style. And as soon as Beavins lets me out of bed, the old tyrant, I'll take you to see the upper meadows. From there it's only a fence and a mile of Victor's land before you're on the sweetest hunting turf you've ever coursed. You'll—'

'Gad's life, boy, take a damper,' said Rotham, waving a lazy hand. 'Beavins will be breathing down my neck for making you too excited, and then your mama will terrify me with one of her scolds.'

'Fudge,' said Neddie, but with an appreciative curl of his lip. 'Mama never scolds. She has *nerves.*'

'Yes, and they upset *mine*,' said Rotham, and with good humor Neddie lay back more quietly upon his pillows. 'Now,' said the duke, turning his attention to Anna, who mentally applauded his adroit handling of the boy, 'I know just the horse for you. A black hunter your bailiff bought from me six months back. The sweetest temper, Miss Templeton, eager to run, and he rises beautifully off his hocks. I've hunted him a couple of times and always found him a steady goer. Never a foot wrong. He'd do nicely for you, damme, he would indeed, eh, Ned?'

'He sounds delightful,' said Anna, brightening.

But Neddie looked troubled. 'I don't think we still have that one.'

'No?' Rotham raised his quizzing glass at the boy. 'Sink me, of course you do. You must. No one else in the county has bought the brute. Only the squire could afford him, and he can't ride a cow.' A droll smile curved the duke's lips. 'Dear me, have I told you about the day he took a tumble? Straight into a puddle of the most *clinging* mire. Such a ruckus he kicked up, too. Quite frightened away his horse, calling it such thunderous epithets, and he was obliged to walk some five miles home. I was never in my life so entertained.'

Anna exclaimed. 'But surely you offered him your assistance, sir.'

'What?' cried Rotham, the glint returning to his eye. 'Carry him pillion like some lusty milkmaid I'd taken a fancy to? What an extraordinary sight we would have presented to the village.' The duke picked a piece of lint from his sleeve, causing the blood ruby he wore on one finger to flash. 'He, black as a Moor, and I in a Weston coat. Gad.' He shuddered delicately.

'You mean,' said Neddie with a snort, 'that he probably cursed you along with his horse. *I* know what his temper is once it's touched off. And his wife is the veriest old gossip-tabby. Why do you let such mushrooms vex you so, Victor? Their opinions don't signify.'

'Don't they?' said the duke, staring into space. Then he collected himself. 'Nevertheless, you must try the black hunter, Miss Templeton.'

'I shall,' she said, too well-bred to betray how eaten she was with curiosity over all of these oblique references the pair of them kept making. What sort of scandal had the duke excited in this placid little community?

Rotham stood. 'Enough visiting. And no protests, Neddie! Sink me, but a sickroom is a tedious place. When you are out of it, you may ride over and see me. And come with him, Miss Templeton. Without Alicia in the house, I utterly rattle about. Good-day.' He swept her a bow and chucked Neddie carelessly on the chin before sauntering out with his quizzing glass dangling from his fingers.

'And who,' asked Anna, still smiling involuntarily when he was gone, 'is Alicia? His sister?'

'Lord, no!' Neddie rolled his eyes. 'His daughter. She is seven and a dead bore. I hope he don't mean to let her come home for Christmas, for if he does we'll never see him here, you know.'

'I . . . I see,' said Anna slowly, turning aside with a faint frown. 'How peculiar of me never to have guessed he is married.'

'Oh, don't look as though you just ate raw fish,' said Neddie rather unkindly. 'He ain't married now. She died years ago. But, Jupiter! I can't think of the horse he is talking about. There *is* a black brute Mollie has, but that's no mount for you. You'd better use my chestnut.'

'And what will you ride if I do?' she asked, thrusting her

curiosity about Rotham away.

Neddie shrugged. 'Hawkins will find me something. Do you play cards?'

'Of course,' she said promptly, grateful for a change of subject. 'Shall I ring for a deck?'

He nodded, and when Beavins had provided them with cards he sent her a shy look from beneath his thick lashes. 'Are you very skillful, Anna?'

She paused in her dealing. 'Why . . . I am competent, I dare-say.'

He looked away and began plucking at the coverlet with his fingers. 'I just wondered if . . . well, dash it all, you seem to be a regular trump like Rotham, and not one to cut up stiff when I fail to come up to scratch. And you don't simper *or* giggle so I feel sure you could keep a secret and not go blabbing about—'

'Neddie, for heaven's sake!' She laughed. 'Cut line, if you please. Whatever is this favor you wish from me?'

He flushed. 'I should like to know how to play cards well, really well, you know, and not like a green flat. Mollie gets so cross when they are obliged to use me as a fourth, and he always lectures me on my cards in a way I hate.' The blue eyes flashed. 'I shan't give him the satisfaction of teaching me how to do anything. But if you would help me, Anna . . . Jupiter, but wouldn't it be famous to see his face if I ever beat him!'

'I can see you mean to twist me around your finger,' she said, but with a smile of understanding. 'The basest flatterer could not hold a candle to you, sir. But yes, I can try, although I promise nothing. You would do better, you know, to apply to his grace.' She glanced down, conscious of a momentary note of scorn in her voice but unable to squash it. 'I am sure he is well-versed in all the tricks of the gaming saloons.'

'Rotham?' Neddie stared at her. 'He's no gamester. Can't keep his mind on his hand long enough to finish a game. He never leaves White's with a full pocket. I need none of *his* skill, thank you.'

They played until time for luncheon, when Anna changed into a walking dress and sat down at table with her father, Lady Edwin, Mr Murvey, and Molineux, who thwarted all her ladyship's attempts to discuss Paris with his own talk of the newest methods of crop rotation.

'Farmer George,' said Mr Templeton beneath his breath while

Anna tried to mask her boredom behind an expression of polite interest.

'Hush,' she whispered fiercely and with a shrug her father pulled a book from his pocket and propped it open against his wineglass. Molineux's brows drew together, but Lady Edwin was leaning forward with her languid smile.

'Dearest Anna,' she said in her gentle way. 'How I admire your energy. Have you truly ridden out with Oliver *and* entertained Neddie? I should be lain down in exhaustion after such a program, and it is barely afternoon. But you must tell me what you think of Victor. Is he not charming?'

The line deepened between Molineux's dark brows.

Anna inclined her head to her aunt. 'I believe I may say, ma'am, that his grace is a complete hand. And Neddie has pronounced me a . . . a Trojan, which I suppose I must take to be the highest of compliments. So I feel quite accepted now.'

This little attempt at humor succeeded in clearing Molineux's expression. He smiled in a tolerant way and said, 'Ah, yes, Edwin is full of sporting cant. One of his schoolmates has a Corinthian for an uncle, and all the boys are infected with the desire to be bucks of the first stare.'

'Indeed? I suppose that must be applauded over a less savory wish to lounge about low gaming rooms and cockpits,' said Anna. She sipped at her glass and forestalled the footman from serving her a second portion of duck. 'We discussed local hunting, and I have been advised that I cannot take part if I am mounted upon Matilda.'

'Really?' One of Molineux's dark brows lifted. 'And did Edwin offer you his own horse instead?'

'Yes,' she replied, trying to take no notice of the condescension in his tone. 'But I am more intrigued by a hunter his grace mentioned. A black horse. He said it would be ideal for me.'

Molineux looked startled. 'Good Lord! Not the one bought from his stables?'

'Yes.'

'It is out of the question,' he said with a curtness that startled her and even caught her father's attention momentarily. 'I have told Hawkins repeatedly to destroy the animal. He is savage, fit for no one.'

'But—' She laid her napkin beside her plate with a frown she did

35

not trouble to conceal. 'I cannot understand why he would recommend the horse if it is not safe.'

'I told you the man is not to be trusted.'

'Oliver, how unkind!' Lady Edwin gazed at him in reproach.

Molineux compressed his lips. 'We all know what he is, Beatrice.'

She dropped her blue eyes. 'Yes.'

'Well, I do not,' said Anna rather crossly.

Molineux rose to his feet. 'Come, put on your pelisse, and I will show you.'

Wondering, she obeyed him, and her frown deepened as they walked around to the stables. It had grown to be a gloomy day, with a disagreeable wind that cut through even the warmest clothing. She shivered and stepped with Molineux into the shadowy interior of the stables with its pungent odours of fodder and horses. The animals stood drowsily in their stalls, now and then shifting a foot or cocking an ear to listen to the muted laughter and chatter of the stableboys as they diced in the loft. The head groom, Hawkins, came hastily to greet them and touched his hat respectfully at Anna.

'We want to see the black,' said Molineux, dismissing him, and with a bow the man stepped back, his eyes following them as they walked down to the very end of the building. There, Molineux motioned her to silence and led her to the half door of a large box stall.

She peered in, cautioned by his behaviour, and her eyes widened at the horse, standing idly in the centre of the stall with one hind foot cocked up. Even in this lazy posture it was obvious his conformation was all that could be wished for. He was perhaps a bit short of bone for a hunter, but made neat and compact, with the look of plenty of spring in his hocks. His coat, despite the natural roughness of winter, gleamed blue-black, and the off forefoot showed his only white marking.

'What a pretty fellow,' she said, and the horse raised its head inquiringly.

'Yes, handsome enough,' said Molineux. 'Irish blood. But—'

At the sound of his voice the horse flattened its ears. It snorted and pawed the ground lightly.

Molineux shrugged. 'You see what I mean?' He moved Anna to

one side and stepped up to extend his hand over the door. 'Here, Dante—'

With a savage squeal, the horse ducked its head and charged. Molineux drew back hasily from the snapping teeth, and with another snort of rage, the horse whirled and kicked the door with a force that shook the heavy oak boards. Anna flinched and took Molineux's arm, feeling shaken.

'You see?' he said calmly, leading her away while behind them angry hooves continued to thud against the stall. 'Not to be trusted.'

'No, indeed,' she said, her voice none too steady. 'I wonder why . . . but surely his grace cannot know—'

'His grace,' said Molineux flatly, 'is aware of everything that goes on at Farrowsleigh. He has even made a pet of the earl, God knows why. To spite us, I suppose. He is a two-faced creature, Cousin. I hope I need not warn you again to be wary of his charm. Neddie is a complete slave to it. See that you do not become the same.'

Despite her distress over the horse and its recommendation, which she supposed must have been an elaborate if cruel prank, Anna bristled a bit at this arrant tone of command. 'Indeed, sir, I hope no one may think my good sense is ever bowled over by cream-pot impressions. I am not a fool.'

'Good.' He smiled as they left the stables and turned the subject, but she had the unshakable impression that her outburst of spirit had not pleased him.

'Fool!' she said to herself later, when she had gained the privacy of her sitting room. He was a man who required a comfortable wife, and she was hardly showing that side of her nature by throwing a mischievous duke in his teeth at every opportunity. Was she a ninny, to be comparing the two men? Rotham amused for the moment, but she could not forgive the prank he had played on her. His, she suspected, was a sadly unstable nature, all very well for drawing-room manners, but nothing upon which to base an admiration. Anna sighed, turning away from the window. She meant, with every inch of her determination, to do her duty, but, oh, if only Oliver Molineux weren't such a pompous bore.

Chapter Four

Lacking any other occupation, Anna dressed early for dinner and took up a lit taper to make her way to the music room. But either she had misunderstood Betty's directions or else she missed her way along the gloomy regions of the house. Being Tudor, it was of course rambling in construction and prone to odd corners. Anna held her candle higher and saw she was walking into an area swathed with dust. The dim light from her taper reflected off the somber, jeweled hues of an enormous tapestry spanning the length of the wall. She paused there, enraptured by its scene of medieval valor, and for a moment forgot her vexation at having missed her way. It was so beautiful; why on earth had it been left to fade with neglect in this abandoned part of the house?

A faint thump from behind the tapestry startled her. It had been too loud to be a mouse; at least she devoutly hoped so as she drew up her skirts from the floor. She lifted the candle again, trying to raise her courage enough to peer behind the tapestry. That was when she noticed the shape outlined behind it . . . a *large* shape.

She lowered the candle so swiftly the flame nearly guttered out. Anna held her breath a moment, pressing her book of music against her bosom. 'Who's there?' she called, none too steadily.

No one answered her, but the shape began to ease cautiously away. Her brows coming together, Anna stepped forward.

'Who are you? What are you doing behind there?' Still no answer was given. Anna grew impatient and laid down her music upon a hall chair. If Neddie had recovered enough to stalk her through the house . . . if he *dared* . . . With sudden resolution she hurried to the opposite end of the tapestry and flung it back, only to gasp as the candlelight fell on the equally startled countenance of a man she did not know.

The dust fogged up from the hanging, and she sneezed violently, stepping back in confusion. 'Forgive me, sir! I . . . but who are you?'

He made no reply, his widened blue eyes still staring straight at her as though he were frozen. She realized now that he was elderly, stooped, and rather thin. He wore a silk dressing gown of brilliant crimson with morocco slippers upon his feet, one of which was twisted. But he was a remarkably handsome man, his face unlined, and gossamer strands of white hair hung over his high forehead.

'I'm sorry,' she said more gently when he went on standing there, his chest heaving. She tried a smile. 'I see I have startled you beyond measure. Do please forgive me, sir. I am Anna Temple-ton, Lady Riddell's granddaughter. Are you—'

'Don't tell Kelby,' he said in a swift, high-pitched voice, quite out of breath. 'Don't tell Kelby!'

'No, if you do not wish it,' she said, completely at a loss. 'But won't you come out from behind there, sir? You are getting frightfully dirty.'

He obeyed, the fright in his eyes being replaced by contriteness. 'I'm sorry. But don't tell Kelby.'

'Is he your valet?'

The gentleman gave a wary nod and watched her rather fearfully.

'He sounds like a perfect tyrant,' she said. 'Here is my handker-chief. You can dust off your sleeve, and this odious Kelby need never know that you've been hiding in the passageway.'

He took the square of cambric and stood holding it as though not having the least comprehension of what to do with it. Anna frowned. She knew enough about gentlemen to know he was not foxed, but what was the matter with him? He was the most peculiar man she had ever met. It was almost as though he were a none-too-bright child . . . She caught her breath and looked at him sharply.

'Are you . . . ' She had to pause and swallow in order to keep her voice steady. 'Are you the earl?'

He nodded, putting his hands over his face to peep out from between his fingers. 'I am Percy. Come and see!' Impulsively he seized her free hand and with a strength that alarmed her, pulled her through a nearby doorway.

Rather frightened, she started to struggle, but he was already releasing her hand.

'See?' he said proudly and pointed.

She was ready to pick up her skirts and flee, but she found herself faced with a portrait of three children, all black-haired, blue-eyed, and laughing vivaciously. The earl stood only inches away from the painting, gazing at it raptly.

'That's me!' he said, pointing a finger that quivered in his excitement. 'And that is Edwin. And that is Louisa.'

Curiosity moved Anna closer. So that was Neddie's father. How strange that Neddie did not appear to resemble him in the least. And the tall young girl must be Molineux's mama. Yes, there was some of his steel in her eye. But as for the earl as a youth . . . how merry, how sprightly he looked. This had been painted, then, before his accident. A chill coursed down Anna's spine, and she knew the first stirrings of pity.

Lord Riddell's lower lip began to quiver. 'I never see them now. They never come. They are mean!'

To her distress he began to cry, his frail shoulders shaking.

'No, please! Do not cry,' she said in some helplessness. 'They don't wish to be unkind. They . . . they are dead.'

'I know,' he said, choking down a sob and making no move to wipe the tears streaking his face. 'But they could still come. They could if they wished to. Even Amelia left me. Only Victor likes me now. Only Victor comes.'

Compressing her lips, Anna dabbed his face dry with her handkerchief. 'Yes, I'm sure Victor is quite a special friend. And you must think of me as a friend, too, Uncle Percy.' The name stuck in her throat, but she made herself say it as normally as possible. Gently she took one of his trembling hands between hers. His fingers were icy cold. 'I am Anna. Can you remember my name?'

'Anna,' he said slowly, sniffing. After a moment the bewildered grief cleared from his blue eyes. 'Anna,' he said more firmly. 'You are pretty.'

She laughed, charmed in spite of his tragic affliction. 'Thank you, sir! But are you not growing cold? I am. And my candle has not much life left to it. Let us go back.'

He stiffened, turning pale. 'Not to Kelby! No! No!'

She held fast to his frantic hand. 'To the drawing room, Uncle Percy. Let us go there. You know the one. It is hung in crimson with clouds painted on the ceiling.'

He looked puzzled. 'Is it Christmas? I go out at Christmas. Victor gives me candy.' He smacked his lips.

40

Anna tried not to give way to distraction. How long had she been here? Surely by now she would be missed for dinner. Summoning her patience, she said, 'It is not many days until Christmas. But tonight is special, because you have met me. Come along, *please*, Uncle Percy.'

To her relief, he did come, hobbling awkwardly along on his crippled leg. She was concerned about finding her way back to some portion of the house that she recognized, but she need not have worried. For when she faltered, Lord Riddell chose the way, and sooner than she expected they were back in the main part of the house. The first person they encountered was Dobbs, who fairly stared.

'Good heavens!' he said, the dignity of his position forgotten. 'Miss Anna! My . . . my lord!'

The earl shrank nearer to Anna, and she pressed his cold hand reassuringly.

'Hello, Dobbs,' she said, sensing the tremors in her uncle, and suddenly knew a fierce protectiveness toward him. It was not right that he should be so fearful, not in his own house. Was he mistreated? Her gray eyes challenged the butler. 'Have I missed dinner?'

'No, indeed. The family, however, has been anxious to know what has become of you, Miss Anna. Especially when Mr Kelby brought word that his lordship had escaped.' Dobbs's stern gaze bore down upon the earl, whose lip began to tremble.

'Not escaped,' said Anna sharply. 'You will not use that word, Dobbs. His lordship left his rooms for a while. And why shouldn't he?' Her chin came up. 'It is his house. Come, Uncle Percy.' And rather haughtily she escorted the earl on by, leaving Dobbs to stare after them in the greatest astonishment.

'I am afraid, Anna,' whispered the earl, his hand nearly crushing hers. 'I'm hungry. I want . . . ' He frowned. 'I'm tired.'

'Yes, of course you are,' she said soothingly and paused at the drawing-room doors to smooth back his fine hair and shake the dust from his sleeve. 'Now here we are. And you need not be afraid.'

Drawing a deep breath, she took his hand and led him inside, only to halt in dismay as the conversation faltered and all eyes turned to stare. There was Neddie with his hair curling over his bandage, and Molineux, rising from his chair with a frown, Papa with his finger in a book, Mr Murvey, Aunt Beatrice, and . . . good heavens! Anna gasped, unable not to stare at the elderly woman sitting regally and straight in a chair with a stick in her bony, beringed hands, and a necklace of fabulous diamonds sparkling at her withered throat. Her carefully dressed hair was snowy white and thin, her cheeks gaunt, her once handsome looks faded, but her gray eyes held steel and they were piercing Anna through this very moment.

Anna's cheeks colored before this silent, censorious group, and she knew not where or how to look, save defiantly.

'Mama!' said Percy, suddenly brightening. He dropped Anna's hand and hobbled awkwardly to the countess, who unsmilingly held out a hand for him to clutch. 'Mama!' he said, smiling. 'Anna is my friend. Where is Victor?'

'His grace did not come tonight, Percy,' she said in a precise, stately way. If cracked with age, her voice nevertheless had lost none of its authority. Her eyes continued to bore through Anna while she spoke. 'I shall inform him you asked about him.' Then her gaze shifted to Molineux, and she gave a slight nod.

He crossed the room and pulled the bell.

An awkward silence fell over the room. Anna saw Neddie fidgeting, unable to look at his uncle, and longed to make him see there was nothing to be repulsed about if one took Percy on his own terms. But the formidable eye of her grandmother was still locked upon her, pinning her to a helpless silence. Mr Templeton, however, was not so quelled.

'Well, my lord,' he said, laying aside his book and standing up to face the earl. He gave his little cough and smiled rather dryly. 'I am Walter Templeton, sir, the man who eloped with your sister Amelia.'

Percy frowned at him a moment, then gave his head a vague rub. 'I'm tired,' he said plaintively. 'Amelia never comes anymore.'

Lady Riddell's eyes closed momentarily, but she betrayed no other sign of emotion. 'Come and sit down, Percy,' she said.

He had just obeyed her when the door opened and a man in a black coat came hastening in, followed closely by two footmen. Lord Riddell saw them and began to cry, huddling in his chair with his hands over his face. Anna would have gone forward to comfort him, but the man in the black coat had already taken the earl's arm firmly.

'Forgive me, my lady,' he said in a quiet, low voice, his sallow face as expressionless as the countess' own.

'This is the third time this month, Kelby,' said Molineux.

'Yes, sir, I'm sorry. It's Christmas that upsets him. Come along now, your lordship.'

'I don't want to go. I don't want to go,' cried Percy, but he gave no struggle as he was led out. He looked gray with exhaustion.

When he was gone there was a collective sigh about the room. Mr Templeton pursed his lips and sat down, folding away his spectacles as he did so.

Lady Riddell's stern gray eyes lifted once again to regard Anna. 'Well, girl,' she said sharply. 'I can see you don't scruple to make a dramatic push to bring yourself to notice.'

Anna's eyes widened at this injustice. 'Forgive me, Grandmama,' she said in a less than conciliatory tone, scornful of all their closed faces. 'But I fear my scruples do not permit me to leave my uncle cowering fearfully in a dark passage.'

Lady Riddell sniffed. 'Impertinent baggage. I see your manners come from your father.' But there was some interest in her gaze thereafter whenever she chanced to glance Anna's way.

Dinner was a stiff affair. Many of the dishes had suffered from being held back, and conversation was stilted under the countess' haughty eye. Unlike many people of great age, she enjoyed a good appetite, and kept the daunted footmen hopping to serve her to her satisfaction. The diamonds clasped around her throat blazed in a myriad of fiery colors taken from the candlelight surrounding them. They quite eclipsed Lady Edwin's rubies, and Anna felt completely underdressed in her modest strand of pearls. Only Neddie seemed impervious to the jewels which Lady Riddell wore so proudly. And if Rotham had spoken the truth about their being her ladyship's to dispense as she chose, little wonder the family was so attentive to her! The jewels should go to Neddie, of course, to be worn by his countess when he married, but Anna could not help but wonder what she would look like in such a necklace.

Pipe dreams, she told herself rather sternly as the ladies rose to withdraw from the table. Neddie, to his considerable chagrin, was

43

not permitted to remain for port and manly conversation. Shoving his hands into his pockets, he followed the ladies at a reluctant distance and refused tea in the drawing room.

'No, I thank you,' he said, scowling. 'I don't care to maudle my insides with the stuff.'

'Oh Neddie, dear, please,' implored Lady Edwin in some anguish.

The countess raised her brows. 'Your son exhibits deplorable manners, Beatrice. Edwin would have caned him for his insolence. Do you let the boy run wild now?'

Lady Edwin shrugged her pretty shoulders in a helpless way. 'I am sure it is better I do not tie him too closely to my apron strings, ma'am. And he has Oliver to emulate.'

Neddie snorted scornfully and flung himself away to one of the tall windows, to stand there fidgeting with the drapery fringe.

Lady Riddell chuckled quietly in her throat and her glance at Beatrice was somewhat contemptuous. 'So, girl,' she said, turning abruptly on Anna, who swallowed her mouthful of tea too hastily. 'Your name is Anna, is it? How do you propose to recommend yourself to me?'

Anna met those formidable eyes directly, refusing to be cowed. 'I must be what I am, my lady, and hope I thus meet your approval.'

Lady Riddell's eyes narrowed. 'Well said. Beatrice, I wish you will not wear that cap again.'

Lady Edwin's hand flew up to adjust the modish scrap of lace pinned to her burnished curls. 'But, ma'am, it is all the kick in London.'

'It looks ridiculous.' Lady Riddell's nostrils curled. 'I detest it.'

Lady Edwin nodded unhappily and at once reached up to remove the offending article. The countess chuckled, and Beatrice smiled, hopeful that at last she had pleased. Anna glanced away, her hands folded tightly together.

At last the gentlemen joined them, without Mr Templeton, however. Lady Riddell looked so scornful of this defection, Anna burned to point out his ill health, but the opportunity was not granted her.

'Neddie, dear,' said Lady Edwin as her son came to throw himself down upon a sofa beside Anna. 'You are looking pulled. I think you've had enough of an evening—'

'Devil a bit,' he said at once, sitting more erectly. 'I mean to—'

'Edwin!' said Molineux sharply. 'Your mother has dismissed you. Go!'

Neddie came to his feet at once, flushing with fists clenched. 'Blast you, Mollie! Leave your nose out of my affairs!'

'Oh, Neddie!' exclaimed his mama, but neither of them paid her the least heed as they stood glaring tight-lipped at one another.

Anna gently laid a hand upon Neddie's rigid arm. 'Neddie,' she said in her calmest way. 'Remember you promised me an outing in the morning. Do go to bed so we can make an early start.'

Unwillingly he turned his blazing eyes from Molineux's and stared down at her as though he would lash out at her, too. Then he bit his lip, the crimson staining his cheeks darker, and let the tension ease from his younger body. 'I'm sorry, Anna,' he said in a low, constrained voice. 'But you do see—'

'Yes. Very well.' She gave him a nod, and with a parting glare at Molineux, Neddie strode out.

Molineux let his angry gaze rest upon Anna for a moment, then he glanced at Beatrice. 'The young cawker needs more than a set-down. He requires instruction from a strap to his back.'

Lady Edwin began to weep into her handkerchief. 'Oh, pray do not dislike him so, Oliver! I shall speak to him. I promise you he will curb his insolence.'

'He had better.' Molineux clasped his hands at his back and walked across the room to the fire. 'Damned whelp.'

'Oliver,' said the countess rather sharply. 'You will please remember you speak of the future Earl of Riddell.'

Molineux whirled as though stung, but his eyes were caught by Lady Edwin's pleading ones, and after a moment he bowed to his grandmother. 'Of course, my lady. Forgive me.'

'Certainly.' Leaning heavily on her cane, Lady Riddell rose to her feet. 'I've had enough. Good-night.'

Mr Murvey hastened to open the door for her and to summon the footman James to escort her upstairs.

Lady Edwin wrung her handkerchief between her hands, her blue eyes glistening in anger. 'Percy ought to be locked up in Bedlam where he belongs. I am persuaded he caused Neddie to misbehave. You know, Oliver, that Neddie is afraid of him. He cannot be held responsible for—'

'By God, Beatrice, he had better learn to be responsible!'

Molineux gestured, his brown eyes ablaze. 'That brat is no more fit to be earl than is Percy. You delude yourself into thinking otherwise.'

She shrank back before his vehemence. 'Don't say such odious things, *pray*! He will steady under responsibility, Oliver. I assure you.'

Molineux snorted. 'You can assure me of nothing.' He nodded at Anna, who sat shocked by this quarrel. 'Even she is cleverer than you! She knows better than to shrink from Percy in Grandmama's presence. And don't think that Lady Riddell did not notice your squirming this evening, for I promise you she did. You are a fool, Beatrice.'

'Oliver—'

Anna rose abruptly to her feet, not bothering to conceal her annoyance. 'Please excuse me,' she said as they paused to stare at her. 'You may brangle better without me, I think. Good-night.'

Molineux started to block her path, but when she met his frown rather coolly, he stepped aside with a slight bow. 'Forgive me. Once you understand the facts—'

'I understand the rules of common civility, Mr Molineux,' said Anna tartly. 'That is sufficient.' She stepped around him and went upstairs to bed, determined that should he not soon show himself to her in a better light she would get herself employment as a governess to support her father rather than ally herself to a man she was growing to respect less and less.

Neddie did find a better mount for her, and in the morning they set off for a spanking gallop, sending chunks of turf flying, and gasping in exhilaration from the sharpness of the winter air. It began to snow lightly, but aside from the small sting of snowflakes flying into her eyes, Anna cared not a snap for the weather as she followed Neddie over the hill, dale, hedge, and wall, her mount lathering and warming her from the work of his muscles. Anna threw back her head and let the wind cut her face. It was marvelous. She could go on thundering across the countryside forever.

But at last they crested a rise, alarming a flock of partridges, and Neddie drew his mount to a snorting, foaming halt. Anna stopped beside him, laughing breathlessly, and sought to straighten her hat.

'Look,' said Neddie, pointing with his crop.

She gazed across the meadow, her laughter fading as the scene grew upon her attention. On a knoll before her stood a house – oh, not a grim stone structure like Farrowsleigh – but a house with the grace of an ancient temple. It was not fashioned with the quaint little plaster rosettes and columns of the present style, built instead substantially of golden limestone, yet with a certain element of airiness as though the architect's hand had possessed a light touch. The central portion was domed and columned with tall Palladian windows, and two wings flanked it generously. Even in the gray merciless light of a snowy winter's day, it seemed to laugh at grimness and misery, its beauty shining like a promise.

Anna stared at it, lost in the sight. 'Oh, Neddie,' she whispered at last. 'How perfect.'

He broke the spell by kicking his mount forward. 'Come on.'

There was no need to ask whom it belonged to. She had guessed at the first moment. Now, however, she hung back when Neddie beckoned, torn between a deep longing to see the house more closely and a despair of encountering the owner again.

'Anna!' called Neddie impatiently over his shoulder. 'Do come on. We have been invited. You can't play missish now. Come on, or I shall leave you here alone.'

'Despicable boy.' She loosened her reins and let her horse follow him.

They joined the main carriage drive and trotted slowly up to the house along an avenue flanked by clipped yew hedge and Italian statues draped modestly in snow.

'How cold they look,' said Anna, deciding there was nothing for it but to throw herself into the spirit of this escapade and have done.

Neddie went into whoops. 'Jupiter, Anna, the things you do say,' he gasped at last and shook his head admiringly. 'There's nothing stiff-rumped about you.'

'Neddie,' she said in alarm. 'Don't you dare repeat my remark.'

St. Byre merely grinned at her and at the steps jumped down lightly from the saddle. He tossed his reins to a groom and waited while she dismounted with more decorum before escorting her into the house.

The hall was a vast area, surmounted by the dome which seemed to stretch upward forever. Its windows let in all kinds of light; there was not a gloomy corner to be seen. Anna glanced about as she removed her gloves, and began to smile.

'Hullo, Ponsby,' said Neddie carelessly to the butler who bowed with a smile of welcome. 'Is breakfast still laid? I'm starving.'

'Neddie!' said Anna, scandalized. 'You must not make yourself so freely at home.'

'Fudge.' He shrugged. 'I do so all the time. Victor!' A door had opened to reveal Rotham, attired in boots, breeches, and a velvet riding coat of the Petersham design. Neddie rushed to him. 'Good morning, sir! I'm so glad you're up and about this early. We've had a splendid ride over, and I'm famished.'

Rotham smiled lazily, swinging his quizzing glass between his long fingers. 'Yes, you always are. Well, Ponsby, take away the savage and feed him! Miss Templeton, I am honored indeed to see you.' He bowed. 'Will you also eat?'

'Watch out, Victor,' said Neddie, laughing. 'She means to stand on her propriety. But you should have heard what she said about the statues.'

Anna's cheeks grew hot. 'Neddie, I warn you!'

'Spare the lady's blushes and run along,' said Rotham with a smile. He patted Neddie on the shoulder and when the boy was gone, lifted a brow at Anna. 'What a wary expression you sport. Come into the library and make yourself comfortable by the fire. You may as well, you know. My cook dotes on the young scamp and will serve him a feast.'

She smiled perfunctorily. 'You are kind, sir, but I cannot be at my ease. We have no right to intrude on you in this helter-skelter way. I *must* stand on propriety.'

'Tut, my dear Miss Templeton.' He shook his quizzing glass at her. 'The boy runs tame here, always has. I assure you I do not regard it.'

'His custom may be very well for him, but it is far different for me,' she said, a frown creasing her brow as she twisted her crop in her hands.

He sighed. 'Yes, I daresay.' And some of the welcome seemed to dim in his face. 'But you are here now. Do try to make the best of it and come in to the fire. I am attending to my correspondence. Dull work, prodigiously so. I'm no good at letters.'

'Are you writing them, or reading them?' she asked, giving way at last and following him into a rectangular room, lined with books and lit by two tall windows.

'Oh, reading them! I never write . . . not a thing. Gad, I fear I can barely draw my name. And as for the labor in describing one's

48

day to someone miles away who has not the slightest interest in it, appalling, my dear ma'am, simply appalling.' He gave a mock shudder, waving her to a comfortable chair, and picked up a paper from the cluttered library table. 'And I fear the chore of reading these labors is hardly more edifying. Still, one is obliged to try. Will you have some refreshment? You look charming, by the way, with mud upon your cheek.'

She accepted some hot chocolate and wiped her face with her handkerchief, slowly relaxing by the fire as he frowned over a letter. She was glad for the chance to sit in silence, not overborne by polite conversation until she could get some of her composure back. It appeared he meant to make no reference to the matter of that dreadful horse. If so, then he was either callous enough not to care or else he had never meant to trick her at all and had forgotten his advice. She wished she could forget it as well.

Her eyes strayed to his tall, lean person as he stood by the window, reading through his quizzing glass. Thus illumined and momentarily in none of his usual foolish poses he made a striking figure, one whom a stranger would take to be a man of purpose and character. The way the light fell upon his cheekbone and jaw, the intent gaze of his light gray eyes as he read swiftly and without the difficulty he professed, and even the unconscious tapping of one foot upon the floor all drew her in some disquieting way she had never experienced before.

To distract herself, she tore her eyes away and studied the room instead, taking note of various busts of famous statesmen and philosophers grouped here and there on their plain marble pedestals. It was, moreover, a library which was used – unlike the musty, tomblike chamber at Farrowsleigh. The desk was covered with papers, inkpots, and books left open at various passages. More books were strewn about the room; several had been stacked on the floor near her chair. Anna balanced her cup and bent down to pick up the top volume. It was Voltaire – untranslated – with numerous observations scribbled tightly in the margins. The book below it was verse, and the last volume a reference work for Greek history.

Anna's lips curved slightly. If he read these, and indeed, who else would put the room into such appalling disorder, then he was neither a fool nor the fop he pretended to be. She wondered idly what her father would make of him.

'There!' he said, startling her by scooping up all the letters and dropping them on the fire, save one brief note, considerably smudged, which he folded thoughtfully. 'From Alicia, my daughter,' he said, catching her eye upon him. 'Are you shocked, Miss Templeton, that I have a daughter? So was I, for a time, but now I have grown used to it.' He looked pensively at the letter. 'Thank God this is short. Her hand is completely unformed. I cannot for the life of me comprehend this word, and she sets such store upon it. Look here.' He thrust it at Anna, pointing out the word, which was scrawled in a large, childish hand.

For a moment Anna stared at it blankly, then realized it was all in French and berated herself for letting her wits lay so scattered. 'Kitten,' she said.

'I beg your pardon?'

Anna smiled. 'She says she has a black kitten. *Chaton.*'

'By Jove, so 'tis.' He sniffed and put the letter in his pocket. 'I guessed château and could not in the least discern what she might be doing with a black castle in Lucerne. Children are so trying.' He smiled at himself, and inclined his fair head to Anna. 'Thank you. Now I shall send her congratulations on the acquisition of her little *bête noire.*' He laughed foolishly and walked over to the table to close one of the books lying there.

Anna stood up, sensing his constraint, yet aware that if she showed no curiosity he would know she had listened to gossip and despise her. 'Why does your daughter live in Switzerland, sir?' she asked with care.

He glanced at her rather sharply. 'It is the safest country in Europe with Napoleon haring about. I won't have her here.'

'Why not?' His lips tightened, and Anna dropped her eyes. 'Forgive me. I should not ask such personal questions.'

'No,' he said quietly. 'But I shall reply. My wife, Miss Templeton, killed herself five years ago.'

Anna gasped. Suicide was something . . . unspeakable, an irreparable stain to the survivors. Little wonder he kept his child away! She looked up slowly at him, to find him watching her, and her gray eyes involuntarily softened.

He raised a brow. 'You do not speak, Miss Templeton. Damme, I have given you a disgust of my company.'

'No!' She stretched out an impulsive hand. 'No. Grant me more intelligence and less sensibility, sir.'

'Should I?'

That checked her a moment, then she said, half laughing in exasperation, 'Yes, *indeed*.'

He smiled with some wryness. 'Very well.' And now his silvery eyes were no longer wary. 'Have you seen Lady Riddell yet, or does she still keep you dangling? Gad, a capricious woman could not keep pace with her, but sink me, she likes me, and in my gratitude I permit her the pleasure of my flattery.' He helped himself to snuff delicately and offered her his snuffbox, which she declined.

'Yes, I have met Grandmama,' she said, her eyes beginning to twinkle. 'And under the most outstanding circumstances. If she was disposed to take me in dislike, I fear her opinion must now be quite confirmed.'

He sat down. 'Ah! You fascinate me. Tell all, dear lady.'

More than willing to take their conversation far away from his pitiable wife, Anna told him of her adventure. 'And poor Uncle Percy! He seems wretchedly terrified of his servant. I hope he is not mistreated. But I quite wished to sink through the floor when I walked in and saw them all staring at me – Grandmama especially, and in those diamonds, too. I am sure she thinks me a miscreant, for dinner was completely ruined and I answered her impertinently.' Anna grew a bit wistful and sighed. 'I fear it is proving harder to be conformable than I imagined.'

'Dear me, it always is.' He smiled lazily. 'That's why I never am.'

'Oh, you!' She sniffed, daring at last to pay him back in his own coin. 'You are shamming, sir!' His brows flew up, and she could repress her smile no longer. 'You should never have brought me into your book room, to let me see what you read.'

He lolled back in his chair, twirling his quizzing glass. 'Alas.'

'Indeed. A shocking fibster.'

He draped a hand over his eyes. 'Your accusations, ma'am, are too harsh. I have no reply, save to admit guilt. Gad's life, I am so blue I must posture or be drummed out of society.'

She gasped. 'Now that, your grace, is coming it far too strong. I warn you to make no such statement in my father's hearing, or he will have you recite Catullus in the original.'

'In the original what?' he asked so innocently a gurgle of laughter escaped her.

'Latin, sir.'

'Dear God!' He got to his feet. 'Would he really?'

'Oh, yes. I am not hoaxing you. Catullus is his measuring rod of all those he encounters.'

'Perhaps I'd better learn a passage. Is this Roman poet a naughty fellow?' Rotham opened a bookcase door and studied the titles within vaguely. After a moment he gave up the search. 'Greer will find it if we have it. Greer,' he added with a twitch of his lips, 'is my scribe. Faithful as Argos.' He regarded her a moment, then said, 'It is his efforts you see scattered about. I barely know which end of a book to read first. Word of a duke.'

Her brows came up. 'And my father never reads verse. Really, your grace, do stop trying to pull the wool over my eyes.'

'And what prodigiously pretty eyes they are, too.' He bowed. 'I concede you are too clever for me, Miss Templeton. I shall learn a poem by this Roman fellow, to entertain you at our next meeting.'

She smiled. 'I shall look forward to hearing your grace's efforts.'

He brought up his quizzing glass. 'Do you know? I believe we have quite chased away that frown from your eyes. Good! You should never be serious, Miss Templeton. When you laugh you are quite . . . striking.'

Something intent in his gaze as well as his words brought up the warmth into her cheeks. She rose to her feet, fighting to hold on to her composure. 'And a shocking flirt as well.'

'I am not flirting, Miss Templeton,' he said.

With a rush of confusion, she believed him. 'I . . . ' She swallowed with difficulty and snatched at her only straw. 'You forget, sir, that I am nearly betrothed.'

His brows came up and he dared smile. 'I haven't forgotten, Miss Templeton. But may I venture to suggest that sometimes . . . you do?'

Her eyes flashed at that, and she was about to deliver a blistering retort when the door flew open, and Neddie burst in with a striped lurcher bounding at his heels.

'I say, sir!' he said, his blue eyes glowing. 'Where did you get such a bang-up dog?'

The lurcher halted by Anna to give her skirts a polite sniff, then sprang over to sit down in front of the duke, his powerful body quivering joyfully, his long tongue lolling out.

'Yes, I see that you are here, Festus,' said Rotham aloofly, but smiled when the dog put a foot upon his booted leg. 'Very well, you incurable beggar.' He petted the animal, laughing at its yawn of delight. 'I won him, Neddie. Imagine bringing home a puppy in my pocket instead of the jingle.'

Neddie looked up in quick disbelief. 'Fudge. You never win at cards.'

'Dice, dear boy, dice.' Rotham flicked his wrist and smiled. 'Now *that* I have the knack of. Festus, be quiet, you brutish fellow. Miss Templeton—'

'I think,' she said rather tightly, 'that we had better go, Neddie. We cannot spend the entire morning plaguing his grace.'

'You may stay for luncheon,' said Rotham, holding Festus by the collar.

Neddie brightened, but Anna shook her head firmly.

'We must decline. Thank you. Come, Neddie.' She turned to gather her hat, crop, and gloves, but Neddie lingered.

'Shall I see you tomorrow, Victor?' he asked in hope. 'You must come to dinner. I'll ask Grandmama to invite you.'

'No need,' said Rotham, putting a hand on the boy's shoulder. 'I have my invitation.' His eyes turned to Anna. 'Ma'am, I shall be going to the village this afternoon if the snow stops. Have you any errand I may perform for you?'

She refused this offer of service and extended a stiff hand for him to bow over. 'Good-day, your grace.'

In a few minutes their horses were brought around, and they rode away into the cold, the snow falling more thickly than ever, and Anna's heart a whirlwind of confusion.

How dared he say such a thing to her? His effrontery knew no bounds, and even if it was true that she was increasingly eager not to consider her betrothal, Rotham still had no right to point this out to her. He might go to the devil before she would let him trifle with her affections! She had promised her father she would wed Oliver Molineux. She could not, in all honor, look elsewhere or even wish to do so. Why must Rotham delight in oversetting her? He had spoiled all her pleasure in his company and yet . . .

'Does his grace come often to dine?' she asked, despising herself but unable to hold back the question.

'Oh, yes,' said Neddie, squinting against the snow. He pulled his hat lower to shield his face. 'Grandmama dotes on his company. I wish you would not cut up so stiff around him, Anna. He doesn't stand on ceremony, you know. Mama says he has the easiest manners of any duke, and that's something.' Neddie laughed, slapping at the snow graying his horse's mane. 'Lord! You'd think Mollie was the duke, wouldn't you?' Then Neddie's blue eyes hardened in a way that gave Anna pause. 'I'd give anything to be able to land him a facer. He has no right . . . Well, just let him watch out, that's all. When Percy dies, I shall take the greatest satisfaction in putting Mollie out on his ear.' He shot a swift look at her. 'You are not to repeat that, Anna!'

'I am no tale-bearer,' she said coolly.

'No, I daresay not, but after all, you're to marry him. Have I your word, Anna?' Neddie's eyes looked suddenly frightened. 'He is my enemy.'

Anna frowned. 'I wish you would not say so.'

'It's true! Promise me, please.'

She relented. 'Of course you have my word, Neddie. I won't betray you. But try for a little patience, I beg you. He is someone you should look to for guidance.'

'I'd as lief turn to a captain-sharp,' said Neddie through his teeth and met her look of reproach defiantly. 'You don't know what he is, Anna.'

She glanced ahead, growing thoughtful. 'Perhaps not.' Suddenly she hated the sight of Farrowsleigh, rising up before her, and longed to be back in that spacious book room at Chevely Hall, laughing over spirited banter with a good fire going and the smell of mellow chocolate wafting over the scent of calf-bound books. What would they discuss today at luncheon? Turnips? She sighed. 'Neddie, please, *please* don't hate Cousin Molineux so much! You make it hard for me, and I fear my resolution fails me too often as it is.'

Neddie reached out to put a hand over hers that was gripping the reins far too tightly. 'Don't marry him, Anna! When I am earl, I shall see you provided for.'

'Oh, Neddie—' She looked swiftly at him, her eyes filling with tears. 'Thank you. But I must. I *must*. Papa's illness will not wait until you are earl and in control of your interests.'

'Do you mean his cough?' Neddie frowned, looking rather startled. 'But that does not seem so—' He broke off as he met her agonized gaze.

Her tears spilled over before she could stop them. She raised a hand to wipe them aside lest they freeze upon her face.

'Jupiter, Anna,' he said, his blue eyes wide. 'I am sorry. I'll try to be good if it will help. I'll . . . I'll do anything you want,' he said fiercely.

'How splendid you are,' she said, touched to the heart by this avowal of support. Somehow she found a smile to give him. 'Thank you, Neddie. That means more than you know.'

Chapter Five

By the time they returned to the house she had recovered herself, and it was as well, for Lady Edwin came to her rooms while she was changing out of her riding habit.

'Her ladyship has sent for us,' she said, trying, not very successfully, to conceal her excitement. 'We are to come at once, if you are ready. How prettily that shade of green becomes you! I should have been utterly frozen from a ride on a day like this. You are the most hardy child.'

'Yes, I have never been in the habit of mollycoddling myself,' replied Anna, taking up a lawn handkerchief as she accompanied her aunt out.

'Of course, I do hope you have not encouraged Neddie to harm himself by so vigorous an exercise,' said Lady Edwin, her eyes looking up at Anna from beneath thick lashes.

'Nonsense,' said Anna, returning her gaze in a direct way. 'He is perfectly fit.'

'He has never been robust.' Lady Edwin's eyes grew just a trifle cool.

Anna sighed and sought to turn the subject. 'Why does Grandmama wish to see us?'

Lady Edwin shrugged gracefully. 'Well, she has yet to receive you, hasn't she? But for my own part I confess I am agog to see if she means to give me the diamonds. I have been devoted to her always, and especially after my husband died.' She sighed, clasping her hands to her shapely bosom. 'And they are beautiful, aren't they? I fancy I do not delude myself when I say I have kept my looks, and only imagine the sensation I should excite were I to appear at Almack's wearing them. There would not be a gentleman present who would not be anxious, nay, desperate to attach himself to my side.' A smile played around her lips, but Anna was privately very much shocked and made no comment. After a moment her aunt looked at her and laughed in a low ripple of silvery notes. 'Oh, dear. I can just see you thinking what a *brassy* creature I am. But when Neddie becomes earl, I must think of myself again. It could not be right for me to remain a widow all my life.'

'No, of course not,' said Anna.

Her aunt laughed again. 'What a sobersides you are! I expect you are terrified of her ladyship, but no more than I. She never fails to cast me into a quake. And last night I was ready to sink when Neddie exhibited that shocking display of misbehaviour before her. She need not think it *my* fault. He is as headstrong as his father.' She broke off rather abruptly. 'Well, here we are.'

A somberly gowned womanservant admitted them into a large sitting room, decorated with heavy furniture and dark hangings. There were a few sporting scenes on the walls, but nothing of a lively nature. Here, they were obliged to sit down and wait for nearly a quarter of an hour. Then Mrs West came out of the bedchamber and curtsied.

'Her ladyship will see you now, Miss Anna.'

Anna rose at once, and with her Lady Edwin.

Mrs West shook her head. 'Only Miss Anna today, my lady.'

'But I—'

'I am sorry, my lady.'

Mrs West, tiny in her starched apron and carefully pinned hair, faced Lady Edwin regretfully but firmly. Chagrin sparked crimson in Lady Edwin's lovely cheeks. She stood there rigidly for a moment while Anna longed for some way to ease her embarrassment.

'I see,' Lady Edwin said clearly. 'I see quite well!' Turning with a rustle of her silk petticoats, she swept out, Mrs West trotting apologetically after her.

Anna drew in a deep breath and walked into the bedchamber. It, too, was furnished in masculine style, mostly in gold and scarlet. The bed quite eclipsed Anna's, being larger and more fantastically made, with a gilded eagle atop it, clutching the velvet hangings in its beak. Anna blinked at it, suddenly smitten with the urge to laugh. The Riddell crest was emblazoned at the head of the bed, and paneling similar to that in Anna's chamber bordered the fireplace. She realized these must be the traditional rooms of the Earl of Riddell, which had not been relinquished to Uncle Percy. And . . . was it possible that she now slept in what had been the countess' room?

She looked at her grandmother, seated in a chair by the fire in formidable puce satin, and curtsied low.

'Gawked enough, have you?' The countess beckoned with one bony hand. 'Come here, girl.' When Anna obeyed, she pointed to a portrait hanging over the mantelpiece. 'Your grandfather. Gawk at him if you like.'

Anna stepped nearer, gazing up at the stern visage of a gentleman in a black periwig. His coat was cloth-of-gold, and an enormous emerald winked from the lacy folds of his shirt front. He had not smiled for the painter, but there was something in the eyes which glinted suspiciously like a twinkle. Anna forgot her nervousness and smiled at her grandmother.

'I would have liked him.'

'Poppycock!' said the countess with a sniff. 'He had a notorious temper.'

'His eyes smile.'

The countess' gaze swung up to Anna's with frank surprise. Abruptly she nodded. 'You'll do. Come and sit down. Where have you been all morning? I am not accustomed to being kept waiting.'

Anna's smile dimmed. She sat down and stared at her hands. 'Riding.'

'Where?'

It was pointless to attempt evasion. 'Neddie and I visited Chevely Hall.'

'So! Not only are you impertinent, you are full of brass as well. Your mother was the same. As,' added the countess with an involuntary smile, 'was I in my salad days.' Her eyes pierced Anna. 'Farrow women have spirit. Thank God the Templeton blood has not watered that out of you. Moreover, you are no widgeon. I am grateful to you for finding Percy. Sometimes it is most difficult to corner him, and he falls ill readily from these escapades. This time, however, he is quite unharmed.'

Anna inclined her head.

'I have no patience with those who fear him. Fear Percy.' The countess snorted. 'Beatrice is an idiot, and her son is little better. But you . . . I depend on you, Anna, to look after Percy if he outlives me.'

Anna looked up quickly, remembering the remarks of last night.

'I would not send him to Bedlam, Grandmama.'

'Thank you.' Lady Riddell looked away, but betrayed no other sign of emotion. 'He was not born this way. Some members of the family have tried to take away the title from him, but it is his and it will remain his.' Her expression grew fierce once more, and she frowned. 'Why do you wear that paltry strand of pearls? They make you look insipid. Where are Amelia's jewels, the ones she took with her?'

'She sold them, my lady.'

'For what purpose?'

Anna met those furious eyes as straightly as she could. 'I am not at liberty to discuss my parents' private affairs with you, ma'am.'

'Indeed?' Lady Riddell's tone turned glacial. 'And whom do you discuss them with? No.' She held up a hand to stop Anna's spirited reply. 'Let us not draw daggers. Go to my dressing table and open the box there.'

Compressing her lips in the hope this was not yet another test of her mettle, Anna did so and gasped at the blazing wealth of jewels within.

'Well?' demanded Lady Riddell. 'Don't stand there like a gapeseed. Choose what you desire.'

Anna whirled, white. 'I could not!'

'Why not?' Lady Riddell's brows drew together. 'Swallow that wretched pride, girl! You will take a dowry of twenty thousand pounds, but not a trinket? Bah!' But she had begun to smile, as though against her will, and said more kindly, 'Please. I wish to make you a gift.'

Unbending, Anna smiled back and suddenly rushed to press her lips to the withered cheek. 'You are so good to me, so kind!'

Lady Riddell sniffed, but she did not look displeased. 'Choose! All you like.'

Anna flew back to the jewel box, her heart hammering with excitement, and at length chose an emerald necklace and diamond ear drops.

The countess nodded approvingly. 'Exquisite. I see you think of what is the most becoming rather than what is the most valuable. Take the topaz necklace too. It will match your coloring. Go ahead. I have no need of it.'

Anna held the necklace against her throat, marveling at how it brought out the golden flecks in her dark eyes. 'It's lovely,' she said with a sigh.

'You must always wear jewels,' said the countess with decision. 'And find a better dressmaker. With your height and looks, you should dress to distinction.'

Anna tried to hold back her mirth, but it gurgled out in spite of her. 'Forgive me, ma'am,' she said unsteadily. 'I sew my dresses.'

There was a moment of profound silence.

'Good God,' said her ladyship at last, frankly horrified. 'And what else has Walter Templeton had you do? Scrub pots?'

'N-no,' gasped Anna, trying her best not to go into whoops. 'I assure you, I have had a proper upbringing.'

'Shabby-genteel,' snapped the countess. 'My granddaughter does *not* wear homemade garments. It is quite beyond the pale of what I will allow. Give your measurements at once to the village dressmaker. She is not to London standards, but she will do for this emergency.'

Anna sighed, but not without a smile. 'I fear, Grandmama, that you are sadly undermining all my notions of pride and independence.'

The countess snorted. 'It is your duty to look your best. I brook no shabbiness.'

'Yes, Grandmama,' said Anna meekly, keeping her eyes down.

'And if you are laughing at me, you need not,' said her ladyship sharply. 'You are no longer merely a tutor's daughter. In this community, you are a young lady of considerable consequence. I will not have you snubbed by mushrooms as an obscure miss. And when you go to London—'

'London!'

Lady Riddell smiled tightly. 'Oliver's interests are not solely confined to managing this estate. He is quite a man about town, as by now you should have realized. If you wish to be worthy of him, you will heed my advice and make a push to please his eye.'

'Of . . . of course.'

'He is compliant to my wishes,' continued the countess, 'but he does have a will of his own. Your betrothal cannot be considered binding until he makes a formal offer.'

'I understand,' said Anna quietly.

'I hope you do,' said the countess significantly. 'Perhaps I should not say this, but when you came I had decided to abandon my idea of having the two of you marry. I confess I had doubts regarding your suitability and meant to award you a competence and send you away. But, Anna, I was most impressed with your mettle last night. You are not repulsed by Percy to an undue length and you know how to govern yourself in a reasonable way. You will make Oliver an admirable wife should he decide to recognize your merits.'

Anna looked away quickly. 'Thank you, Grandmama,' she said in a flat voice, unable to bring herself to speak further. If only she had never found Uncle Percy!

Shortly thereafter Lady Riddell dismissed her, and by the time luncheon concluded the snow had stopped falling. Anna watched her father accept Mr Murvey's challenge to chess and knew she could not endure Oliver Molineux's company for the afternoon. Her composure was so thin she was certain she would blurt out something ruinous.

Lady Edwin – whose absence from luncheon had been pointed – sent down a message declining to go with Anna to the village, but Neddie agreed and dashed off to get his hat. Anna turned to Molineux with some constraint.

'Of course we would be delighted for your company, Cousin.'

He shrugged. 'Shopping for feminine furbelows is not to my taste, I fear. Will you forgive me if I decline your company this time? I have been outdoors all morning and, unlike you, do not care to brave the cold again.'

'Very well,' she said coolly and left him to don her bonnet and pelisse. It was a relief to know she might depend upon being left to her own devices, but she was piqued as well. Molineux was far too indifferent to her. He knew she would marry him for money, and he was just conceited enough to put no romantic overtones on a most cut-and-dried business. Certainly this suited her. She had no desire to suffer his attentions.

She and Neddie set out in the countess' closed carriage behind a good pair of bays, and once he found out he was to have an afternoon's complete freedom, Neddie brightened considerably and called her a good 'un.

'Thank you . . . I think,' she said, her frown clearing as she her troubled thoughts aside. 'Do you need a loan?'

'Devil a bit,' he said cheerfully. 'I'm quite plump in the pocket just now, on account of Christmas, you know.'

'Why, yes. I'd forgotten just how near it is.' Anna reached into her reticule and felt of her two carefully hoarded guineas. She was not quite sure if she knew how to comport herself like an heiress.

The carriage deposited them in front of the linen-draper's shop.

Neddie looked at it and shook his head. 'Deuce of a place to spend all your time in. I'm off.'

She let him go with a smile, noting his attempt to imitate the walk of a town buck. Before she could enter the shop, however, a familiar voice hailed her.

'Sink me, but is it not Miss Templeton?'

He was astride a deep-chested gray and swept her a bow from the saddle. 'Charmed, my dear ma'am. Now I see why you declined my assistance. Your errand involves more than a man on horseback could carry.'

'Good afternoon, your grace.' Anna saw glances of passersby being turned their way and colored. 'Do, pray, let us not talk in the street.'

'Ever to oblige.' He dismounted with easy grace and summoned an urchin to hold his horse before offering Anna his arm and escorting her into the shop with the manner of being delighted to do so. 'What is our quarry, ma'am?' he inquired, nodding at the proprietor, who hastened forth to greet them. 'Ribbons? Trimming?'

She drew him aside, suddenly thankful for his presence despite her previous annoyance with him. 'Grandmama says I must have better clothes. I have not Aunt Beatrice for advice on what is the newest fashion, and I hardly know how to begin—'

'What?' He raised his brows. 'A lady in perplexity over a new dress? How extraordinary you are, to be sure.'

He looked serious, but she decided he was roasting her and replied in kind:

'Yes, but you forget I am very blue.'

'Gad, so you are.' He appeared much struck and promptly turned to snap his fingers at the proprietor. 'Tell me, Mr

Smyth. What happened to that charming young woman who used to work here? Does she still sew? Or has she gone to London to open shop?'

'Oh, indeed, your grace,' said Smyth with a bow. He smiled and puffed out his chest a bit. 'In fact, your grace, I married her.'

'Ah,' said Rotham, enlightened. 'Congratulations! But has she retired her needle?'

'Well, your grace, not for certain *valued* customers.'

'Splendid!' Rotham helped himself to snuff. 'Miss Templeton finds herself in need of some new gowns rather, er, unexpectedly. The holidays, you know. And if Mrs Smyth would be so obliging—'

'Yes, your grace! I'm sure of it. With your leave I'll run and fetch her now.' Bowing, beaming, breathless, Smyth hastened out without his hat or greatcoat.

'Dear me,' said Rotham, flicking shut his ornate snuffbox and pocketing it before the awed eyes of the remaining clerk. 'It appears we have caused a furor. Well, Miss Templeton, let us not be idle. My good fellow,' he said to the clerk, beckoning with his quizzing glass. 'Be so good as to bring Miss Templeton a chair and some cloth to look at.'

In short order Anna found herself surrounded by silks and satins that defied description. Velvets enticed her. Sarcenets shimmered before her dazzled eyes. Delicate cambric and muslins enchanted her. Overwhelmed, she had just chosen a length of pink satin when the Smyths returned. Mrs Smyth proved to be a petite, comely woman, with a rounded figure, a pretty ankle, and a shrewd eye. She curtsied to Rotham and shook her head at the pink satin.

'It would do,' she said, 'but if miss wishes distinction—'

'Yes,' said Anna with such decision Rotham's lips twitched.

'Then this perhaps . . . ' A piece of rose-shot silk was held up.

'Ah, delightful,' said Rotham, raising his glass, and Mrs Smyth smiled.

She then had the clerk clear away the overwhelming profusion of bolts, keeping only the very best of the stock.

'I still cannot decide,' said Anna helplessly. 'They are all so beautiful.'

Rotham smothered a yawn and walked over to a bolt of bronze velvet. 'It appears to me that this would do for a riding habit. Bring out those eyes, don't you know.'

Anna's cheeks colored, but she remembered the effect of the topaz necklace and agreed to it with a sudden choke of laughter. 'Only think of it . . . on Matilda,' she said unsteadily.

His eyes laughed back although he contrived to keep his countenance schooled. 'Matilda is a horse,' he said to the mystified Mrs Smyth and waved an airy hand. 'It appears that since you cannot make up your mind, Miss Templeton, you must have them all.' Behind him Mr Smyth was heard to breathe audibly. Rotham smiled. 'I'm sure Lady Riddell will not object.'

Slowly Anna gave a nod, both thrilled and alarmed by the daring of such extravagance.

Mrs Smyth came forward. 'Then we must take your measurements, miss, and look at fashion plates.' She sent the duke a pert glance. 'And there, your grace cannot assist us.'

'Alas,' he said. 'I have been given my *congé*. Your servant, ma'am.'

Anna gave him her hand, raising her eyes to his. 'Thank you. I am excessively grateful.'

'A trifle, I assure you. Damme, I'm off.' Cocking his hat at a rakish angle, he strolled out of the shop, looking rather pleased with himself.

'Come this way, miss,' said Mrs Smyth, and Anna was led to the back of the shop.

At the end of an hour, she emerged on to the street with a clerk who deposited three large boxes into the carriage. They contained a new pelisse trimmed with fur and two readymade walking dresses that had required only minor alterations to make them serve. The rest of the order was promised by the end of the following week. Quite pleased with the result of her expedition, Anna went down the street to the glover's and recklessly purchased a pair of French kid gloves. The milliner's shop she resolutely passed by, feeling she had been quite extravagant enough for one day, and occupied herself with choosing gifts for Christmas.

It was relatively a simple matter to select a book of verse for her father and a fan for Aunt Beatrice. A beaded reticule took nearly the whole of a guinea, but she meant not to be miserly toward Grandmama. After much thought she selected a brightly colored puppet for Uncle Percy. Cousin Molineux would get handkerchiefs, which she would embroider. That left Neddie, who was neither child nor man and thus at that impossible age to buy for.

A hunting print in a shop window caught her eye, and she hesitated over it, wondering if it or a new crop would please him the more.

'More difficulties, Miss Templeton?' drawled Rotham's voice in her ear.

She looked around at him with an involuntary smile. 'I fear I am quagmired in them today, and usually I am such a managing sort of female. But I was thinking that print would do splendidly for Neddie to hang in his room at school, to remind him of the sport he loves best. But perhaps he would not wish to have it.'

'There is more depth to Neddie than many suppose,' said Rotham. He bent forward to view the print through his quizzing glass. 'You have a good eye, Miss Templeton. Buy it.'

She drew in a breath, mentally counting her remaining shillings. 'Very well.'

But to her surprise, Rotham was waiting when she came out. She lifted her brows at him.

''Pon my soul, don't look as though you mean to snub me,' he said. 'May I carry your parcels?'

'Thank you. They are getting numerous.' But such prolonged attentiveness in full view of Linwick was beginning to put a line between her brows. She glanced up at him. 'It grows late. I need to find Neddie and—'

'Ah, look! I must buy you a tart in that charming little bakery over there. What marvellous smells it's putting out.' He inhaled with relish as he put her parcels in the carriage. 'Tempting as a guinea in the gutter. Ambrosia to the gods. Are you not famished?'

Anna smiled, but without much warmth. She was growing tired and cold. She wished to go home. 'I fear I must decline, your grace. You are very kind to—'

'But I have no doubt the pastry shop is where Neddie is to be found,' he said, cheerfully brushing aside her refusal. He proffered his arm, a glint in his gray eyes. 'Shall we search for him there?'

She gave way, reflecting ruefully as he led her safely across the muddy street, that he was equally adroit at handling her as he was most everyone else. But Neddie was indeed in the cozy little establishment, his hair tousled, his cravat awry, and his contentment apparent as he munched on a vast sugar bun. His pockets bulged with undisclosed items. Rotham quizzed him on these, and Anna found herself thankful for the chance merely to sit quietly a moment amidst the heavenly smells of cinnamon, currants, and fresh bread baking in the ovens. Neddie had room to eat a second sugar bun, as enormous as the first, and upon Rotham's urging Anna accepted a treat as well.

When it was at last time to go, she bought a pie for their coachman and sent Neddie ahead with it.

'Miss Templeton,' said Rotham, standing with his hat in his hand as she paused by the shop door to pull on her gloves.

She looked up inquiringly and was startled to see him serious of countenance, his affected expression quite absent. 'Yes?' she faltered.

'I was unkind this morning,' he said quietly. 'What I said was . . . unwarranted.'

Her brows drew together. 'It certainly was.'

'Please.' He moved to block her way. 'Mockery has become one of my many unfortunate habits. I forgot you are not of my circle, and thus hardened to darts and jests that are less than kind. This afternoon has given me some hope that you will forgive me.'

She sighed, taking refuge in impatience. 'I expect no apology, sir.'

'But I am making one.' His eyes met hers, frankly for once, and she saw in their silvery depths sincerity . . . and incalculable loneliness.

'I . . . accept,' she said, shaken.

He inclined his fair head unsmilingly. 'Thank you,' he said, and let her go out.

Chapter Six

That evening when Anna came down for dinner in the yellow satin gown she had worn before, Lady Edwin's set expression cleared, and graciously she beckoned Anna to her side when they had finished eating and sat alone in the drawing room.

'Did you think me cross at you, dearest Anna? I assure you I am not.' She smiled in her gentle, radiant way. 'What did Lady Riddell find to talk to you about?'

Anna hesitated for an instant. To speak of her incomplete betrothal plans would be presumptuous, and she refused to boast of largesse. 'Why, she told me of my grandfather.'

Lady Edwin stared, then burst out laughing, her relief obvious. 'Why, how dull for you!'

'I did not find it dull,' said Anna stiffly. Her eyes flashed as she forgot her desire not to offend. 'You may be at your ease, Aunt Beatrice. She did not give me the diamond necklace.'

Lady Edwin's laughter faded, and her elegant brows arched up. 'No,' she said coolly. 'It could not be expected.'

They might have brangled in earnest, but just then the gentlemen joined them, and Molineux came over with one of his faint smiles.

'Have you noticed the addition to the room, Cousin?' he asked. 'I had the servants bring the pianoforte here from the music room. Now you may practise all you like without fear of getting lost again.'

This unexpected thoughtfulness touched her. She gave him a smile. 'Why, how kind of you! I have been missing my music sorely.'

He bowed. 'Will you play for us?'

'The very thing!' said Lady Edwin, clapping her hands together.

'What? Are you to play?' Mr Templeton glanced up from his conversation with Mr Murvey. 'Something graceful, I beg you. My digestion will not condone a ponderous dirge.'

Anna laughed, quite restored to good humor. 'Papa, you are insufferable! I never play dirges. How unhandsome of you to say so.'

He smiled in his dry way, peering at her over his spectacles. 'Just putting you on your mettle, my dear.'

Meanwhile, Molineux had been opening the pianoforte for her. 'Do you have music you wish brought downstairs?'

She seated herself, pulling off her gloves and laying them aside. 'No, thank you. I'll endeavor to play from memory.'

Again to her surprise, he stood beside her to watch her play, his serious dark eyes fixed upon her. Anna fought down a ripple of nervousness and began a Mozart sonata. This effort was applauded, and she next played country airs, singing in a voice that was low and sweet. After a moment her father joined in with his tenor and punched a discomfited Murvey to do likewise. Lady Edwin smiled and added her voice, one well-trained but rather breathless. Neddie came into the room with his spaniel at his heels and stopped, grinning at the sight.

Then they all sang old wassailing songs, Molineux's baritone joining in at last. The company grew quite merry with laughter and song, and Neddie persuaded his mother to dance a lively reel with him. By ten o'clock they were all exhausted and indulged in a cup of tea brought in by Dobbs.

'Heavens!' cried Lady Edwin, collapsing on the sofa and fanning herself vigorously. 'What sad romps we all are. I've never seen the company this merry . . . . not at Farrowsleigh. How prettily you play, Anna.'

'Yes,' said Molineux, allowing his fingers to touch hers as Anna handed him a cup of tea.

She blushed. 'Careful,' she said, her eyes dancing. 'My head is being quite turned with praise. I am persuaded, Aunt Beatrice, that you are far more accomplished than I.'

'Well,' said Lady Edwin, graciously inclining her head, 'I did have the benefit of instruction from the best musical masters. Perhaps another evening I shall contrive to play.'

'I wish his grace had been here,' said Neddie, pulling the ear of his dog. 'It stands to reason he must be prodigiously fond of music, for he was never seen last year in London without that Italian singer on his arm—'

'Neddie!' cried Lady Edwin, making an unsuccessful attempt to pretend outrage while Mr Templeton went into silent whoops behind his hand. 'Darling, that is just the droll sort of remark I have warned you repeatedly not to make.'

Neddie grinned. 'Yes, but she was a diamond of the first water. I saw her—'

'That is not to the purpose.' Not in the least amused, Molineux frowned at him. 'You've caused enough mischief for one evening. Make your apologies at once.'

Neddie jumped up, clenching his fists, but before he uttered one of his fierce retorts his eye was caught and held by Anna's. She shook her head slightly. He turned bright crimson, but held himself in check.

'Forgive me. Come, Pepper!' He hastened out with a slam of the door.

Molineux looked at Anna in astonishment. 'I had no idea you had gained such influence over the brat,' he said.

'Why, yes,' said Lady Edwin in some pique. 'You checked him far better than I have ever done. I applaud you. He appears to be quite in your pocket.'

Anna gave her head a self-deprecating shake. 'You make too much of it. I—'

'Perhaps this influence is mutual,' said Molineux thoughtfully. His dark eyes regarded her in a steady manner she found disquietening. 'You rode with him to Chevely Hall this morning, did you not?'

Anna colored. 'Yes. I—'

'You must understand,' said Molineux with gentle firmness,. 'that to do so is not at all the thing. Rotham is not fitting company for an unchaperoned young lady, and please do not say that Edwin's presence is adequate protection. I ask you not to go there again.'

Anna stood up, her eyes flashing at this unnecessary homily. 'I had not intended to return, sir,' she said evenly and left the room with her father.

'Temper, Anna,' he said mildly as they passed up the stairs.

She sighed, resting her head momentarily on his stooped

shoulder. 'I know, Papa. I'm sorry.'

'He is a fine man, my dear. No popinjay, but rather a gentleman of sound sense and judgement. You must allow those qualities to outweigh his faults.'

'He was rather agreeable tonight until he climbed on his high ropes.' Anna gripped her father's thin, dry hand. 'But you married for love.'

He laughed rather wheezily. 'So I did, my dear. But I confess I miscalculated Lady Riddell's stubbornness in refusing to relent and forgive her daughter.'

Anna halted, pulling away to stare at him. 'Papa, no!'

He returned her widened gaze for a moment with world-weary eyes, then smiled ruefully and put his arm around her shoulders. 'No,' he said softly. 'I loved Amelia to distraction, and if you had found someone for whom you felt . . . well, I would not have objected. But you have not, and so I must see to your future this way. It is one thing to be a hot-blooded young suitor and another to be a father. Good-night, my dear.' Gently he kissed her forehead and walked on.

She saw nothing of the duke for three days, and caught no more than a glimpse of him lounging in the Chevely pew in church Sunday morning. His apology at the close of their last encounter continued to linger in her thoughts; she need not deny she thought better of him for it. But Molineux had at last exerted himself to please her, bestowing his attention and conversation upon her, even greeting her entry into a room with his rather grave smile.

He did so that frosty Sunday afternoon, rising when she came downstairs for tea, and taking her hand to lead her to the chair nearest the fire. The others had not yet come down; nor had Dobbs yet brought in the tray. Anna frowned slightly to herself over this unexpected tête-à-tête, then gathered her unsettled emotions tightly in hand and cleared her expression.

Molineux took a stance by the hearth, leaning one elbow upon the mantelpiece. The firelight gleamed softly upon the polished gloss of his Hessians. He commented on the sermon, to which she returned a dutiful answer, then he said with some abruptness, 'I have a confession to make . . .

Anna.' He glanced at her as though to note how she might react to this familiar use of her name. She returned the look steadily. He cleared his throat. 'It is true that I have found the affairs of the estate in their usual snarl, but I have used this work as an excuse also to keep my distance from you.'

Anna's brows came up at this frankness. 'Indeed.'

He appeared not to hear the satiric note in her voice. 'Yes, pray do not let your surprise close you to what I wish to say. I am not quick to make acquaintance. My judgement of character is purposely deliberate, for I hate error. Admittedly at first I found your tendency toward laughter and jest peculiar and somewhat of an irritant, and certain other of your actions bespeaking a sad want of stability. But on the whole, I am not displeased in you, Cousin.'

Her gray eyes lowered desperately lest he should read them. 'I am . . . overcome,' she murmured.

He bowed. 'Believe me, I do not dispense compliments lightly. You are quite devoted to your father, and show yourself dutiful in every respect to attending his wants and commands. Your intelligence is good, and your behavior generally decorous. I applaud the modesty of your attire, and find your manners pleasing enough. Grandmama has not yet confided to me her opinion of you, but I should like to hope it a favorable one.'

He paused as though expecting some expression of gratitude from her. Anna cast about for one, and found herself unable to do more than lift her eyes briefly to his brown ones and drop them again.

'Yes,' he said with some amusement, 'I agree that it is trying to wait upon the capricious whims of an elderly, infirm woman. But I am patient, Cousin, and time will tell me to what degree you possess this quality.'

Her eyes flew up at that, and she saw him smiling down at her with unconscionable assurance. She drew in a hasty breath, but before she could speak Lady Edwin came in, trailing a paisley shawl.

'My dears! That fire looks positively *heavenly*. I shall never understand why churches must be damp. My very bones feel sodden.'

71

Mr Templeton entered, his hand upon Neddie's arm, and the servants brought the tray. To Anna's relief, her aunt took on the task of pouring, with a dainty display of elegantly turned wrists. The conversation was desultory, mostly wavering between criticisms of the state of the church roof and plans for the Christmas festivities. Neddie yawned frequently and cast looks out the window, and Mr Templeton was soon buried in a book, cake crumbs sprinkled unheeded down his flannel waistcoat. As soon as she could, Anna made her excuses and slipped out, pausing in the hall to grip the newel post and heave a deep breath.

Her brows came sharply together. 'Pompous blow-bag!'

Dobbs paused in startlement on his way to the nether regions. 'I beg your pardon, Miss Anna?'

She turned in equal startlement, then had to laugh at herself. 'Forgive me, Dobbs. I promise I was not referring to you.'

He bowed and went on his way. Anna's smile grew rueful and slightly vexed. She heard the door open behind her and hastened up the stairs, pretending not to hear Molineux's call.

But the next day was better. The gardener and his assistants had sent forth a holly-cutting expedition, and the morning was spent agreeably in watching Mrs West supervise the footmen's efforts to strew the mantelpieces with greenery. Yew boughs were tied to the banisters with great red velvet bows, transforming the gloominess of the stairs into welcoming cheer. A Yule log was selected for the dining-hall fire and waited outside at the servants' entrance for Christmas Eve when it would be carried in and lit. There were to be festivities in keeping with Farrowsleigh traditions, and accordingly the doors to the dining hall were thrown open, the draperies pulled back, and quantities of beeswax brought out with which to polish the vast mahogany table. The ballroom mirrors were washed, the chandelier supplied with a hundred new candles, and chairs lined up against the walls. Baking was begun in the vast kitchen oven and now and then delectable odors escaped upstairs into the rest of the house. Neddie and his spaniel went shooting to supply the table with game suitable for cook's · more inspired efforts, and Molineux and Dobbs held long conferences. over the sufficiency of port and claret in the cellars.

Into all of this pleasing confusion was delivered a numerous quantity of boxes from Mr Smyth's shop, and Mrs Smyth herself came to secure the final fittings. Anna dropped the length of scarlet ribbon she was holding for James to tie according to Lady Edwin's instructions and excused herself to hasten upstairs.

'Mrs Smyth! I am all astonishment at your powers,' she said, laughing as she rang for Betty and began pulling open the boxes. 'How did you finish so many so quickly?'

Mrs Smyth smiled, gratified. 'As to that, miss, I have an assistant, a very clever girl who's eager to learn her trade. Try on the habit first, if you please. There was a bit of trouble with the bodice and I wish to make it exactly right.'

More boxes were being brought up – to Anna a seemingly incomprehensible number – and she and the seamstress retired to the privacy of her bedchamber.

The habit was a vision of bronze velvet, frogged in the new Polish style, and fashioned very tightly in the waist. Mrs Smyth went deftly to work on a troublesome seam while Anna stared enraptured with her reflection. Clothes might be vanity, but what a difference a becoming garment could make! Rotham's judgement had been flawless in the color. Anna's eyes glowed with more depth; her skin took on a new translucence. She smiled with special warmth at her dressmaker.

'It's beautiful, Mrs Smyth. You're a wonder. And now I need not shrink from taking part in the hunt.'

Mrs Smyth accepted this praise and whisked her into the next dress. Their work took up the entire morning, and during luncheon Anna sat at table in a new afternoon dress of Italian cut worn loosely over a cream petticoat, frankly so dazzled by her new acquisitions she barely knew what she ate.

Her aunt was staring at her in frank surprise. 'Why, Anna! I confess I myself have not yet dared take up the Italian mode. You quite *astonish* me, and yet . . . you do look perfectly ravishing. You eclipse all of us. Here I sit in this old gown I've had for an age.' She made a deprecating grimace at the gown of pink satin, trimmed with Brussels lace and garnished with rosettes of fluttering ribbon. 'So *jeune-jeune*, and look at Oliver and Neddie in shooting coats.' She sighed and turned her blue eyes back to Anna. 'I wonder what next you may surprise us with.' Abruptly she met Molineux's gaze and laughed in a gay titter rather unlike her usual rich tones. 'Do you also waltz, my dear? Oliver would be *shocked* to hear you say yes.'

Anna, thus brought forcibly to earth, managed an easy smile with some effort. 'Then I shall say no,' she said sweetly and glanced at Molineux, who was watching her in considerable speculation. At once she colored and looked down, dropping her teasing manner.

'I say, Mollie,' broke in Neddie, to her relief. 'Do you mean to hunt? For my part I think we all ought to participate.' He threw a glance around the table as he spoke.

'No, I thank you!' said his mama with a pretty shudder. 'A bloodthirsty, dangerous sport with everyone riding in the most heedless way as though getting mud thrown over one was the principal object.' She threw up her hands with a glance of appeal that her son ignored. 'You know I have never liked it, Neddie. Not since your dear papa broke his neck.'

'I do not cram my horses, Mama,' said Neddie flatly. 'I have no intention of taking a rattling fall.'

'Anyone can take a fall, cawker,' snapped Molineux. 'Of all the preposterous statements . . . do try, if you please, to respect your mother's sentiments on this head.' When Neddie had been quelled to scowling silence, Molineux leaned his forearm upon the table. 'Is Rotham getting up the pack?'

Neddie's blue eyes met his warily. 'Yes.'

Molineux nodded. 'Suggest to him that we gather here, will you? It will be less distance for the Hardcastles to come. And, yes, you may count on my participation.' He motioned for James to refill his glass. 'Someone must keep an eye on how fast you take your fences.'

Neddie bridled. 'I'm not a baby—'

'Teasing, you block.'

'Oh,' said Neddie, subsiding with obvious discomfiture. 'I beg pardon. One can't tell with you, Mollie. You're always so dashed serious.'

'Not always,' said Molineux with surprising mildness. 'Were you not so violent in your admiration for the duke, you might notice the less blatant of us.' He smiled at Neddie's puzzled blink. 'Moderation, my boy. Moderation in behavior, dress, and thought. That is what you should cultivate. Extravagance is never to be sought or admired.'

Neddie began to toy with his fork. 'And gambling?' he asked innocently.

Molineux's dark eyes narrowed. 'Have you taken it up?'

Neddie shrugged. 'Rotham said you were heavily gapped by Devonshire two months ago. Is that why you sold your town carriage?'

The other conversations around the table stilled. Anna sat holding her breath, wishing she might stop Neddie from this dangerous fencing he had undertaken. But her curiosity kept her silent. *Was* Molineux a gamester? Would he deny it?

'Rotham *says!*' Molineux slammed his fist down upon the table, making the glasses jump. 'Rotham says far more than he knows. I do not always win at the faro table, but then neither does anyone. I was *not* gapped, and if you mean to spread this slander further, my boy, you will think again.' His voice had become icy, his brown eyes flaming coals under their black brows. 'As for my lord duke, his word is worthless! We all know that. And if you persist in believing otherwise, Edwin, it shall be to your cost. Excuse me.' Rising, he strode out.

'Well!' said Neddie with a toss of his golden head. 'That—'

'Neddie, you will quit the room at once!' cried his mama, clenching her fists upon the table. 'Why must you persist in brangling with Oliver at every turn? And especially when you know what is said about Victor in the gossip circles

75

. . . oh, I am sure I shall go distracted from the strain of watching you bait your cousin.'

'I shall be earl, not he,' said Neddie hotly. 'I—'

'You go too far! I shall brook no more of this shameless behavior, do you hear? Go away! You are dismissed.' She looked near tears, and as he ran out, she had to press one hand to her heaving bosom for several minutes. 'It is dreadful,' she whispered, pale as the damask upon the table. 'I cannot make him see sense. He has no notion of prudence, and he will not heed me. If this goes on, he'll ruin everything.'

'I cannot believe his grace would deliberately tell Neddie lies,' said Anna with a perplexed frown. 'Or perhaps he would.'

Lady Edwin shook her head. 'No, no! You do not understand. Of course Oliver gambles, and heavily. It is his weakness, which he cannot shake off. He loathes mention of it.'

'Then he was hypocritical to lecture Neddie,' said Anna indignantly. She turned to her parent. 'Papa, did you hear? A gamester!'

He coughed and shook his head, but she was too angry to pay heed.

'It is beyond anything shabby,' she said, throwing down her napkin. 'He has no place to rip up at Neddie if he cannot govern his own behavior. As for this slander against his grace—'

'Pray, do not defend *him*,' said Lady Edwin coldly. 'Victor does not require the championship of a penniless chit.'

Dashed, Anna drew in a slow deep breath, seeking her lost composure. 'I beg pardon,' she said at last.

'Anna—' Her father suddenly bent over in a spasm of coughing, his hand oversetting his glass and sending the crimson stain spreading across the white damask cloth.

She rushed to his side in alarm. 'Papa!'

The horrible coughing subsided, and he leaned weakly against her, breathing heavily. His face was gray and spent.

She put her arms about him, her heart hammering with a fear that did not fade.

'You must go upstairs and rest,' she said, looking at Mr Murvey, who at once summoned James and another footman to her assistance.

Together they supported Mr Templeton upstairs to his chamber and laid him down upon the bed. He refused to let the doctor be sent for, and knowing argument would only upset his temper, Anna gave way to his wishes and sent everyone away. Then she took out her handkerchief and wiped her eyes before summoning a wan smile.

'Oh, Papa,' she said.

'Fustian,' he said, his voice rasping as he lifted his head a bit off the pillow. 'I shan't be wept over.'

'Very well,' she said gently and got out a book of verse to read aloud until his harsh breathing eased and he slept, freeing her at last to lower the volume and let her tears come.

By evening his color had returned and since he desired only to lie quietly, she had no scruples against leaving him. With a rather haunted expression in the depths of her dark eyes, she thought of what Lady Riddell had told her about striving to please Molineux's eyes. Anna had never in her life dressed to catch a gentleman's fancy, but now quiet sobriety must be laid aside. Duty dictated, and she must not hesitate further against complying with it.

Accordingly, she had Betty bring out a new evening gown, the one made from rose silk that was cut off the shoulders in a décolletage that made her blush each time she saw her reflection. Her dark hair was pinned up with loose waves allowed to frame her temples, and with a sense of considerable daring she drew a rose from the vase on her dressing table and fastened it in her hair. Then, with held breath, she clasped the emerald necklace about her throat and stared at the stones winking their dazzlement upon her creamy bosom. It was as though a stranger gazed back at her. She had never dreamed she could look so . . . so appealing.

For a moment she drew on her resolution along with the new gloves of French kid and made her way downstairs. It had been her hope to quietly dazzle Molineux, but when she entered the drawing room it was to find Rotham and Lady Edwin there before her, with Mr Murvey pacing by the fire. For a moment she felt a sharp pang at the sight of her aunt and the duke with their golden heads together.

Mr Murvey saw Anna first and came forward with his brows anxiously together. 'My dear Miss Templeton, I do hope your father is feeling more the thing.'

'Yes,' she said, rather relieved now that her cousin was not yet in evidence. 'Thank you. He asked that you be kind enough to look in before you retire.'

'Of course. Of course.' The rotund little solicitor patted her hand.

'Anna,' said Lady Edwin, staring at her at last with a blink. 'Good heavens! You are ravishing.'

Anna curtsied. She did not mean to, but as she rose her eyes went to Rotham for his reaction. To her inestimable chagrin, he was busy polishing his quizzing glass and did not even appear to notice her. Then, before she could look away, his eyes came up to meet hers, and the expression in their depths made her cheeks burn.

He came forward with one of his elaborate bows. 'Ah, you have become a vision, Miss Templeton. Sink me, but I am your slave.'

'Slave?' inquired a sharp, quavery voice. 'What nonsense are you nattering now, sir?'

They all turned to see Lady Riddell entering upon the arm of Molineux. Bows and curtsies were made; she sniffed.

'Bah! I see we are not complete. Why not?'

It was explained that Neddie had been banished to his room for his conduct that day and that Walter Templeton was feeling under the weather.

The countess raised her brows. 'Then we need not wait. Your arm, Rotham! I am glad to see you.' Her shrewd eye fell on Anna as this arrangement was made, and she gave a slight nod which spoke volumes of approval.

Anna's chin lifted.

'May I have the honor?' asked Molineux, proffering his arm.

She started to accept, then checked with a swift glance at her aunt. 'Should you not—'

'I prefer to go in with a Beauty on my arm,' he said and smiled slightly as she blushed. 'You do not cease to surprise me, Anna. As soon as I come to appreciate your retiring modesty, you appear as a . . . as a *goddess*.'

She laughed. 'Oh, no! That's doing it far too brown.'

'I speak truth, not flattery,' he said forthrightly. 'So Grandmama has taken a fancy to you. You may count yourself a fortunate young woman indeed.' He cast a speculative glance ahead at the countess, who was rapping Rotham's cheek lightly with her fan over one of his sallies. 'Who knows? Those diamonds she wears may one day belong to you.'

'I think not,' said Anna quickly.

'I disagree.' He inclined his dark head. 'You would wear them with distinction as Beatrice never could. That you have been given other jewels and . . . ' His eyes traveled slowly over her person. 'And an allowance of considerable generosity speaks much to your credit. Yes, she likes you a great deal. As do I.'

Anna's eyes flew to his, wondering at his sincerity.

He pressed her hand gently and smiled. 'Does this surprise you? Then I fear I have been too cold. I told you once I tend to be formal. Will you forgive the fault if I seek to correct myself?'

She just managed a reply, her heart thudding, before she was seated at the table and conversation became general.

Rotham leaned forward in a lazy manner, his cool gray eyes hooded so that only an occasional glint showed from beneath his lids. 'Stap me, Molineux, it's awfully good of you to let the hunt start here. Do you mean to ride?'

'Yes,' said Molineux with civility that was too careful. He was seated on Lady Riddell's left and seemed a trifle discomfited by the proximity to her piercing eye. He did smile, however. 'St. Byre has bullied us all into taking part.

I find it most odd in the boy, this sporting craze. Certainly he did not get it from Beatrice, and no one could have called Lord Edwin a Corinthian.'

Lady Edwin choked on her ratafia, and Lady Riddell's gaze narrowed.

Rotham curled his lip. 'Probably Neddie has acquired it from that set he keeps at Eton. But do, pray, Molineux, mount Miss Templeton on something that will survive the course.' Now he smiled at Anna with all of his charm. 'I wish I might give you the pick of my stables, dear ma'am.'

'You need not put yourself out,' growled Molineux, sending Anna a speaking glance.

'Rotham, you absurd creature,' broke in Lady Riddell abruptly, 'cease throwing my grandson into a pucker and tell me news of Alicia. I wish you will bring her home. I should like to know the child.'

He shrugged and eyed a dish of creamed vegetables through his quizzing glass. His coat tonight was actually spangled and fashioned with an absurdly high collar. He was obliged to turn completely about to address her ladyship since the starch and excessive style of his cravat prevented the slightest movement of his head.

'Alicia?' he said vaguely, still peering at the dishes before him and making fastidious little grimaces. 'Alicia. Heavens, the name falls well on the ear, does it not? Am I supposed to know her? Is she the newest belle of the *ton*?'

Lady Riddell snorted rather severely, but Lady Edwin gasped and quite stared at him.

'Victor!' she said in tones of deepest reproach. 'You cannot be so beastly as to make us think you have forgotten your own daughter.'

He laughed foolishly. 'Think? My dear lady, I never think. Too fatiguing by half. 'Pon my soul, the place seems to be positively reeking with yew. How festive you do become. Is it to be the usual sort of thing on Christmas Eve with feudal fires and hordes of tenants?'

'Yes, of course,' said Molineux.

Rotham dropped his fork upon his plate and leaned back in his chair. 'Gad's life! If it's to be as *usual*, then we shall be obliged to suffer through your abominable punch.' He held up a hand, shuddering, as Molineux started to speak. 'Zounds, man, don't defend it.'

'Mr Molineux makes a very tolerable punch,' put in Mr Murvey loyally.

'Tolerable? My dear fellow,' said Rotham, raising his brows as he twisted about to gaze at the solicitor. 'Forgive me, but you are hardly a judge of these matters.'

'Fie!' Lady Edwin hunched a prettily revealed shoulder. 'Who cares about silly old punch?'

'If Molineux makes his, Farrowsleigh stands to lose its reputation of fine hospitality,' said Rotham, crossing his arms.

'Rubbish!' snapped the countess. 'Rotham, you are being ridiculous. What is wrong with the punch?'

Rotham waved his long fingers contemptuously, the lace falling back from his wrist. 'One may as well drink milk. Gad, madam! I insist on *punch*, punch that will make the cat speak!'

'Oh, John Bull stuff,' said Mr Murvey, brightening.

'Exactly.' Rotham's eyes glinted at Molineux, who had tightened his lips. 'A wager, my glowering fellow. Shall we venture a monkey on whose bowl is emptied first, mine or yours?'

'Done!' said Molineux as though wishing he was at liberty to cast the duke out by his collar. 'Yours will be undrinkable in your effort to make it potent. I'll lay odds it will smoke in the bowl.'

'As you like,' said Rotham mildly and took something from his pocket to record the bet upon. 'Shall we do anything about the hunt?'

'Enough!' said the countess in annoyance. She glared at them both, her withered lips compressed as the diamonds she wore winked and blazed in the candlelight. 'You may conclude your gaming over your port. For now, have done!'

Soon thereafter, she rose from the table and accepted her cane from a solicitous footman. Anna and Lady Edwin accompanied her to the drawing room.

'I'll say this for you, girl,' said the countess with her

cracked laugh. 'You do know how to take advice. Very prettily done.'

'Yes,' said Lady Edwin, her eyes upon Anna's emerald necklace. 'You are uncommonly lovely, my dear, now that you've gone to some effort. The gentlemen could not take their eyes from you.'

'Not to your liking, was it, Beatrice?' The countess seated herself heavily. 'Why don't you remarry? I'm not likely to reward you for these years of devotion to me.'

Lady Edwin whitened, and Anna took a step between them.

'Please—'

'You need not champion me, Anna, thank you,' said Lady Edwin with a brittle smile. Her eyes met those of the countess. 'It would not be natural of me, ma'am, if I did not try.'

To Anna's relief, this fraught conversation was interrupted by the arrival of the gentlemen, who had not been congenial enough to linger over their port. Molineux hesitated and bent his dark head to attend to Mr Murvey's remark, but Rotham sauntered on in and led Anna away to a corner.

'At last! A moment of privacy where I can tell you how greatly you enchant me.' He said this seriously, but before she could take alarm he had drawn on a satirical smirk as one might draw on a glove. 'Beatrice is green. Heavens, what a Friday face she has worn all evening.'

'It is *not* sour grapes,' said Anna, her nerves beginning to fail her. 'She has been dealt several unkind cuts this evening. I beg you not to be horrid to her as well.'

His eyes glinted down into hers, making her feel as though all her limbs had melted to water. At a loss to understand what was the matter with her, she put out a hand to grasp the back of a chair. Molineux, she knew with a pang of distress, was glaring at them, but she did not dare leave Rotham abruptly.

The duke had noticed Molineux's glance too, for he loosed his foolish laugh and with an audacity that shocked her, tapped her emerald necklace lightly with his quizzing glass. 'Engaging little bauble, this. Oh, don't scruple to blush, my sweet. It's plain as a pikestaff Molineux and the fair Beatrice think the countess means to give you *all*. I think, however . . . ' His smile broadened. 'Yes, upon occasion I do think. But I believe you have been thrown the scraps.'

Anna frowned, rather jolted out of a more elemental confusion. 'I do not understand you.'

'But you should. I warned you of your grandmother's capriciousness. And she does hold grudges. Just because she appears to favor you at present does not mean she will ever forgive your father for eloping with her daughter.' He smiled and aimed his quizzing glass once more at Anna's necklace. 'Scraps. What an inelegant word, but sink me, how descriptive. I hope you have not set your cap for the diamonds.'

'I wish you will go away,' whispered Anna in a crimsoned fury. 'Stop ogling me, or I swear I'll box your ears in front of everyone.'

'Gad, a devilish threat.' He dropped his glass to the end of its ribbon and turned to see Molineux advancing upon them with a purposeful air. 'And here comes that bit of fog. Why must the pestilent fellow feel obliged to dampen everyone? He is most depressing. I daresay he is going to be dog-in-the-mangerish and deny me further conversation with you.' Rotham sighed and faced Anna once again while she fought to snatch her lost composure.

'I did learn a line of verse with which to impress your father. Mollie, you glowering oaf,' he added fondly, taking her cousin's rigid arm. 'Do you know I spent all afternoon in the most tedious labor, striving to have some means of making myself agreeable to Walter Templeton, and here he does not even deign to come down to dinner. I am crushed.'

'You are drunk, sir,' snapped Molineux.

'On table wine?' Rotham cocked his golden head. 'No, I do not believe so. Shall I recite, Miss Templeton? Catullus was a naughty fellow at times, I must say.'

Her eyes widened as he struck a pose. 'Please do not!' she

said hastily, certain he meant to say some wicked line of Latin which would in all likelihood get him knocked down by her cousin. 'I beg you, sir, do not put yourself out.'

His eyes gleamed, but he shook back the lace gracefully from one wrist and said, while she held her breath, 'Damme, it's left me. What a cursed bother.' He lowered his hand with a faint smile which quizzed her so thoroughly she knew not where to look.

Molineux snorted. 'You, sir, are nothing but a mincing Tulip.'

'Am I?' Rotham smiled. 'Well, it's good of you to say so. But do not, I beg, seek to place me in the bow-window set, for I am far beneath their level.'

Anna was able to smile at last. 'Punster.'

Rotham bowed. 'Thank you. It is really too good of you not to roast me on my lamentable loss of memory.' He raised one brow, his eyes daring her to smile back. 'But, you know, I never can recite in the damp. Excuse me. I must go and be agreeable to the countess.'

He sauntered away, leaving Anna desperately trying not to go into whoops.

Molineux frowned after him. 'What kind of ridiculous remark was that? This room is never damp.'

She carefully avoided his eyes. 'Surely, sir, you know better than to attach any meaning to his prattle.'

'Yes, of course.' Molineux's expression cleared. 'He is a cursed chatterbox. It's all affectation, of course, adopted after the death of his wife. I quite dislike it. Anna,' he said abruptly, taking her hand. 'Come with me to the library. I have something to discuss with you.'

She drew back involuntarily. 'Tête-à-tête?' Then she sighed and gave him a resigned nod. 'Yes, of . . . course.'

Lady Riddell's sharp eyes seemed to burn right through her back. Anna held her head high and tried not to show how mortified she was to be going out on Molineux's arm in bold view of everyone. Why could he not have chosen a private moment tomorrow? But tomorrow was the hunt. There would be no private moments.

A fire burned in the library grate, casting soft light over the calf-bound volumes. The few lit tapers did not dispel much of the shadowed gloom. Anna frowned, disliking it to be so dark, and to her relief Molineux lit more candles.

'Now, then,' he said, turning at last to face her. She had not sat down, and so he, too, was obliged to stand, muscular and dark in his maroon coat and gray breeches. He was not a bad-looking man, she told herself. If only he would smile. If only good humor would lighten that somber gaze. Her breath tightened in her throat, trapped there so that it could neither go up nor down into her aching lungs.

'I am a sensible man, Anna,' he said in his grave way. 'And you are a sensible woman. You are surely aware that if I choose to marry you, our grandmother will reward us both handsomely.' His dark eyes studied her with approval. 'You have quite surpassed all my expectations. Shall I inform her ladyship that we will marry?'

Relief surged through her. She was so thankful at being spared impassioned, hypocritical declarations she could only nod.

He bowed. 'Then we are agreed. I think we shall suit very well, Anna.'

She drew in an unsteady breath. 'Yes . . . Oliver.'

He smiled then and took her hand between his. Suddenly he did not seem quite so aloof. Looking up, she read ardor in his eyes and tried, too late, to draw back.

'Please—' she gasped, but then his lips were upon hers and his hand hard against her back, pressing her so firmly to his powerful chest she was crushed, breathless, powerless to escape the unwelcome tumult rising within her. She could not breathe. She was going to swoon. Panic gripped her more ruthlessly than his hands.

'Sink me,' drawled the coolest, most welcome voice she had ever heard. 'What have we here?'

With an oath, Molineux released her to stand glaring at Rotham, who had his quizzing glass to his eye. 'How dare you intrude, sir?'

Rotham sighed and lowered his glass, still looking, however, at Anna, who was grasping the back of a chair with both hands and feeling dangerously close to tears. 'The lady appears distraught.'

'The lady,' said Molineux angrily, 'has just accepted my offer.'

'Dear me,' said Rotham, helping himself to snuff. 'Has she really? I thought this point had been settled long ago. What a slowtop you are to be sure, Mollie.'

'It's no concern of yours, sir! I ask you to keep the news to yourself until the official announcement is made on Christmas Eve.'

'Hmm?' said Rotham vaguely and turned his gaze away from Anna's scarlet profile. 'I fear I was not listening.'

With a flash of his eyes, Molineux repeated himself.

The duke smiled, although his eyes remained cold. 'Oh, certainly. I'm demmed discreet. Word of a duke.'

Molineux snorted. 'Well, see that you keep it.' Then as Rotham went on genially standing there, Molineux growled, 'Have you a reason to linger?'

'By Jove, yes.' Rotham raised his brows. 'My hat, you know.' He walked past Molineux to the library table where a chapeau-bras was lying upon one corner. 'I can't imagine why I left it in here, but I did. I'm making an early departure. Don't want to oversleep and be late for the hunt. Bad form, don't you know. My very dear Miss Templeton.' He bowed to her, his smile so gentle she could have thanked him for it. 'You really are most lovely. When you are married, I shall have to set up a flirtation with you. Good-night.'

He ambled out, still smiling, and Molineux slammed the door behind him.

'Jackanapes!'

Anna turned, clutching her sangfroid like a shield. 'Yes, he is very odd. I wish to bid you good-night, too, Cousin. Will you make my excuses to Grandmama? I have the headache coming on.'

He did not look pleased, but he let her go out. ''Till tomorrow, Anna,' he said, his eyes burning into hers.

She sent him a troubled look. 'Yes.'

He watched her go up the stairs, but when she had reached the landing and knew he could no longer see her, she gathered up her skirts and ran the rest of the way to her room, where she flung herself inside, panting, and bolted the door with a vengeance.

Chapter Seven

However she might try to be sensible and shrug it off as merely something one must expect from a full-blooded man one had just agreed to marry, Anna could not rid herself of lingering agitation. Molineux had never before given her the slightest indication that he was a sensual man. But his display of passion had thoroughly frightened her, and she realized there would be more to marriage than merely changing her name and residence. Thank God the duke had entered when he did!

After three-quarters of an hour she wearied of her pacing about the sitting room and gave way to the exhaustion of her nerves and the true beginnings of a headache. She did not bother to ring for Betty, who would be agog to know how the evening had turned out. Duty, Anna told herself as she unclasped the emerald necklace and put it carefully away. She had done what was asked and expected of her. But she could not help but wonder, as she tied the ribbons of her nightgown and banked the fire before climbing into bed, what Molineux's reaction would be did she not receive the gift of the Riddell diamonds.

Sometime in the night, a sudden sharp draft of icy air across her face awakened her. Her eyes flew open, and with a start she saw that the bed curtains were parted just enough for the dim ruddy glow of the hearth to be seen. She frowned, recalling she had shut the heavy curtains completely. Or perhaps not . . . Her eyes widened, and suddenly she could not breathe. A hand was holding the curtains open! Terror jerked her upright, the bedclothes clutched to her chin. She tried to scream, but nothing more than a strangled gasp escaped her.

The hand fell away, and the curtains swung together, shutting her into darkness like a tomb. Anna clenched shut her eyes, her heart pounding so madly she could not hear or even think. Was she dreaming? No. With a trembling hand she reached out and touched the curtains. They still swayed lightly. Someone was in her room.

'Who's there?' she blurted out. 'Betty?'

No answer came and in desperation she jerked back the curtains.

She could see no one. Holding her breath, almost too shaken to command her limbs, she pushed herself out of bed – gasping at the chill in the air – and crept across the room to light a taper with trembling fingers. There was no one in the room but her. Slowly she took the poker in her right hand and with the candle held before her, went through the sitting room and even the narrow dressing room. No one.

She frowned, her breath coming easier now. Was Uncle Percy loose and wandering about again? She flew to the door, but it was bolted securely from the inside. And there was no servant's door, no other means of access.

Anna dropped her hand from the knob, swallowing with difficulty. She had not dreamed it. She had not! She was not prey to superstitions, so she need not even consider something so silly as a ghost. But who could it have been? Who could have any reason to frighten her out of her wits in this clandestine way? And most importantly of all, how had this intruder entered and left her rooms?

Shivering in the cold, she snuffed out her candle and returned to bed to lie down rigidly. Suppose the intruder came back?

As she lay there with her ears strained for every sound, she heard the slow hissing of the embers in the grate and the shriek of the wind outside. Somewhere far away, a loosened shutter banged with hollow repetitiveness. The house was built of stone and had stood perfectly solid for two centuries, but it had its internal creaks and shifts, each of which made her start. Old tree limbs rubbed against the walls outside and clawed at her window. Earlier thay had all been normal sounds; now each seemed full of the most sinister implications. But time dragged on in the darkness, and eventually her lids grew too heavy to keep open.

She was still sleeping soundly when a knock on the door awakened her. Anna dragged her eyes open, disoriented at first, then she realized it was morning. Yawning, she threw back the covers and left her bed to unlock the door.

Betty stood there, a tray in her capable hands and a frown on her face. 'I'm so sorry, miss! It's such a bother, there being no servant's door, and I wouldn't have disturbed you, especially with the door bolted, but the hunt—'

'Yes, of course.' Anna moved back to let her enter. 'You were right to waken me.'

Wrapped in the warmth of her dressing gown, Anna breakfasted thoughtfully, her expression somber. The frightening incident in the night did not fade with morning as she had expected. Every detail stood out clearly in her mind, disturbing her.

She dressed in the bronze velvet habit and was putting up her dark hair when she noticed the folded piece of paper lying atop her dressing table. Anna laid down her comb and unfolded the stiff vellum. On it, written in bold, disguised letters, was, 'Leave this house.'

She frowned, struck by a faint chill across her spine, and turned rather abruptly to Betty, who was plumping pillows on the bed.

'Did you bring me this note, Betty?'

The maid blinked at her and shook her head. 'Why, no, miss.'

Anna frowned again at the letter. Or should she call it a threat? There was certainly an air of menace to it. And her intruder had been merely a messenger. Anger stiffened Anna, and she finished her hair swiftly, her lips compressed. She would not be frightened away so easily by this impudent prankster. She would—

Just then a footman tapped on the door and brought in two hatboxes, which Betty directed him to leave in the sitting room. Anna laid down the paper and went at once to see what had been brought. The milliner's name stamped upon the lids brought her brows together.

'This is a mistake,' she said. 'I purchased no hats.'

But her name was scrawled upon a card affixed to one of the boxes. Anna plucked it off and turned it over, to read:

I could not resist pandering to the secret vanity of the most charming bluestocking of my acquaintance.   Rotham

An involuntary smile quivered upon her lips. She pulled off

the lid of the first box and drew out the confection with a shedding of silver paper on to the floor. It was a mannish hat, with a short veil and a pleasant feather sweeping off the brim. Anna had no need to run to the mirror to see how well it set off her new riding habit, but she did so nonetheless, observing the effect with a pleasure that could not be denied.

'Wicked creature,' she murmured, her spirits unaccountably rising, and flew back to see what the second box contained. The poke bonnet inside was fashioned of blue velvet, lined prettily with satin, and trimmed with matching ribbons. It was the very thing with which to replace her shabby old shovel bonnet. She laughed, then sobered and lowered it back into its box.

Surely Rotham knew better than to send her such gifts, which were far from proper for her to accept at any time, much less now when she was bound to Molineux. They must be returned. Resolutely she shut the lid on the bonnet and returned to the mirror to unpin the riding hat. But as she reached up, she could not help but adjust the veil first just to observe the effect. She sighed. It was the most becoming hat she had ever worn. But, no, she must not even dare to think of keeping it.

A thunderous pounding on the door made her whirl around, her eyes wide. Betty threw open the door to reveal Neddie, who did not enter or apologize for nearly startling her out of her wits, but instead said curtly, 'Well, come on! Are you ready? We're half mounted, and the dogs are hot to start. You can't preen all day and expect us to wait on you.'

'But, Neddie!' said Anna, flustered. 'I must talk to Papa and . . . Betty, where is my hat?'

'It's on your head,' he broke in. 'And your gloves are in your hand if only you'll pick them up off that little table. Jupiter, Anna, don't go gooseish on me now! Come on!'

She had little choice but to snatch up her gloves and crop and hasten out after him, struggling just a bit to catch up with his purposeful stride. 'Neddie, for heaven's sake, *do* slow down! I don't wish to appear before your friends gasping for air like a landed fish.'

His lips twitched into a grin, and he altered his pace a fraction. 'Beg pardon. But I don't want people to think you're the lady they must always wait on. Oh, Anna! The weather is perfect. No more than a hint of fog, and plenty of solid footing. Rotham's dog—'

'Never mind Rotham's dog,' she said as they headed downstairs. Neddie's pace was quickening by perceptible degrees and she picked up the train of her habit in some vexation. 'Neddie, are there secret passageways in this house?'

'What?' His spaniel met them on the landing, and he knelt to pat the barking creature. 'No, no, you old beggar. No hunting for you, Pepper boy. What did you say, Anna?'

She sighed, and went on into the hall. 'I asked,' she repeated, when he had left his whining spaniel in James's care and caught up with her outside, 'if there are any secret passageways—'

'Lord, I don't know.' His eyes swept over the assemblage already present, his nostrils quivering against the raw bite of the wind. 'I say! There's his grace now. Victor!' He dashed down the steps, waving his crop to the considerable annoyance of a raking bay hunter.

Rotham paused well out of the way of the shying animal, his brows up, then said mildly, 'Terrifying wart. You had better ask Mrs Hardcastle's pardon, for she won't thank you if she is thrown in the drive.'

Neddie colored and rushed off to do so, leaving Rotham to hand the reins of his mount to a groom and walk up to Anna, who was looking at him with all the reproof she could muster.

He removed his beaver and bowed, his light gray eyes warm. 'Good morning, Miss Templeton. You look delightful.'

She tried hard to keep her lips compressed, but they began to quiver. 'Man-milliner.'

He smiled and raised a hand as though to acknowledge a hit. 'Yes, I suppose I am. Cleverly said. But . . . ' He ventured another, warmer smile. 'You *are* wearing it.'

'Yes, I am, and feel like the boldest piece in England,' she said, but without much force. 'Wretch! It is too bad of you to tempt me in this manner.'

He bowed and proffered his arm. 'I knew it would suit you to perfection. Let it be our secret. Come, ma'am. Allow me to help you mount.'

By this time Molineux had noticed her presence, for he came riding through the jovial crowd and touched his hat with a hint of narrowness in his dark eyes as he saw her hand on Rotham's arm.

'Hawkins is bringing your horse,' he said.

Anna nodded, and Molineux sent Rotham a dark glance. 'I understand your grace desires her to ride that black you foisted on to us.'

'No—' said Anna, not wishing to bring up that unpleasant matter again, but the two men ignored her as they locked eyes.

'You appear to have something against the animal,' began Rotham, his drawl rather cool in tone. He glanced down and flicked a bit of mud off his boot toe with his crop. 'I can't imagine why. Is it because I once owned him?'

'Don't be a dolt,' snapped Molineux. 'You know very well what is wrong with it.'

Rotham looked up at that remark, but before he could respond a burly man of middle years well set up on a raw-boned chestnut hailed Molineux, who wheeled his horse away to reply.

'What sort of plaguey game is Mollie trying against me now?' murmured Rotham, half to himself.

Anna stepped forward to take the reins of her mount, but as she did so the duke touched her arm.

'Please, Miss Templeton! You frighten me to death with that beast of yours. Straight-shouldered to a fault. He'll give you a spill if you aren't careful.' He affected a shudder as she glanced at him in some exasperation.

'I must ride him, your grace,' she said, her words nearly eclipsed by the eager yelping of the hounds. 'There is no other.'

Servants were bringing out offerings from the cellar, and Rotham stepped out of their way, taking up a glass of brandy as he did so. He swallowed this and left his glass between the stone paws of one of the lions.

'Demmed cold,' he said and grasped her elbow before she could put her foot into the hand of her groom. 'No, my dear ma'am. I am determined to show you there is nothing wrong with that black horse.'

Being steered away from the others very much against her will, Anna sought to free herself as civilly as possible, but with a firm shake of his head Rotham took her on around the house and across the graveled stable yard.

'I have seen the horse, sir!' she said, becoming quite vexed with him. 'Pray, unhand me.'

'If there is something amiss with Dante I want to know it,' said Rotham, gazing about the dim interior of the stables. 'Bred him myself, you know. Now where is the creature kept?'

'In the box stall,' said Anna. 'But I assure you he is all Molineux says.' She hastened after Rotham, who had strode away toward the end of the stables. 'Why will you not listen to me? I do not wish to ride that animal!'

'Fudge, my dear Miss Templeton,' said the duke, unlatching the door of the stall.

Anna put out a hand, horrified. 'Do not go in there!'

'Why not?' He walked into the stall with the easy sureness of movement required around horses. 'Hullo, Dante, my fellow! Why, yes, I have sugar for you. Do you remember me still? Good boy!'

With held breath, Anna peered over the door and watched him slide a hand around the glossy neck and rub the alert ears. Dante nickered softly and nuzzled Rotham's waistcoat.

The duke smiled at Anna, his hand stroking Dante's arched neck. 'Now, you see? Perfectly docile.'

She blinked, nonplussed. 'Yes. So he is. But—'

'Miss!' It was Hawkins who came hurrying up to her. 'Come away from that door . . . oh.' He saw the duke inside the stall and came to an uncertain halt. 'Beg your grace's pardon. But you'll want him tied, sir.'

'No, there's no need for that,' said Rotham. 'Damme, I'll ride him if you're afraid to, Miss Templeton. You may use my gray. Hawkins, be so good as to change the saddles.'

Hawkins stared at him. 'But your grace—'

Rotham's cool eye met his, and the groom turned reluctantly away to do his bidding.

'He seems quite sweet today,' said Anna, still frowning. 'But you shouldn't—'

'What's this?' said the duke suddenly, his hand pausing on the horse's withers. His brows came together, and he took a closer look at Dante's back. The horse snorted and put up its head, the white forefoot shifting restlessly.

94

'Do be careful!' said Anna, gripping the door.

Approaching footsteps made her turn her head, and with relief she saw Molineux coming with Hawkins in tow.

'Cousin!' she said. 'I cannot persuade his grace—'

'Rotham, are you mad?' snapped Molineux, coming up to grasp the top of the stall door. 'Come out of there!'

Dante's ears flattened and he backed up a step.

Rotham shot Molineux a furious look. 'I might ask you, sir, what you have done to—'

'Get out of the stall, you fool.' Molineux gestured. 'Hawkins, put a rope on that brute. Now—'

But with an enraged squeal, the horse suddenly reared, its forefeet striking out, and whirled, knocking Rotham against the wall. He staggered and fell to his knees, trying to dodge the aroused horse.

'Damn!' Molineux opened the stall door and tried to go in, but he seemed only to upset the beast further. It charged, snorting, and he barely had time to leap out and slam the door before murderous hooves hammered against it.

Helpless, horrified, Anna stood there, clenching her fists, her eyes unable to look away from Rotham, who was trying to drag himself into a corner. Hawkins had returned with the ropes, and others had come running to help, but Dante was a wild fury, rearing, plunging about the stall so fiercely no one dared go in. Molineux was still shouting instructions, but Hawkins kept shaking his head.

'It's murder to go in there, sir. You know what he is. You—'

'Damn your eyes, Molineux!' shouted the duke, bracing himself in a far corner, his face white and his coat torn. 'Be quiet—'

But the horse spun about, maddened by the voices, and struck the duke down. Anna screamed and covered her face with her hands, unable to watch further.

'Get her out of here,' snarled Molineux. 'Someone get her out! I'm going for my firing piece.'

A hand tugged at Anna's shoulder. She looked up wildly into the kindly, anxious face of the burly gentleman, then

95

shook her head at him and glanced back into the stall, too horrified not to watch. Rotham lay face down in the straw, motionless, and mercifully the horse had turned from him to face the men gathered about the door. It blew a challenge, pawing, and Anna gasped at the blood staining the white forefoot.

'No!' she cried, so breathless the protest was nearly inaudible.

'Not the duke's,' said the burly gentleman quickly, his own eyes wide. 'Brute cut himself, lashing out. Come away, ma'am. Come away. By God, it's an awful thing to watch a sound horse be shot, but there's nothing for it. Come away, I beg!'

Anna had no intention of going. Her whole being seemed to be in that stall with Rotham, but suddenly her strength to resist left her. Trembling, she stumbled outside, the burly gentleman's arm supporting her.

'What on earth is amiss?' demanded Mrs Hardcastle, dismounted now, as were most of the rest of the company. 'Squire?'

'Rotham,' said the burly gentleman gravely. 'Trampled in a stall. Dash it, what the deuce do these Farrows think they're about, keeping such a savage on the premises? Beg pardon, ma'am,' he said in sudden discomfiture to Anna, who barely heard him.

'Anna, you'd better go into the house,' said Neddie, coming to her and looking as pale as she felt.

She shook her head, her eyes fixed on the wide doorway of the stables. 'No! Send for a doctor, Neddie, please!'

'I'll go myself.' Choking, he hurried away.

'But what happened?' Mrs Hardcastle was demanding when a loud report crashed out, deafening them all and sending several horses shying frantically.

'My God,' breathed someone. 'They've shot the horse. Poor brute.'

Anna closed her eyes, quivering, her hands twisted together with painful force. Was he dead? Was he?

After several interminable minutes, a group of men came out carefully bearing the duke's limp form. He was white as death, his face bruised and bleeding, his fine clothes torn. One hand dangled, the lace falling muddy and draggled over it. Anna pressed her hands to her lips, her heart motionless within her.

'Well?' demanded the squire, stepping forward. 'Well, sir?' .Molineux gestured, still carrying his spent pistol in his hand. 'Alive,' he said grimly. 'Someone fetch the doctor.'

The world swirled about Anna for an instant, then she drew a deep breath and every frozen nerve within her seemed to return to life.

A clamor broke out among the guests, all demanding to know how such an accident could have happened.

'Foxed,' said the squire severely. 'Always is. He was bound to come a cropper some day.'

'If the black had wanted to kill his grace,' muttered the head groom darkly as he supported the duke's head, 'then, aye, it would have damned well done so. Poor brute.'

Anna gasped. 'Do you mean—'

'That's enough, Hawkins!' snapped Molineux. 'If you please, Anna—'

'Yes,' she said, pulling her attention back to the immediate matter at hand. With one last glance at the duke's drawn face, she turned sharply on her heel and hastened into the house.

'Dobbs!' she said sharply, startling the butler into a hasty appearance from his pantry. 'His grace is grievously injured. We must have a room prepared at once to put him in. See to it. And send someone to Chevely Hall. Oh, yes, and ask Mrs West to do what is required in the way of bandages and hot water.'

The duke was brought in and laid down in a comfortable bedchamber. With the help of Neddie's valet, Beavins, Anna shooed out those who would have crowded in.

'I don't dare undress him, miss,' said Beavins, his usual manner stripped by anxiety. 'If there's ribs and things broken—'

'More than that, I expect,' she said, fresh worry clutching her. 'As soon as Mrs West brings the water we shall clean up his cuts. More than that we must not attempt without the doctor's instructions.'

They did agree to remove his grace's boots, and Anna was

sitting beside him, gently sponging at the cut on his cheek, when Rotham's eyes flickered open. He stared at Anna a long moment, then made a poor attempt at a smile.

'Damme,' he said, his voice a feeble thread. 'Thought I'd cut my stick, but I guess . . . not.' His breath caught sharply, and he clenched shut his eyes.

A tremor ran through Anna. She laid a hand upon his shoulder. 'You must be quiet until the doctor comes.'

He managed a nod, not opening his eyes. Such ready compliance only increased her anxiety. She and Beavins exchanged glances.

The waiting seemed to go on forever, but at last Neddie came striding in with his face blue with cold and his boots splattered. 'I brought the sawbones as quick as I could pry him along. How . . . does he still . . . ' Neddie swallowed hard, his blue eyes searching hers.

She nodded reassurance as the doctor came in, shedding his hat and coat. He was a trim, black-haired individual who spared her no more than a glance for courtesy before bending over Rotham.

'Well, well, your grace!' he said coolly. 'Still alive, are you?'

Rotham managed a smile, his gray eyes heavy with pain.

The doctor began feeling his limbs. 'You are alive, and conscious, but silent. That is most unusual of your grace.'

'Devilishly painful,' said Rotham with a gasp.

'Oh?' The doctor frowned. 'I'd better sound your chest. My bag please, Mr Beavins.' He glanced across the bed at Anna and said in his brusque way, 'You've been sensible, ma'am. Would you be kind enough to go now?'

She stood up, laying aside her cloth. 'Yes, of course.' But her eyes went to Rotham's face, searching it, before she put her arm about Neddie's shoulders and went out.

They nearly collided with Molineux in the doorway. He halted and backed up a step, looking thunderous.

'How dare you cast propriety to the winds in this bold-faced manner?' he demanded in a voice hard and cutting. 'Have you no shame, mooning over him in a private bedchamber? I can see what comes of letting you make sheep's eyes at him unchecked—'

'Jupiter—' began Neddie as Anna hastily shut the door behind her. She silenced the boy with a hand on his arm and met Molineux's blazing eyes with her lips pressed tightly together. His outburst had at first taken her aback, but now something within her snapped at this unwarranted outburst of choler.

She lifted her chin and said in the coldest voice she could muster, 'Question your conduct before you presume to question mine, sir! That poor horse was perfectly docile before you came about, upsetting it. I do not know what you may have done to savage it in that way, but be assured that I blame you for this accident.'

Neddie's mouth fell open, but the flame in Molineux's eyes abruptly faded. He stared at her with a gaze so black and cold it struck her to the heart with its menace.

He said, in a tight, clipped voice, 'You blame me? You are hysterical.'

'No.'

'I see.' His gaze flickered down, but its implacability did not lessen. 'Our understanding is—'

' —finished,' she snapped. 'Quite.'

Only then did he smile, in a brief chilling manner. 'Oh, no,' he said softly with a shake of his dark head. 'You are quite mistaken on that score, Anna.' Then abruptly he glanced at Neddie. 'I've dismissed the pack. Will you see that Rotham's men have assistance returning the dogs to Chevely Hall?'

'Yes,' said Neddie. He sent Anna a troubled glance as though reluctant to leave her, then shoved his hands deep into his breeches pockets and strode away.

Molineux watched him go with a frown. 'I'll not brook his insolence much longer.'

'Nor will I *yours*,' said Anna and walked away, her heart seething with anxiety, anger, and fear.

Chapter Eight

When Anna entered the drawing room, it was to find Lady Riddell sitting there, with Lady Edwin, Mr Templeton, and Mr Murvey gathered around her like a court. The countess lifted her chin at Anna and said in her imperious way, 'I do not believe this faradiddle. Victor Chevely is not doltish enough to get himself trampled to death. You will explain.'

He might still die, and if so . . . With an effort Anna collected herself and faced their eyes, longing to throw herself into her father's arms and weep. But she stood there as calmly as she could, and replied:

'He was trampled, But he is not dead. The doctor is with him.'

'Thank heaven!' cried Lady Edwin and ceased squeezing a silk sofa cushion. 'I all but swooned when I heard of it. How could you bear to be there, Anna? And Neddie—'

'Quiet, Beatrice,' snapped the countess, her gray eyes never leaving Anna's face. 'What happened, girl? Oliver will tell me later, but I want to hear it first from you.'

Anna dropped her eyes, wishing she could clear away those horrible scenes branded permanently upon her mind. She swallowed with some difficulty. 'May I . . . If I could have a glass of sherry?'

'Yes, of course!' Mr Murvey hastened to ring the bell.

'Sit down, Anna,' said her father with his faint smile. 'You've done splendidly. We get no missish vapors from you, thank God.' And as he spoke he threw a speaking glance at Lady Edwin, who looked affronted.

Sherry was brought to Anna, and after drinking it down she did feel better, sufficiently so to tell them of the incident. Her aunt had recourse to a vial drawn from her reticule, but the countess listened with her brows together.

'It seems—' she began, but the doors opened and the doctor entered with his impatient step.

He checked as they all looked at him. 'His grace is a most fortunate man. Only some ribs broken, and I think none have touched the lung. Of course I shall return in the morning to sound his chest again, just to be sure.' He paused, and the countess raised her head.

'Is that *all*, Dr Gibbon?'

He frowned. 'I think it sufficient, my lady. His grace is in considerable pain. I was not able to persuade him to take laudanum, but he should do so.' His eyes moved to Anna, who was sitting limp with relief. 'Perhaps you will have better success.'

'I'll try, of course,' she said at once.

He inclined his head. 'Thank you. He should remain here for a few days, my lady. Even the short carriage ride to Chevely Hall would be inadvisable at this time.'

Lady Riddell raised her brows. 'Very well, Dr Gibbon. Do you intend to see the earl while you are here?'

'Yes, if you desire it.'

She met his eyes unflinchingly. 'I am not entirely satisfied with this newest servant, this Kelby person.'

'He was Mr Molineux's choice, ma'am, not mine,' said Dr Gibbon coolly. 'Nevertheless, I'll do as you request. Ah, Miss Farrow—'

'I am Miss Templeton,' said Anna, rising.

'Forgive me.' He handed her a vial and paper. 'I have mixed the drops and written out instructions for their administration. You may give these to his valet when that person arrives. But his grace should take a dose now. I prefer him to sleep as much as possible.'

Anna nodded. 'Very well.'

He took his leave, and she turned to her grandmother with a slight frown. 'Is it improper of me to go to his grace, Grandmama?'

Lady Riddell snorted. 'What a missish question! A man with broken ribs is in no shape to ravish anyone, my girl.'

Anna colored, but looked at her father. 'Do you object, Papa?'

'Certainly not,' he said, putting on his spectacles and regarding her through them. 'Why do you suppose I should?'

Anna lifted her chin. 'Cousin Molineux has a poor opinion of my doing so. We have quarreled on the subject. Excuse me,' she said as her father and grandmother exchanged glances, and went out.

Wishing she had dared tell them the betrothal was broken, Anna paused in her chambers to change out of her habit into a dress of blue crêpe with a prettily gathered flounce and ruching at the bodice. Then she returned to the duke's room, where Beavins admitted her. A good fire blazed in the grate, and Beavins had been straightening up the disorder. He held the duke's ruined coat over one arm.

'He desires his own man, miss.'

'Yes, of course.' Her eyes moved past the valet to the bed. 'He has been sent for. Thank you, Beavins. That is all for now.'

Beavins bowed and accepted his dismissal.

Clutching the bottle of laudanum in her hands, Anna went quietly forward to the bed. Rotham, now clad in a borrowed nightshirt, had been propped up high on a quantity of pillows. He lay there with his eyes shut, a frown upon his brow, and his mouth still drawn. One hand rested clenched upon the coverlet, and the ruby upon his finger glowed balefully.

'Your grace,' she said softly, touching his hand.

He looked up at her and smiled, less wanly than before. 'By Jove,' he murmured. 'I have seen the way past your reserve. Shall I endeavor to make a cake of myself more often?'

'Don't tease,' she pleaded, seating herself beside him. 'You have given me the most nightmarish morning of my life.'

He sobered. 'You knew Dante would—'

'Yes,' she said unsteadily, the horror of it still constricting her throat. 'Cousin Molineux had me look at him the other day.'

'Molineux, yes.' He frowned. 'I thought I heard him bellowing at you a short while ago. Demmed rude fellow—'

'But he was right,' she said, seeking to mistake his reference. 'If only you had listened to me.'

'Well, I rather wish I had,' he said ruefully. 'Dash it,

though, the brute wasn't soured six months ago. I'd stake my life upon it.'

'You did stake it,' she said and looked quickly away to hide her tears.

'Anna—'

She shook her head to silence him and with a great effort brought her emotions under control. 'You needn't fear I am going to be womanish and weep copious tears over you,' she said, throwing up her head. 'Besides, I think it's time you had your drops.'

His expression grew wry. 'I see you mean to bully me like the usual female in charge of a sickroom. Gad's life, and I haven't even my quizzing glass with which to defend myself.'

'You do not need it,' she said with a smile. 'You're going to have a shocking black eye that shan't want to ogle anyone.'

He was plainly tiring from their banter but managed to put up one eyebrow. 'Daresay the chambermaid shan't mind how I look as long as, stap me, I *look*. Eh?'

'Wretch.' Anna's lips quivered, but his evident exhaustion forced her not to encourage him further. She unstoppered the bottle and started to pour laudanum into the spoon when he put out his hand to stop her.

'I need none of that, thank you. Gad, I'm not an old dowager on the verge of vapors. Take it away, dear ma'am.'

She lowered the spoon with mild vexation. 'Do, pray, be quiet. I must count the drops.'

'No drops.' He tried to shift his weight upon the pillows and winced. 'Damn Gibbon! The cursed leech has bound me far too tight. I'm surprised he didn't try to cup me as well.'

'Stop acting like such a baby.' She eyed him severely. 'Open your mouth, sir, and swallow your dose.'

He frowned. 'Where the devil is Wilkes? No, Miss Templeton, I shan't. I have the greatest dislike of potions. Brandy I might accept.'

She set down the bottle sharply. 'You shan't have any. Of all the ridiculous notions . . . I wonder you do not accuse me of wishing to poison you.'

He flinched and looked away. 'No,' he said in a low voice. 'Not you. Did Gibbon give you that bottle?'

'Yes,' she said, frowning. 'With his own hand. Why—'

'Very well,' he said, sighing. 'I'll take the infernal drops. But only if you agree to give that bottle to Wilkes when he comes. Don't be leaving it about—'

'Yes,' she said, catching his restless hand and forcing it to lie still upon the coverlet. It felt dry and rather warm. Her eyes regarded him in fresh concern. 'Now you must rest. Please.'

To her relief he laid his head back against the pillows and remained silent while she counted the drops. He swallowed them, making so horrid a grimace she laughed.

'It could not be that bad. Really, your grace—'

He caught her hand. 'Wilkes *is* coming? I cannot stay here without him, you know.'

'Certainly,' she agreed, watching him fight his growing drowsiness. 'He will come.'

'Anna . . . ' He pressed her hand. 'I'm not such a paltry fellow, you know.'

'I know.'

'No, listen to me, please. I must apologize for getting in the way of things last night. Daresay you didn't want rescue—'

'Yes,' she said softly. 'I did.'

But his eyes had fallen shut, and she did not think he had heard her. She sat there, holding his hand until Wilkes did come at last. Carefully she drew her fingers from his slackened grasp and stood up.

'When he awakens, will you follow these directions from the doctor?' She handed the valet the paper. 'And also, please tell his grace that I gave the laudanum personally into your keeping.'

Wilkes, a small individual with neat carrot-colored hair, bowed and permitted himself a faint smile. 'Indeed, miss. His grace has a profound distrust of medicines. I shall follow Dr Gibbon's orders to the letter.'

She thanked him and went out. Luncheon had been served without her and she did not regard it for she could not bring herself even to think of food, but after having lain down for a while in her room, she came downstairs for tea and found herself ravenous at the sight of the laden tray in the upper saloon.

'Anna!' Neddie stood up, his blue eyes stormy. 'Only guess what Mollie has done now.'

Anna sat down with a sigh and accepted a cup from Mr Murvey, who was the only other person present. 'I have no idea, I'm afraid.'

'He has dismissed Hawkins.' Gesturing, Neddie paced about the room. 'Just like that. Turned him off without a reference, not that he needs one around here. But all the same, it is the shabbiest thing imaginable. Mollie can't be such a scabster as to blame Hawkins for what happened today! Anna, can't you tell him so? He won't listen to me.'

Anna put down her cup on a small table by her elbow. 'He isn't likely to listen to me either since I have blamed him for it.'

'Oh, Jupiter! I had forgotten that.' Neddie frowned.

Mr Murvey cleared his throat. 'Dear me, we seem all to be distraught. I fear you must have made your remark too hastily, Miss Templeton.'

Neddie turned on him with a glare. 'Dash it all, you're the man of business! Haven't I any way of stopping him? I hate how he runs roughshod here, as though Farrowsleigh belongs to him!'

Mr Murvey pursed his lips. 'I fear, my lord, that you are quite powerless until you become earl.'

'It isn't fair!' Neddie rammed his hands into his breeches pockets, scowling. 'He proses on and on about duty and responsibility, but it is all a hum with him if this is anything to judge by! But at least you've come to your senses, Anna, and thrown him over. Jupiter, but he looked queer when you sent him to the devil.'

Something twisted sharply within her, and she suddenly realized that in a moment's hysteria she had thrown away that which was most necessary to her and her father's futures. Had she been mad, to speak to Molineux in that ungoverned way?

She lifted somber eyes to Neddie. 'I spoke unjustly to him, Neddie, and must seek to make amends. You know where my duty lies.'

'Ah!' said Mr Murvey, sending her a smile.

'And I'd as lief you eloped with a Lascar!' said Neddie

hotly. 'You cannot make me believe that you like him. Money can't mean that much to you.'

His words hit her rather forcibly, but angered her all the more for their truth. Her brows snapped together. 'It is none of your concern whom I marry or why. You have stated your objection, Neddie. I beg you to be silent on the matter.'

'But, Anna—'

'No!' Abruptly she rose to her feet and walked out. For a moment she could not think of where to go or what to do, she was so vexed. Then she grew a degree calmer and felt ashamed of losing her temper with the boy. As she had done, he was letting his agitation rather than his good sense speak for him and could later regret it. For a long moment she stood there, frowning and still resistant, then she went on purposefully until she found James and asked him for Molineux's whereabouts.

She was directed to the library. Molineux stood at the far end of the room, a book open in his hand, his frowning gaze locked in the distance. He turned at the sound of her footsteps.

'Well!' he said and snapped the book shut. 'Neddie has sent you to cajole me into keeping that worthless groom. The boy is a sentimental fool.'

She took another step forward. 'I have not come at Neddie's bidding.'

'Oh, I see.' He smiled, not pleasantly. 'To apologize, then.'

Her fists clenched at her sides, but she said evenly, 'Yes. I was unforgivably rude to you, and I wish to beg your pardon.'

'I thought reflection would bring you around.' He laid the book aside and crossed his arms over his chest. 'Let me say this. I don't appreciate shrews, and you had better control that sharp tongue of yours in the future.'

Anna's eyes flashed at this exhibition of churlishness, and her notions of duty flew out of her head. 'You may go to the devil!'

'Really?' He came forward and seized her wrist before she could evade him.

106

She stiffened. 'If you *dare* foist your unwelcome advances upon me again, sir, I swear I shall box your ears. Of all the rude, arrogant, overbearing creatures in this world, you are by far the worst. Release me at once!'

He did so, looking thunderous. 'You go too far, ma'am. I don't brook insolence from mere chits—'

'No!' she burst out, 'you are far too conceited to accept a set-down you thoroughly deserve. I could say a great deal of my opinion of you, sir, but I shan't waste my breath. To be brief, Cousin Molineux, I shan't marry you! Not now. Not ever! You may look elsewhere for a compliant wife who will suffer your odious behavior.'

'Are you finished?' he asked in a low, menacing voice.

She lifted her chin. 'I believe I have been plain enough.'

'Plain, yes, and remarkably stupid.' He sneered. 'You see, I know all about your father. He can't live in this climate, can he? You've been fairly adept at winning Lady Riddell's favor, I'll grant you that, but she'll cut off her generosity quickly enough if you thwart her wishes.'

'I have no doubt of that,' replied Anna with contempt for his toadying notions. 'But I won't be bribed into going against my principles. You, sir, offend every sensibility, and I would sooner exist on a governess' wages and keep my self-respect than sell myself to you for twenty thousand pounds.'

His fists clenched as he narrowed his dark eyes. 'And your father?'

She had no intention of letting him see how deeply that shaft pierced through her. 'No, sir,' she said defiantly. 'We have lived in dun territory before. I have no doubt of being able to go to Italy and survive. And do stop brow-beating me! I know you think I am to be given the diamonds and thus you pursue me for no other aim, but you may rest easy on that score. I am not likely ever to receive them. Nor do I much care!'

'Don't be a fool,' he said sharply. 'They are priceless, and not to be whistled down the wind. Besides, who told you about them? Beatrice? No.' His eyes narrowed as Anna flushed. 'No, it wasn't her. Rotham has been chattering in your ear.' Suddenly he smiled in a way that chilled her. 'So that's your game. Why, you mercenary little jade! You think a duke is a better catch, don't you? You've thrown out lures to him since your arrival.' He laughed, his contempt cutting her on the raw. 'Good God, what a bird-witted ploy! He might give you *carte blanche*, Cousin, but never marriage.'

Her cheeks flared scarlet. 'How dare you say such a thing to me! Rotham is a gentleman who has never, *never* passed the line. While as for you—' She broke off, her expression sufficient to finish for her.

His eyes raked her. 'I kissed you. Yes, and you have been hysterical ever since. I suppose the caresses of a duke are more genteel, somehow more agreeable. Well, dream all you like, my dear, but you've cast your cap after a will-o'-the-wisp, and will never—'

She slapped him, with stinging force that numbed her hand and left red marks across his cheek.

For a moment he stood there tight-lipped and motionless save for the flame in his eyes. Then he inclined his head and said in a cold, deliberate voice, 'You leave me no choice. Doubtless, in your widgeonish, feminine way, you've felt sympathy for Rotham because his wife killed herself, and he is left haunted by scandal with a motherless child to raise. How touching.'

'I have heard, Cousin,' she said, equally coldly, 'that the scandal would have faded long ago had you not kept it alive.'

'Indeed, ma'am? I'll tell you why I do not let it go. Ellen Chevely did not die by her own hand. She was poisoned deliberately by her devoted husband, yes, the charming Duke of Rotham, who loathed her to the bottom of his soul.'

'No!' cried Anna, staring at him in horror. '*No!*'

'Yes!' Molineux glared at her, and try as she would she could read no lie in his face. 'He was riddled with debt and married her for her money. Only when the vows were spoken, it was revealed she had no more funds than he. You see only charm and wit of his manner, Cousin. You blind yourself to his deceit and cunning. Did I not tell you once he is my enemy? Do you know why? Because he has done all he can to make Neddie hate and distrust me. He has succeeded. As soon as Neddie becomes earl, my capable direction of his affairs will be thrown away, and Rotham will be free to sponge off the Riddell fortune. Yes, Anna! He is a murderer, and a liar, and a rake. Ask anyone if you can't believe me.' He gazed levelly into her stricken eyes. 'Ask Beatrice. Ask the squire. If you dare, ask them! But I tell you this, my girl. For my part, he deserved what happened today and far worse. And the sooner he leaves this house, the better.' With that, he brushed by her and left her standing alone and numbed in the vast shadowed room.

Chapter Nine

That evening Anna dressed early for dinner, dismaying Betty by donning her old yellow sarcenet. She took the emerald necklace in its case and went to her father's room, interrupting him in the midst of tying his cravat. He turned from the mirror long enough to raise his brows at her.

She smiled wanly. 'Poor Papa. What a struggle you are having.'

He grunted and went back to wrestling with his neckcloth. 'Fashion is a devilish beast. I cannot for the life of me discover what Rotham does with the ends of his cravat. They are never in evidence.'

'Perhaps you should ask him.'

'Not I,' he said with a snort, tugging gingerly at a fold with his chin thrust up at an unnatural angle. 'You know I never descend to discussions of fripperies.'

'Yes, Papa,' she said kindly. 'But it would be the easiest way to learn how to manage your neckcloth.'

'This will do.' He coughed and turned his back on the looking glass, hunting in his pockets for his spectacles. 'Well, Anna, what are you about? Don't you mean to dress for dinner?'

That cut her so sharply it was a moment before she could answer. She looked down. 'I am . . . Papa, we must leave Farrowsleigh.'

'Leave? Why?' He stared at her in considerable displeasure. 'I thought Molineux popped the question.'

'He did,' said Anna in some desperation.

'Well, then! We—'

'Papa, please. I cannot marry him. I will not.' She drew in a deep, miserable breath. 'I do not respect him.'

Mr Templeton paused to frown intently at her. 'Anna! Good God! Have you been weeping?'

She lifted her eyes to his, intending to deny it, but under the sternness of his gaze she nodded instead.

'Missishness,' he said. 'It does not become you. I vow, you

110

have acquired the habit from that dreadful aunt of yours.'

'I have done nothing of the sort.' She compressed her lips, a spark kindling in her eyes. 'I shall never forgive him for what he said to me! He is a vicious backbiter, and believes in nothing save his own ruthless ambitions. I'm sorry, Papa, I realize I have whistled all your plans down the wind—'

'What you have done is whistle twenty thousand pounds down the wind,' he said tartly. 'Heavens, girl, when I taught you not to love money, I did not mean for you to become an utter ninny. You must go at once and tender your apology.'

Her chin came up. 'I have jilted him, sir. I'm going now to tell Grandmama.'

For a moment Mr Templeton did not speak, then he threw up his hands. 'Bah! We may as well go. You have thrust a spoke in the wheel with uncommon thoroughness. Did I once say a daughter was to be preferred over a son? I must have been mad.'

'Oh, Papa!' She rushed to embrace him. 'I'm sorry! Truly I am. But we can contrive without the Farrow money. We have always done so.'

He sighed and gave her shoulder an awkward pat. 'And what is to become of you when I die?'

'Papa!' She jerked back.

'Well? All men die,' he said fiercely. 'I don't wish your future to be spinsterhood. You aren't clever enough or rich enough to be an eccentric. God knows I'd as lief grow two heads as see you become a drudge of a governess. That leaves marriage. Why must you be so stubborn?'

There was no answer she could give him. He returned her gaze, thin and just a bit stooped with his spectacles perched on his nose and his gray hair rumpled, then snorted and turned away.

'You are a headstrong child. I suppose I'd better ring for my trunk.'

She released her breath. 'Thank you, Papa!'

'Thank me? Why thank me? You are the one who shall suffer for it.' He waved a hand, avoiding her eyes. 'Run along.'

At her grandmother's door, her courage nearly failed her, but she took herself in hand and knocked. When she was at last admitted to the countess' presence, Anna found her grandmother sitting swathed in a lace peignoir in the process of having her snowy hair dressed. Lady Riddell acknowledged Anna with a stony glance.

'You are a fool,' she said.

Anna tightened her lips. 'Perhaps,' she said clearly and laid the necklace case upon the dressing table. 'I have disappointed more people than merely you, Grandmama. I'm sorry, but it is impossible for me to carry out the wishes of you and my father.'

Lady Riddell lifted a hand, and her maid went into an adjoining room, closing the door noiselessly behind her. 'Oliver tells me you have been making sheep's eyes at Rotham. Is that true?'

Anna did not bother to hide her anger. 'It is not,' she said with something of a snap. 'I enjoy his grace's company and find his sense of humor diverting. Anything else is Cousin Molineux's imagining. I had hoped to be able to talk to you before he came with whatever he has chosen to say, but I see I am too late.' She met her grandmother's frowning eyes. 'Papa and I will be going in the morning.'

'Is this why you are dressed in that shabby affair and bring back the jewels I gave you?' demanded the countess in a harsh voice, her nostrils flaring.

'I do not *sponge*, Grandmama.'

'That pride of yours will land you in the basket, my girl. Show a little sense! What is there in your cousin which you find so exceptional?'

Anna made a slight gesture of repugnance. 'Need I—'

'Yes! Speak up. I will have your reasons for this flight.'

'Very well,' said Anna. 'First of all there is his treatment of Neddie—'

'Poppycock! The boy is an insolent puppy.'

'Neddie is spoiled, certainly,' said Anna firmly. 'But he need not be treated with contempt.'

The countess snorted. 'What else?'

Anna's cheeks flushed again. 'I will not be treated with contempt either.'

The countess smiled in a knowing way. 'Tried to kiss you, did he? That, girl, you will grow used to.'

'A gentleman does not embrace a lady against her will,' said

Anna with a flash of her eyes. 'Did you know Cousin Molineux has dismissed your head groom without suitable grounds? Did you know he despises you because you will not let him run the estate entirely as he wishes? Did you know that when I sought a reconciliation with him this afternoon he sneered at my apology and cast all the wrong on me?' Anna clenched her fists. 'I shan't be ridden roughshod over by an arrogant, conceited, pompous block, nor treated as though I am a possession. Furthermore, I do not care to be accused of throwing myself at Rotham's head. And as for the slander Cousin Molineux cast against his grace, I can only label such tactics despicable and beneath a gentleman.'

'You mean you fear what he said is true,' said the countess grimly.

Anna turned her face away. 'You have been kind and most generous to me, ma'am,' she said with a slight break in her voice as Lady Riddell went on glaring at her. 'For that I thank you.'

'Do you expect me to beg you to stay?' demanded the countess haughtily.

Anna frowned. 'No. Why should you? I have not kept my part of the bargain.'

'You have not! Well? If you have no more to say for yourself, you may go.' The countess waved a curt hand. 'All I have could have been yours, you fool. But go. Go!'

Anna curtsied and went out with her head rather high.

Dinner that evening was a constrained affair. Molineux sat looking like a thundercloud, and Anna was not disposed to attempt conversation. Mr Templeton showed no appetite for buttered crab, and every time Anna glanced at him and his untouched plate a pang of remorse struck her. Only Lady Edwin seemed in high spirits, but a terse remark from Lady Riddell soon dampened her. As soon as possible Anna excused herself and went upstairs to supervise the packing of her trunk. The Christmas gifts she had bought reproached her, and at last she stuck them all away in a drawer. It would not be a festive holiday for her father and her, travelling along some damp road, unwanted and thrown on their own meager resources once again. And even should she contrive to find employment in London, where was Papa to go?

It was only then that she recalled her mysterious visitor the night before. Wryly Anna threw the note on the fire and walked slowly about her sitting room, which had become so familiar to her. *Leave the house*, the note had said. Well, someone was getting his wish.

But in the morning when she rang for the footman to carry down her trunk, the summons was not answered. And when she hastened downstairs in considerable dudgeon to see what was the cause of this delay, she found no carriage waiting at the steps and no one willing to bring it around.

'Point nonplus, my dear,' said Mr Templeton and gave his hat to Dobbs before escaping into the library.

Her brows together, Anna turned on the butler. 'What is the meaning of this?'

He did not meet her kindling eyes. 'Orders from Mr Oliver, Miss Anna.'

'Orders indeed.' She drew in a deep breath. 'Where is my cousin, Dobbs?'

'He has driven to Plover, Miss Anna, in the chaise, and is not expected home until late afternoon.'

She withdrew then from the hall, as expressionless as Dobbs, although within she longed to smash something over her arrogant cousin's head. No doubt he thought himself clever, but she was not defeated yet. Gathering up her skirts, she went upstairs with a determined set to her mouth and knocked on Rotham's door. Wilkes admitted her and somewhat to her surprise she found his grace propped up on his pillows in a dressing gown of scarlet brocade, a breakfast tray across his knees, and Neddie seated on one corner of the bed in the process of reading aloud from a book.

Both of them looked up at her entrance. Rotham lifted his quizzing glass to one eye, the other being as black and swollen as her prediction.

'Stap me,' he drawled, not yet with his usual strength. 'What a pleasant way to start one's day. Do come in, Miss Templeton, and visit with us.'

She had been able, until that moment, to force to the back of her mind what Molineux had said about Rotham. Now, with the duke looking at her in that glinting way of his, she had to wonder.

114

Whatever else he might be, her cousin was a square and truthful man. Could Rotham be that wicked? Was he a killer, this man who endured young chubs like Neddie and sent hats to inexperienced young women of his acquaintance? She searched his lean countenance, able to read no answer, and in her heart despised Molineux for having cast this doubt in her way.

Rotham raised his brows. 'Sudden scruples over your intrusion, ma'am? Put them aside, I beg you.' He smiled in self-deprecation. 'I am quite bound here to helplessness and in no condition to ravish anyone. By the by,' he added as her cheeks flamed. 'The chambermaid is muffin-faced and prone to spots.' He affected a shudder, only to wince and abruptly close his eyes.

Anna came forward in concern, but almost at once he lifted his head and raised a hand to ward her off.

'Do not put yourself in a pucker. I am getting along very well, thank you.'

'No, you are not,' said Neddie, tossing his book aside. He saw Anna's eyes go to it and added defensively, 'Yes, it's yours, the one you left in my room. I thought if I read to him he would not talk. He isn't supposed to, not much anyway. And he won't eat any of his breakfast.'

Anna lifted a cover on the tray. There was a bowl of broth, cooling, and a bit of soft egg, all untouched. She frowned slightly and glanced back at the duke, noting now the heaviness about his eyes and a faint flush on his cheek.

'You are looking positively haggard,' she said, but did not place her hand on his brow to check for fever as she would have done yesterday. 'Perhaps we had better all of us leave you in peace.'

'No,' he said quickly as Neddie stood up. 'That is, will you go away without mentioning what brought you here in such magnificent color?'

The ease with which he complimented her and even the faint suggestion of a smile upon his face as his eyes looked up into hers struck her with a consciousness heightened by Molineux's spiteful words. Had she grown too at ease in Rotham's company?

'You're dressed for traveling,' said Neddie, suddenly, his blue eyes lighting up. 'Are you leaving Farrowsleigh then? Capital!'

She looked at him, hurt. 'Do you like me so little, Neddie? I had thought we dealt well enough together.'

'Lord, I didn't mean that!' Crestfallen, he gestured. 'Of course I like you, Anna, for you never rip up at one, or make a fuss one don't like. It's just that . . . well, if you're leaving, then you aren't going to reconcile with *him*.'

'Oh, Neddie.' She sighed. 'You are incorrigible.'

'So it's farewell, is it?' said Rotham rather coolly. He eyed her through his quizzing glass without his usual smile. 'Damme, I'm surprised. I confess I did not think you would give in so easily.'

Her chin lifted. 'I have not given in. I am leaving because I cannot bring myself to remain.'

'To marry Mollie, you mean,' said Neddie with glee. 'I *knew* you'd never stomach it.'

'Neddie, *please*,' she said in exasperation and met the duke's hooded eyes. 'I came here, sir, to ask for your help.'

'My help?' he murmured in displeasure. 'Dear me, I'm no good at remembering stagecoach timetables. Ask Wilkes. Ask Dobbs. Wilkes! Be a good fellow and remove this.' He waved fastidiously at the breakfast tray. 'I am quite tired of it.'

She watched the valet obey, then said with some stiffness, 'Your grace mistakes me. I came to ask . . . I wish for . . . ' She twisted her hands together. 'Cousin Molineux has gone to Plover in the carriage. May I have the use of yours to take myself and Papa to the coaching office in Linwick?' She flushed slightly beneath his cold gaze. 'Indeed, it is perhaps presumptuous of me to make such a request of your generosity, but I—'

She broke off because with a yawn he had begun to study his nails. When she stopped talking, he lifted a finger.

'Neddie, be good enough to step outside with Wilkes a moment.'

Anna frowned as the two threw her glances of curiosity and went out, leaving her to stand there constrained and not quite sure where to look.

'He told you, did he not?' said Rotham in a cold, curt way completely unlike his usual languid tones.

She looked up with a blink, and his expression hardened.

'I thought so. You have that look of wanting to pity me but not quite daring to.'

Her breath seemed to leave her. She stared at him. 'Is it true?'

He laughed, but broke off with a gasp of pain, his hand clenching hard on the coverlet. 'I am not stupid enough to reply to that question,' he said harshly, still struggling for breath. He let his head drop back upon the pillow.

She was torn between the desire to seek some way of easing his discomfort and a growing sense of revulsion. She had not known him at all. He was a stranger . . . a monster. He did not even trouble to deny it. Dear God . . . her lower lip began to tremble, and she bit down upon the inside of it in desperation to betray nothing. What was she to do? What was she to say? Quite suddenly, as she stood there dumb and stricken, staring at him as she never had before, she realized she loved him and with such intensity the ache of it had become a part of her. Molineux had been right. She loved Rotham! And he lay there sneering at her.

'And now I have lost your friendship, Miss Templeton,' he said in a cutting way. 'Well, it does not surprise me. There are few who do not blench at rubbing shoulders with a murderer.'

Wretched, she lifted her eyes to his. 'If you do not deny it, I have no choice but to believe what I am told.'

His gaze fell. 'Some believe. Some do not. My denial, Miss Templeton, makes little difference to either group.'

'It would to me!' she cried.

His eyes flew up, and for a moment he searched her scarlet face. 'Yes,' he said gently at last, 'it would. Tell me first, before I answer, would the truth make you give up this notion of going away?'

'I cannot marry him!' she cried, feeling as though she were being sucked deeper into a quagmire of doubt. What did he want her to answer? What might he say?

'Such a marriage would be greatly to your advantage,' he said in a quiet voice, wounding her to the heart. 'Mollie is not a man I admire, but that signifies nothing. Dash it, you would have all the freedom marriage gives a woman. You could do as you like.'

Her head snapped up. *He will offer you carte blanche,*

Molineux had said. Anger burned through her, and she turned her back on the duke.

'It is true, then,' she said furiously. 'You will not deny it, and you evade giving your answer. You *did* kill your wife, and I—'

'No!' he said so sharply she was silenced.

She stared at him, but he had turned his face away so that she could see nothing but the working of his jaw.

'I wish Ellen at the devil,' he said after a moment, his voice rough. 'Alive, she made my life miserable and, damme, in the grave she contrives to continue the business.' He struck the coverlet with his fist. 'I did *not* kill her! I wish to God you would all let her lie.' Abruptly he turned his head back to glare at Anna with more anger than she had ever seen in him. 'Does that satisfy you, ma'am?'

She bit her lip. 'Please. I wished only to know—'

'Yes, and if you are at such outs with your cousin, I fear I must wonder why you persist in believing every word he utters. Did he tell you I married Ellen for her money?' Rotham gave a scornful laugh, pressing a hand to his side. The faint color which had tinged his face was gone, leaving his skin gray against the furious bruise on his cheek. 'For love, ma'am, for what I thought was love. But marriage is no arena for sentiment.' For an instant the anger glazed in his eyes as swift and as sharp as a rapier's point, then he let his lids fall half shut. 'You had better follow the dictates of duty,' he said wearily, 'and wed someone you care nothing for. It is less wearing on the emotions.'

'How odious you are,' she said in a low, intense voice. 'How odious, and wretched, and cruel.'

He raised his brows at her. 'What is it you expect of me? I cannot believe your father willing to let you have your way in this matter, and even if he is, for me to lend you my carriage would give Molineux the right – nay, the obligation – to call me out. And he is a far better shot than I am.'

'Pray, do anything but make a joke of it!' she said so fiercely he broke off in surprise.

'Do you dislike the notion of dueling? Gad, so do I—'

'You know very well to what I refer.' She gestured bitterly, her eyes filling with tears she was too proud to shed. She had been a fool to come to him. Oh, but she had been a stupid, stupid fool! 'I

. . . I see I was mistaken in expecting your grace to help me avoid humiliation. You are quite right. The shackle of duty must stay on. Good-day, your grace!' Choking, she ran out, and slammed the door on his attempt to call her back.

Chapter Ten

'This is the second time you have come to beg my pardon for your behavior,' said Molineux the next morning when she finally was able – after hours of stormy raging and tears – to leave her room and her pride and go downstairs to him. He sat across from her in a wing chair, his dark blue coat neatly brushed, his linen and pantaloons flawless. His expression was set, his dark eyes cold.

'I am not appreciative of being jilted, Cousin,' he went on in a hard voice. 'You appear to enjoy blowing hot and cold. Such games do not appeal to me. Nor will you find Lady Riddell inclined to view you with much leniency.' He let his eyes linger upon her rather contemptuously. 'All the same, you are easily managed. I'm surprised you did not appeal to the duke for his carriage yesterday.'

Anna's eyes lifted at that barb, but fell again without answer.

Molineux smiled for a moment, then said like a lash, 'And what if I do cast you out, my girl, as you wish me to? Give you use of the carriage indeed. Where do you mean to go?' He leaned back in his chair to cross one booted leg over the other. 'As you said, there are plenty of women more compliant of nature than you. I should not suffer from your stupidity.'

She bit her lip, struggling to hold down her temper. He would like to crush her spirit to extinction by making her beg for permission to leave this house, and in her heart she despised him.

'You are silent. That marks a decided improvement,' he said with feigned approval, making her long to strike him as she had before. 'But I do not intend to let you go, Anna. Surely you understand that.' He adjusted one of his cuffs. 'Did you know our grandmother will give me an equal sum to yours if we marry? Forty thousand pounds is a considerable increase in the stakes. And I intend to win them, even though it means enduring an over-educated giantess with a shrewish disposition.'

Anna gasped. 'You vile brute—'

'Silence!' He glared at her. 'Have a care, my girl, for you are in no position to give your temper free rein. Here.' He drew out a square of paper from his pocket and tossed it on to her lap.

She frowned at it, beginning to hope. 'A stagecoach ticket to London?'

'A one-way fare, you will note.' He gestured. 'Give it to your father. He is leaving in an hour's time.'

'But—'

'In London he is to take a letter to Murvey's office. Murvey is writing it now. It authorizes a draft to be written on our account, establishing a quarterly allowance payable to Walter Templeton. And also, he'll be given ship's fare to Naples. Well? That is what you want, is it not?'

An awful sensation of dread swept over her. She frowned, unable to answer him.

'Is it not true his health is seriously endangered?' Molineux raised his brows. 'I thought the sooner he reached a more salubrious climate the better. And now that the French blockade has been broken, he should have a safe and speedy journey.' Molineux snapped his fingers. 'Come, come! You have no choice in the matter now. I can add years to his life with that ticket. What can your stubbornness give him save an early grave?'

'Stop!' She pressed her hands over her ears. He smiled faintly, his eyes growing arrogant as he watched her distress. But even as she realized there was no escaping the trap he had laid for her, pride stiffened her. She lowered her hands to her lap and stared past him. 'Thank you,' she said in a low, unsteady voice. 'I agree that Papa should go.'

Molineux stood up. 'You do understand, do you not, that if you exhibit more of these lamentable lapses of temper, your father shall find himself cut off without a penny. I have been told that penury in Naples is not a pleasant state. Italian rabble are not—'

'Very well!' She, too, rose and met his gaze stormily. 'I understand what you mean, sir. I . . . ' Her eyes fell as she struggled to retain mastery over herself. 'I agree to your terms.'

'Good.' He stepped closer and stood staring down at her. His forefinger traced the outline of her jaw, stopping at her chin, which he tilted up.

Anna stiffened, but the look in his dark eyes told her she must submit now . . . and forever. Oh, Rotham! cried her heart, but then Molineux's lips crushed hers with a force so bruising and masterful every thought was shocked from her. Despite her re-solution she would have pulled free had his powerful arm not held her fast. The dreadful moment seemed to last an eternity while he kissed her shut eyes, her rigid lips, and the hollow of her throat where the pulse raced so madly it seemed her veins must soon burst. Nausea heaved within her at the shame of his touch. And when at last he released her, she was trembling with the effort of submission.

He smiled, his eyes lingering possessively upon her. 'I think there will be no more trouble between us. And, in time, you'll learn to like my kisses.' Arrogantly he tapped her aching lips with his fingers. 'In time you may even learn to beg for them.' She stiffened, and he laughed. 'Go now and say farewell to your father. The banns will be read this week.'

She inclined her head and walked out with a good semblance of composure, but as soon as she was away from him and in a secluded corner, a dry sob escaped her and she rubbed and rubbed and rubbed at her lips, trying to erase the imprint of his own still lingering upon them.

The sight of the footmen carrying her father's battered hand trunk into the hall reminded her that time was fleeing. In sudden desperation, she ran upstairs and met him at the landing.

'Papa!' she cried, her eyes pleading. 'Oh, Papa, please—'

'Now, now, Anna,' he said sternly, holding her at arm's length. 'No vapors, if you please.' Then he paused and continued in gentler tones, 'I must go, my dear, without you. When I was young, I was a devil-may-care fellow. But now I am an old man. Yes.' He put up a hand as she started to protest. 'An old man, useless and crotchety. I've always indulged you, my dear, and I suppose I would have done so again against my better judgement. But Molineux has spoken to me like a sensible man.' He coughed harshly with a rattle deep in his chest. 'They're deuced generous, you know.' He met her eyes then, in an apology he could not speak.

She gazed at him, seeing the lines carved so deeply in his face and the weariness in his eyes. For a moment she hated him as she hated Molineux, but then reason returned to her, and she knew she must not go on being selfish.

Tears welled up in her eyes. 'Oh, Papa, I shall miss you—'

He kissed her cheek and gave her hand a pat. 'Keep your wits, girl. Remember you're a Templeton and can read Greek. Don't learn to simper. Good-bye.' He blinked at her rather fiercely, and thrust a small book at her before going on downstairs.

Slowly she followed, and even braved the cold to stand on the steps outside with the wind plucking at her hair and dress. A few half-frozen droplets of rain stung her face while Mr Templeton was settled in the chaise with a thick lap robe tucked about his shanks and a hot brick placed by his feet. Then, all too suddenly, the steps were put up, the door slammed, and the horses started. She hastened forward, holding out her hand, but the chaise was already turning down the drive. Mr Templeton's handkerchief fluttered from the window briefly before he was gone, leaving her behind . . . frightened . . . and very much alone.

Returning inside, she paused in the hall to look at the volume he had given her. It was bound in shabby calf and held a collection of verses written in the sentimental vein he usually scorned. On the inside cover was written a loving inscription from Lady Amelia Templeton to her husband, the date that of their elopement. Slowly Anna closed the book, her lips compressed. No, she did not blame him but she was far too conscious of the irony of his actions in stealing her mother from Farrowsleigh only to return his child to its walls like some long overdue apology. She sighed and went upstairs to her rooms, cold inside with anger, hurt, and a certain measure of unforgiveness at this final abandonment.

A formal dinner party was to be given that evening to celebrate the beginning of the days of Christmas. Anna found the necklace casc lying on her dressing table, and opened it with the air of donning a slave's collar. She gazed about the candlelit chamber, gleaming softly with velvet hangings and rich woods. Betty was going about her work, laying Anna's gown out with great care. The jewels sparkled and glowed upon the table. Anna lowered her eyes. She would never again know material want, but just now she felt as though she had been flung to the very depths of poverty. Her father was gone, and she must compromise everything within her heart for now and all time.

More importantly, she must put the duke from her heart permanently or she could never survive her future with Molineux. Rotham had no deep liking for her in return, at least not the sort she craved. Were she married and a woman of the world, he might choose to trifle with her, but she wanted more than that. She wanted . . . Her cheeks flamed, and with fumbling fingers she clasped the topaz necklace around her throat. She belonged now to Molineux; she could have no hope of anyone else. Sighing, she began to get ready.

An hour later when she entered the drawing room, only a certain tightness to her lips could have given her away. She wore russet silk over a frilled petticoat with soft kid slippers dyed to match. The golden jewels gleamed at her throat with the same muted fire as that in the depths of her dark gray eyes. Several of the guests were already assembled, most of them as close as possible to the blazing fire. Anna recognized Mrs Hardcastle and Squire Wetherby. The rest were strangers to her. Lady Edwin sat on a sofa, charming in spangled net worn over blue tulle. Her rippling laughter floated above the other conversations, and the gentleman talking to her edged noticeably closer to her side.

Molineux was not yet present. Relieved, Anna smiled as Mr Murvey came hurrying forward to greet her and curtsied to the squire, who followed him.

'Hah, Miss Templeton,' he said in his bluff way. 'We meet in better circumstances this time. I've brought London guests . . . m'wife's brother and his wife.' He gestured at the gentleman so engaged with Lady Edwin, frowned, then glanced past Anna. His brows flew up. 'Why . . . your grace!' he said, bowing.

Anna turned in astonishment to find that Rotham had entered the room. The conversations broke off one by one as they all gave him bows or nods of courtesy. He stood there rather haughtily, resplendent in a coat of apricot silk, his cravat the Waterfall, the painful-looking bruise surrounding the cut upon his cheek dimmed by powder. For an instant she thought he had left his buffoon mannerisms behind him, but even as it crossed her mind, he lifted his quizzing glass with the lace spilling back from his hand and curled his lips into a smirk.

'Stap me,' he drawled. 'A positive crowd. Comstead, my dear fellow, you've lost weight.' He nodded to a tall gentleman in regimentals. 'Does Wellington keep you run ragged? How very disobliging of him.'

Major Comstead returned a civil answer, and conversations

resumed. Rotham advanced slowly into the room, warding off the approach of a plump matron with a languid wave.

'No, no, madam. I beg you will not curtsy, for I cannot bow.' He smiled graciously at her flustered expression and came up beside Anna. 'Miss Templeton. Squire. I assure, you, dear sir, I am not being stiff-rumped. This style of cravat prevents me from moving my head, so I cannot nod to you unless I bow, and I cannot bow for I cannot bend.' He sighed. 'How very tedious it is going to become, tendering constant apologies.'

The squire frowned. 'What the devil are you doing here, your grace? For my mind, you look like something the cat dragged in. Aye, and then abandoned.'

Rotham laughed softly. 'Blunt fellow. How you delight me, sir! I assure you I am perfectly well, however deplorable I may look.'

But Anna thought his eyes still looked unnatural, and he was far too pale and drawn. She could not help but ask, 'Did Dr Gibbon give you permission to be up and about, sir?'

His gray eyes flicked to her, and he lifted a brow. 'Permission? I greatly fear I never permit myself to ask the permission of others. Will you give St. Byre my thanks for fetching over the mail from Chevely Hall? I was asleep when he brought it, and it was most kind of him to ride out in this miserable weather.'

She nodded, as cool in manner as he. But as soon as the squire had moved away, Rotham came down from the lofty heights.

'Gad, John Bull in the life,' he murmured, causing her to choke involuntarily. He glanced at her with a glint in his eyes. 'Obviously you chose to heed my advice. I'm glad.'

Her brows drew together and she looked swiftly away. 'You could have saved your breath, sir, for my cousin has arranged matters precisely to his satisfaction.'

'Has he indeed? I wonder.' Rotham surveyed the assembly through his glass. 'Where is the diverting Molineux?'

'I assume he is escorting Grandmama downstairs,' said Anna. The sense of hurt welled up within her again, causing her to send him a curt glance. 'Excuse me. I have a word for Aunt Beatrice.'

She walked away and joined the small court around Lady Edwin, who greeted her with marked coolness. Soon engaged with introductions and small chatter, Anna only once had occasion to glance the duke's way. He had gone to lean rather heavily against the fireplace. Concern sent a pang through her.

Lady Edwin also looked his way. 'Poor Victor looks dreadful. I am persuaded he ought to be in bed.'

Then the double doors swung open, and Dobbs announced in stentorian tones, 'Lady Riddell!'

The company rose as she came slowly into the room upon Molineux's arm. Her piercing eyes swept the faces, and she nodded graciously. Then she spied Rotham at the fireplace and smiled with unfeigned pleasure.

'Your grace!' she said, holding out a thin beringed hand.

He came forward to gallantly raise it to his lips. 'My lady.'

She snorted. 'You do not look to be on your deathbed. I see my concern has been wasted.'

He smiled, returning a witty answer, but Anna had no more occasion to listen to their repartee for Molineux had come to her.

'Cousin.' He smiled and bowed over her hand, pressing her fingers.

She won the brief inner struggle not to snatch them from his clasp and forced herself to meet his dark eyes. 'Good evening, sir,' she said levelly.

He tucked her hand inside his arm. 'Come and speak to Grandmama.'

Conscious of all the eyes and the faint murmurs behind fans, Anna allowed herself to be led over to the countess. She curtsied deeply, her hand still in Molineux's.

Lady Riddell tapped Anna's shoulder with her fan. 'Very sensible. I confess, however, that I lost my wager with Rotham. I thought you would leave us.'

Anna gasped, her eyes flying in a fury to the duke, who curled his lip. So he had said those things about marriage and duty merely to win a bet! The miserable, lying wretch!

'Dinner is served, my lady.'

Anna's burning eyes fell as the countess turned to place her hand on Rotham's arm. Silently Anna let Molineux lead her to the dining hall, where a fabulous repast awaited them. To Anna's further dismay, she was seated on her grandmother's left, with Rotham directly across from her, thus leaving her at the mercy of his quizzical gaze. Anna ate the first course without having the least notion of what she swallowed. They had all warned her not to trust Rotham, and she had ignored their advice. He was a capricious, heartless devil!

The squire kept most of the talk centered on poachers, boring them all save Molineux and another gentleman. Somehow she got through the intolerable meal, even overcoming the flaming desire to hurl her glass at Rotham's head. He kept up his banter with the countess, frequently causing her to utter her sharp laugh. Anna noticed he drank more than he ate and told herself she hoped he made himself ill.

Then mercifully at last it was time to withdraw. Anna gave a sigh of relief, hoping for a moment of solitude, but Lady Edwin came to sit beside her in the drawing room.

'You have surprised me very much, Anna dearest,' she said in cool accents. 'I was certain you meant to leave us.'

Somehow Anna dragged out a smile. 'The misunderstanding has been cleared away.'

'Yes, but how odd of Walter to go off without seeing you wed.' Aunt Beatrice raised her delicate brows. 'Of course he is an eccentric so we must not expect him to behave as we would like, but aren't you terribly disappointed?'

Unable to decide if her aunt were merely tactless or the most malicious creature alive, Anna dropped her eyes and admitted to disappointment, but said, 'His health is more important. Cousin Molineux has shown such generosity to Papa.'

'So that is how it is!' Lady Edwin looked much struck. 'You poor dear. If only I—'

She broke off then with an apprehensive glance over her shoulder as the gentlemen came in. Puzzled, Anna had no more chance to talk with her, for they all went away to the ballroom and danced into the small hours. Anna found herself gratifyingly popular, and although she was obliged to stand up twice with Molineux he made no remark out of the way to overset her precarious composure. As for Rotham, she had no chance to put a flea in his ear, for he did not attend the dancing and made no further appearance that evening.

In the late morning, however, as she was going downstairs for a ride with Neddie she was waylaid by Wilkes. At once, despite her vexation with the duke, a pang of alarm clutched her.

'Yes?' she said quickly. 'What is wrong?'

127

Wilkes inclined his bright head. 'His grace wishes a word with you, miss.'

Her brows came up. 'Is that all? Give him my excuses, for I have not time—'

'Please.' Wilkes' eyes met hers with an appeal that undermined her annoyance. 'He is most upset. He suffered a bad night, as I told him he must after coming downstairs and rushing things. And now with the news that's come to him, he won't rest, and I fear we shall have to send for the doctor—'

'Very well,' she said, drawing in a deep breath. 'Let me send word to Lord St. Byre that I shall be a few minutes delayed.' This done, she followed Wilkes upstairs to the duke's chamber, stripping off her gloves as she went.

From what the valet had said, she expected to see his grace pacing about, but, no, when she entered he was propped up in bed with his eyes closed. Before she could turn on Wilkes, however, Rotham raised his golden head.

'Miss Templeton! The very person I require. And dressed for riding. Excellent.'

Frowning, she drew nearer, not liking his pallor or the nervous movements of his hands. 'Have you been taking your drops?'

For answer he picked up a litter of correspondence scattered over the coverlet. 'This has brought the most appalling news. It is from my daughter's governess, the wretched woman wishing to inform me that she and the child expect to arrive today.'

Anna smiled. 'How delightful—'

'No!' he said sharply, flinging the letter aside. 'It is not at all delightful.' He paused a moment, his jaw working, and pressed a hand to his side. 'Damn!'

'You must strive for a little calm, sir,' she told him worriedly. 'Are you in much pain?'

'Blast the pain,' he said, regaining his breath after a moment. 'Please . . . ride to Chevely Hall and inform Greer that he is to say I have left.'

She frowned. 'I do not understand. Don't you wish to see your little girl?'

'Gad, no! I . . . ' He paused, frowning. 'Yes, yes, of course. But she will want to stay, and we shall be obliged to go through another scene of tears and deuced unpleasantness.' He swallowed, his eyes

128

half shut as he clenched a fist. 'I do not wish to explain these private matters at length, Miss Templeton. Please . . . just tell Greer what he is to do. I said good-bye to my daughter six months ago. I do not wish to go through all that again.'

'But what has brought her home so unexpectedly?' asked Anna, seeking to divert him to less agitation. Fine beads of perspiration had broken out across his brow. She took out her handkerchief and began dabbing gently at them. 'Perhaps there is something—'

He clutched her wrist. 'Please, Miss Templeton?'

She drew back, but he did not release her. His gray eyes held an appeal she could not refuse.

'Please do this for me.'

Uncertainly she glanced at Wilkes, then back to the duke. Her frown deepened, but she gave in. 'Very well. But could you not send a boy over with your instructions?'

He shook his head, letting his hand fall wearily from her wrist. 'It is my hope that perhaps you may see her arrive. Greer is not good at observation. I should like to be told how she looks . . . if she is well.'

Anna looked down, her anger against him fading. 'Yes, I shall stay as long as I can,' she said quietly and turned to go.

'Miss Templeton.'

She looked back over her shoulder.

'Thank you,' he said with a faint smile. 'You are a true friend.'

'Do not.' She put out a hand of repudiation. 'I fear we shall never be friends. Friends do not treat each other as you—' Abruptly she broke off and hastened out.

Chapter Eleven

It was bitterly cold outside, the air like knives in the lungs. Neddie set a blistering pace to Chevely Hall, and Anna was glad of it for she neither wished to think or talk. But as they came trotting up the drive with its yew hedge and statues, she released a sigh of relief that no carriage stood yet at the door, then grew fiercely ashamed of herself for having agreed to come on this despicable errand. Why was it, that no matter how angry she became at the duke, he could still with a look and a smile turn her to his bidding? It was dreadful to be so much wax in his hands.

'Anna, why are you glowering so?' asked Neddie as they dismounted and started inside. 'Don't you like coming here?'

'Was I?' With an effort she shook off her thoughts and schooled her features into a more pleasant expression. 'I'm sorry. Of course I like this house.' Removing her hat and gloves for the butler, she glanced around at the spacious, well-lit hall. It was indeed lovely here, a home where no one ought to be sad or unkind.

The ring of hastening footsteps turned her and Neddie about to face toward the stairs. A plump young man in neat tailoring was coming.

'Welcome, my lord,' he said, bowing to Neddie. Then he looked at Anna and smiled involuntarily.

Introductions were made in Neddie's casual way, and Anna held out her hand with a smile.

'How do you do, Mr Greer. No, thank you, I require no refreshment but I am sure Neddie does.'

Grinning, Neddie admitted he was a bit peckish. 'But I say! Where's Festus? Still moping in the library, I'll wager. Do you think we might take him to Farrowsleigh with us, Anna? Victor would be no end surprised.'

Mr Greer blinked in some horror. 'I daresay! But, er, I doubt if his grace needs the companionship of a very energetic dog just now. Suppose your lordship gave him a run over the grounds—'

'Yes, all right. You mean to be rid of me, I see,' said Neddie cheerfully, and took himself off.

Mr Greer smiled. 'An engaging boy, his lordship.'

'Oh, indeed!' Anna laughed. 'Quite incorrigible, and *always* hungry.'

'Cook will ply him with gingerbread, providing he doesn't loose that dog in the kitchen.' Mr Greer gestured. 'Do come into the saloon, Miss Templeton. Are you sure you won't have some chocolate or tea to warm you?'

This time she accepted and while he rang the bell, she went to the fire to warm her hands. Above the mantelpiece hung a charming portrait of the duke, sitting unsmiling but elegant in a winged chair with a young girl leaning on his knee. She had his pale gray eyes and something of his smile, but her long ringlets were dark and her face heart-shaped. When grown, she would be a beauty.

'Gainsborough came last year to paint that,' said Mr Greer, joining Anna. 'He made quite a pet of Lady Alicia.'

'She's a pretty child.' Anna abruptly looked down. 'That is why I've come this morning. I fear his grace received a letter from the governess, informing him of their arrival here today.' She met Greer's suddenly alert eyes. 'He wishes you to say he is . . . away.'

Mr Greer frowned, turning to pace slowly to one corner and back again. 'Oh, dear,' he said. 'I should have been more careful with the letters I sent yesterday to Farrowsleigh. I'm afraid I took no notice of . . . ' He sent her a troubled look. 'Was his grace much disturbed?'

Her brows rose with emphasis. 'Yes.'

He sighed, fingering his watch chain. 'What a mull it shall be. I cannot say he has gone to Bath or to his seat in Oxfordshire, for they are likely to seek to follow. Mademoiselle Dubret is a determined woman when she sets her mind upon a course of action. It will have to be a shooting party in Yorkshire, then.' He frowned, pacing again. 'I wonder why they have left Lucerne. Napoleon's army is not advancing on the Swiss.'

'Forgive me,' said Anna, unable to hold her tongue any longer. 'But it seems so harsh of his grace, not to wish to have his daughter with him. He cannot surely dislike her or be indifferent to her, for he asked me to see her and tell him if she is well.'

Mr Greer eyed her a moment. 'His grace regards you as one of

131

his few – very few – valued friends, Miss Templeton. So I shall not scruple to tell you that he is devoted to Lady Alicia. It quite breaks his heart to send her away with only occasional visits home.'

'But why—'

'He does not wish her to grow up in England, listening to what is whispered about him and the late duchess. If only he might remarry! That would hush the scandal, but I fear he is quite determined never to repeat the experience.'

Anna frowned. 'It is quite ridiculous that people think he killed her grace. I, for one, refuse to believe it.'

'Yes.' Greer pursed his lips. 'Certainly it is all nonsense, spread by malicious gossip-mongers. But it is harmful, and he wishes to protect Lady Alicia.'

'But she is bound to hear of it one day,' said Anna. 'Can't he see that to keep her away only—' She broke off, realizing she was going too far. 'I hope you do not mind me being underfoot this morning. Please do not neglect your duties in order to entertain me. I can sit here quite comfortably, or amuse my wait with a book.'

But he would not hear of it, and insisted on giving her a tour of the main rooms. Since she was eager to see them she did not refuse. Every aspect of Chevely Hall pleased her. There was no room ill-lit or gloomy. The furniture was as light and graceful as the architecture, and covered in the finest pale brocades. Nothing looked shabby, and she realized Molineux had lied in telling her the duke was run off his legs. After the ponderous interior of Farrowsleigh, just to stand here and gaze about brought an immediate lift to the soul. She found herself wishing she could call this house her own, and hastily banished the thought.

Even the appearance of Neddie, struggling to hang on to Festus's collar as the beast bounded across the polished marble floor of the hall with enormous muddy paws, did not vex her as it might have had he made such a disgraceful exhibition of himself at Farrowsleigh. She bade him apologize, both to the butler and to Mr Greer, and a footman took difficult charge of Festus, leading him away with mutters of 'Bad, *bad* dog.'

Anna gave Mr Greer her hand. 'Thank you for whiling away the time so agreeably. I fear we cannot dawdle any longer—'

But just then the butler came forward to say a carriage was

coming up the drive. Mr Greer frowned, then mastered his expression.

'What?' said Neddie, glancing around. 'Is it Alicia coming? Oh, Lord, we don't want her.'

'Hush,' said Anna severely, turning on him. 'You are not to vouchsafe a word. Mr Greer is about to tell a shocking fib and does not require you muddling things up.'

'As though I would,' began Neddie indignantly, but by this time the job-chaise had reached the steps, and the occupants were getting out.

'Jupiter,' said Neddie, staring as the servants opened the doors wide. 'Look at that. Did you ever see such a mountain of luggage?'

A tall thin lady emerged, tightly clutching the hand of Lady Alicia, whose face was prettily framed by a bonnet trimmed in white ermine. She carried a muff to match, and from one side of it the black head of a kitten was peering out with enormous eyes. A maid followed them carrying a draped bird cage and a dressing case. The top of the chaise was mounded with a collection of trunks and portmanteaux.

At the door the butler bowed his welcome, but Lady Alicia broke free and scampered inside calling, 'Papa! Papa! Monsieur Greer,' she said, coming to a halt before the secretary and fixing him with an eye of authority. 'Where is Papa?'

Gravely he gathered himself to reply, but before he could do so Neddie had stepped forward.

'Hullo, Mouse,' he said nonchalantly.

'Neddie!' Clapping her hands, she raced to hug him and began chattering at once, even pulling out her terrified kitten to thrust into his hands.

Behind them Mr Greer had begun a stilted explanation to Mademoiselle Dubret, who eyed him stonily. The kitten broke free and raced away, its tail fuzzed, and Alicia and Neddie took off in pursuit.

Mademoiselle Dubret frowned. 'I see,' she said in flawless English. 'This is unfortunate. Lady Alicia has been ill, and only the promise of coming home has induced her to recover. She will be most unhappy, but it cannot be helped.' Mademoiselle Dubret's eyes moved to Anna.

Mr Greer turned and said at once, 'Forgive me. Miss Templeton, may I introduce Mademoiselle Dubret? Miss Templeton is Lady Riddell's granddaughter.'

'*Enchanté.*' The governess curtsied and Anna returned something civil. Then she said, 'Monsieur Greer. May we remain here the night? The journey has been long, but since you have not yet closed the house—'

'Of course.' He beckoned to a footman, who led her upstairs. Mr Greer took out his handkerchief and mopped his brow. 'Dear me,' he said. 'It is not always easy to serve his grace.'

'No,' said Anna, her brows together. 'I am going on. Neddie will have to catch up with me.' She gave the secretary a smile. 'Goodday, sir. I shall inform his grace how capably you have acted.'

He bowed and escorted her outside to her waiting horse, appearing to take as little pleasure in receiving the compliment as she had felt in giving it.

Back at Farrowsleigh, as soon as she had changed and eaten luncheon, Anna made her excuses and presented herself at the duke's door, ready to tell him just how shabby and heartless she thought him. But Wilkes denied her entry, saying his grace had finally been driven to take laudanum and was now asleep. Restlessly she made her way downstairs once more and installed herself in the library with a book of fashion plates since Molineux's impatience to have the wedding directly after Christmas made it imperative that she order her trousseau as soon as possible.

It was here that Neddie found her. 'I say, Anna. What made you hare off like that? You must have ridden hell-for-leather all the way home for I never even sighted you.'

She tossed the fashion plates aside and frowned. 'Perhaps I should just say I was vexed over how the duke treats his child.'

'Oh?' Neddie considered this. 'I suppose it is rather shabby, although if I weren't feeling the thing I shouldn't want her about either. She never stops talking and as for that dratted cat of hers—' He thrust out a scratched hand. 'But, still, you oughtn't to ride alone, you know. With these poachers loose—'

'Neddie, for heaven's sake,' she said, half laughing. 'I do not fear poachers. They are after rabbits, not young ladies.'

'Yes, but as a rule, they're devilish wild shots. You must be careful.'

Smiling, she started to say that because there were stray shots flying about, his presence could hardly protect her, but she saw he was earnestly concerned and patted his hand instead. 'You are quite right. Forgive me. From now on I shan't set a foot out of the house without a gentleman's protection.'

He grinned. 'Bamming me, aren't you? You're not afraid.' Then he sobered. 'Did you know Hawkins has found work at the Hall? I wonder why his grace never mentioned it. Or perhaps he doesn't know yet.' Neddie's frown deepened. 'Hawkins told Billings – that's Victor's groom – that Mollie ruined the horse. It threw him one day on the shy, and from then on he was monstrous to it.'

Anna sat quite still, cold suspicion sinking through her. 'I *knew* it was he who set the horse in such a rage. Rotham was getting on splendidly until he came and . . . ' She let her voice trail off.

Neddie gripped her arm, his eyes wide. 'Anna! You don't think he did it on purpose, do you?'

For a moment she was tempted to let her suspicions run wild, but then common sense took over. She shook her head. 'Certainly not. He had no way of knowing Rotham would do something as henwitted as going into the stall.'

'I don't know—'

'Oh, Neddie, really!' She eyed him in reproof. 'You are letting your imagination carry you into Machiavellian realms. If Cousin Molineux ever grew to dislike his grace that strongly he would simply find some pretext on which to call him out and they could shoot at each other. It was an accident, and you must not persuade yourself into thinking otherwise.'

He scowled. 'I daresay you don't want to think Mollie might be a cowardly blackguard just because you're to marry him. But I shall think what I like!' He strode out, slamming the door.

Anna glared after him a moment, then turned, only to gasp as she saw Molineux rising from the depths of a tall-backed wing chair in the far corner of the room. She stared, gripped with dismay as he came toward her.

'Thank you for that piece of championship, Anna. I abused the horse because it abused me, but I was not responsible for Rotham's mishap. I am glad you have come to realize that.' His dark eyes narrowed. 'Neddie, however, is another matter.'

Far from reassured by his grim expression, she managed to rise to her feet. 'How . . . how dare you eavesdrop,' she said unsteadily. 'Good manners, sir, should—'

'Good manners?' He snorted. 'I came here directly after luncheon to nap and was quite comfortable till Edwin woke me up.' He clenched a fist. 'I am glad I heard his opinion of me.'

She put out a hand. 'Please! Do not face him with it. He is young. He doesn't realize—'

'No,' he said with a significance she did not comprehend. 'He does not *realize* anything. Perhaps it is time he did.' And with a dark look, Molineux left her.

That evening when Rotham came down for dinner, his color was much improved although for the most part his manner was quiet. Still rather piqued with him, Anna made no move to impart her news of his child, and the force of his gaze upon her merely firmed her resolution to be aloof. After dinner Molineux persuaded her to sing for them. Her performance was credible despite the distraction of her thoughts, and when she was finished Rotham came to her, twirling his quizzing glass between his fingers. He let his hand fall quite naturally over hers when she would have closed the keyboard.

'Play again,' he said, his eyes gazing down into hers in a way that made her heart race.

She looked down shyly, hoping her color was not betraying her. Clearing his throat, Molineux came to stand on her other side. This doggish manner annoyed her into playing a complicated movement from Bach rather than a country tune Molineux might sing with. When she was done there was uncertain applause, and Molineux bowed to her in an affronted manner before moving away.

Rotham curled his lip. 'Was that formidable display of skill calculated to drive me away as well, Miss Templeton? I don't mean to go. Ah, you fix me with a withering stare. How have I displeased you?'

'How can you treat your child in so horrid a way?' she asked in a low, intense voice. 'She was brought home because she has been ill, and if you could have seen how eagerly she came in—'

'Ill?' His brows came together for a moment. 'But she must be recovered or she could not travel. Come, come, Miss Templeton! I am not an ogre.'

'Aren't you?' she asked hotly. 'Much of my childhood was

motherless, too, your grace. And whenever Papa was hired to escort a young gentleman on his Grand Tour, I was stuck away in schools or else left with an out-of-elbows friend who could scarcely afford to keep me. The death of a parent is hard, sir, but not nearly as hard as to be ignored by one who is living.' Anna stood up, meeting his troubled gaze squarely. 'She is sleeping under your roof tonight, knowing that you still do not want her. Are you going to let her leave on the morrow? Are you?'

He did not avoid her eyes, but neither did he reply, and in exasperation she abruptly walked away and went to sit by the fire.

Molineux smiled at her. 'I see you have learned to give him his set-down. Splendid, my dear.'

Her fists clenched in her lap, but she was spared the effort of trying to make a civil reply by the approach of the duke.

'Mollie, you sly creature,' he said, raising his quizzing glass. 'You've put Miss Templeton to the blush. What a trifler you are. Do say, are you ready for our wager to be put to the test? Tomorrow night is Christmas Eve, or have I lost a day in my invalidish confusions? I am right? Good.' He smiled and gently patted Molineux's rigid shoulder. 'Then it's my punch against yours. So much more refined than pistols, don't you think?'

Molineux glared at him. 'You, sir, are a Bond Street fribbler. A popinjay!'

But Rotham merely shrugged off the provocation. 'Insults,' he murmured, turning away to smile at Lady Edwin, who was pale. 'Dear me. Sometimes I think you dislike me, sir.'

'I do dislike you,' said Molineux with heat. 'You need not speculate upon it. And the sooner you are able to leave my—'

Rotham shot him a sudden icy glare. 'Do strive to recall, Molineux, that it is *not* your house, and not likely ever to be. Now how can that possibly offend you so?' Smiling sweetly, he sauntered from the room.

Chapter Twelve

Again, Anna was awakened deep in the night by the sudden flinging open of her bed curtains. Icy air rushed across her like a blow. Crying out, she sat bolt upright, staring and breathless with the clutch of fear, and barely glimpsed what looked like the closing of a portion of the wall through the dim shadowy light cast off from the ruddy coals in the grate. One of them hissed and flamed from the icy draft still lingering in the room. Anna sat there, huddled with the bedclothes to her chin, until the wild pounding of her heart eased and she was able at last to draw a breath again. Then she pushed herself out of bed and ran barefoot across the chilly floor to the wall, pushing upon it without success. The satiny wood of the panel had no knobs or architectural features, and after a moment she abandoned it. To be truthful, she was not quite sure her courage could carry her into a mysterious passageway after the intruder. Her brows drew together. *Was* it Uncle Percy? But surely he was not capable of . . .

Not wishing to return to bed just yet, she lit a taper and wrapped herself in her dressing gown. Then, as she lifted the chamberstick to go into the sitting room, she happened to glance over at her dressing table, and her heart chilled within her. Five golden sovereigns were stacked neatly upon a folded piece of paper. She snatched it up, scattering the coins, and read:

'Now you are no longer poor. *Go away!*'

Anna frowned. It made no sense. Who in this house wanted her to leave? Neddie had said so, but she had not taken him seriously . . . until now. She must discover what was going on.

In the morning, considerably to her vexation, she overslept and after dressing in a haste rushed downstairs, only to find that the viscount had gone out with Molineux.

Anna sighed, a line between her brows.

'Sink me, a damsel in distress.' The duke came strolling out of the breakfast parlor and smiled at her. 'May I help? Or am I still in your black books?'

She made an impatient gesture. 'I am no end vexed at missing Neddie. I particularly desired a word with him.'

'You look rather as though you would prefer to eat him,' observed Rotham and took her hand. 'Stop glowering and come along to the Gold Saloon, where Dobbs has had a good fire built.' He led her into an opulent chamber, whose blaze of golden and russet colors could not overcome a decided scent of mustiness.

Her nostrils crinkled. 'Must we?'

He sighed, looking equally repulsed. 'I fear we must, unless you prefer the Stygian regions of the library. Whoever built this house apparently possessed a remarkable dislike for natural light.' He strolled over to lift his quizzing glass at a small rendering of plump goddesses gamboling in various stages of undress.

Suddenly reminded of the cupid atop her bed, Anna turned away with a blush.

'The drawing room has been overrun by a bevy of parlormaids and stalwart footmen,' he went on, still examining the painting. 'Preparations for the evening, I gather.'

'Oh, yes,' said Anna somewhat coolly. 'Your punch.'

'Ah.' He turned then with a lift of his brows. 'Greer is bringing over the requisite ingredients later today.'

To be civil, she said, 'I must watch you make it. What a pity I shan't have any to drink. My curiosity is afire.'

'Is it?' He aimed his quizzing glass at her, and rather sharply she averted her head. 'Greer sent word this morning that Alicia was put to bed in tears last night. Despicable fellow. I am convinced that you have persuaded him to help you make me feel like the most brutish parent alive.' He paused, letting his bantering tone fall. 'I . . . . I did think over what you said. I have decided to let her stay.'

Anna's eyes flew to his, and reading only sincerity there, she came forward to press his hand. 'I'm so glad of it.'

His smile was faint. 'I am pleased to make you happy. Let us hope I have made Alicia so. If only I can be sure she does not encounter Molineux. He is likely to tell her—' Abruptly he broke off. 'Forgive me. The engagement is settled, is it not?'

A knife seemed to plunge through her heart, but she did her best to nod calmly. 'Yes. The announcement is to be made tonight and the banns read tomorrow.'

'So soon?' Something flickered in his eyes, but he turned away before she could read what it was. He went to stand rather tautly at the window. 'I must send to London for a suitable wedding gift.'

Her pain grew too cutting. 'No!' she said too forcefully, then sought to soften the protest as he glanced at her. 'I prefer you do not, sir.' Her eyes suddenly brimmed with tears she was obliged to blink back hastily. 'Please do not.'

'Anna.' He came to her then, frowning. 'Are you so desperately unhappy?'

Yes! she wanted to cry. But pride held her silent. If he could not see for himself that she lived for the sight of him, if he felt nothing for her . . . well, she could not throw herself at him.

Seeking something to change the subject, she produced the letter and the gold sovereigns from her pocket and thrust them at him. 'This was put in my room last night by someone. I do not know whom, but I suspect Neddie is playing pranks. A few nights ago the same thing happened. My door was bolted, and I could not see how anyone could enter save through a secret passageway. I asked Neddie if the house had such things, and he gave me no proper answer. But last night I just glimpsed the panel closing, although I have not discovered the trick of making it open.'

'And just as well,' he said, frowning at the note. 'You have no business scampering off down some black passageway and losing yourself forever in the walls.'

Her eyes widened. 'Is it likely?'

'Yes, of course it is,' he said with some irritation. 'Gad, ma'am, have you no timidity? But, yes, the place is riddled with passages. There used to be a joke about the riddles of the Riddells. Who fathered whom in 1610? But in your grandfather's day the passages were boarded up on account of Percy.' His gray eyes narrowed. 'It dulled house parties considerably, no doubt. But I wonder who has opened them again? Molineux?'

'But *he* does not wish me to leave,' said Anna with considerable bitterness. 'He is convinced Grandmama will give me the diamonds.'

Rotham's brows shot up. 'Well, won't she?'

'I do not believe it,' Anna's eyes grew troubled. 'We have fallen out with one another . . . but, no, it can't be Cousin Molineux. Either it is Neddie being a prankster or—'

'No, I think not.' Rotham gave the coins back to her. 'He isn't this plump in the pocket. And he could never disguise his hand in such a manner.' The duke stared at her in rather a hard way. 'I do not like this.'

'Well, it is alarming,' admitted Anna, somehow reassured by his concern although the solution was no nearer. 'I do not enjoy midnight visitors.'

'You had better have your Abigail sleep in your room,' he said, taking her hand.

She met his eyes, wonderingly. 'Is it necessary?'

'I would feel better if you would.'

Her eyes fell. 'Very well. I'll give Betty instructions to set up a cot.'

'Anna.'

'Yes?' Again she looked up, breathless at something in his voice.

But he glanced away, shaking his head. 'Nothing, I . . . Be careful, won't you? And promise you shan't go exploring.'

For a moment her chest was so constricted she could not speak. Then she gave him a dull nod.

'Good,' he said, and abruptly left her.

She spent much of her day tying up her Christmas gifts, choking when she was obliged to put her father's aside. His departure had been so sudden she had had no chance even to think of giving it to him. And now . . . there was little likelihood she would ever see him again. She doubted Molineux would let her travel to Naples, for although he had expensive personal tastes, he did not seem excessively plump in the pocket.

Throughout the house hung a definite air of excitement as well as suspense. Mr Murvey wore a smug, knowledgeable expression, and the servants were forever gathering in corners to whisper to each other. The drawing room smelled of yew and beeswax, and the footmen cursed and sweated while carrying the enormous Yule

141

log into the dining hall. At tea time Dobbs brought in a tray laden with mouthwatering cakes and cinnamon pastries, and they all made merry, stuffing themselves to repletion while Molineux sought to make the solicitor tell them Lady Riddell's plans, Rotham flirted with Beatrice on the sofa, and Anna fed Neddie's spaniel tidbits by the fire.

Then James came in, attired in new livery, and bowed. 'Her ladyship wishes to see you, Miss Anna.'

Conscious of all their eyes, save those of her aunt, who was carefully staring at the floor, Anna rose and followed the footman out. A nervous qualm shook her as she wondered what this interview was to be about. Did Grandmama truly mean to award her those diamonds? How she wished Molineux might have the jewels without her! But such thoughts were too unsettling, and she pushed them away as she entered her grandmother's sitting room and curtsied.

Lady Riddell was seated erectly by the fire, gowned in rose-colored satin, her rings glittering upon her thin fingers, a cap of soft Valenciennes lace pinned to her carefully dressed hair. Her gray eyes stabbed at Anna, and she sniffed.

'You made no delay in coming, I see, but from the looks of you, your stubbornness is not yet completely stamped out. I trust you are going to keep your word to Oliver and subject us to no more tiresome scenes?'

Anna's eyes dropped a moment, then lifted slowly to meet her grandmother's piercing gaze. 'I intend to keep my word, ma'am,' she said in a low, controlled voice.

Lady Riddell's withered lips curled in a dry smile. Then in an abrupt change of subject she said, 'Percy is to join us tonight. Do you understand that he is to be present?'

'Yes, I have his gift—'

'I hope it is not candy.' The countess frowned. 'Rotham gives him French bonbons every year and has so spoiled him he will eat no other kind. Have you something different?'

Anna nodded her head.

'Good.' The countess sighed and waved a hand at her dresser, who now came forward with a large box in her hands. She gave it with a curtsy to Anna, who took it with a frown of curiosity.

'For you,' said the countess. 'No, don't open it now. It has just arrived from my dressmaker in London, in time for you to wear tonight.' Lady Riddell nodded as Anna's lips parted. 'My gift to you . . . no, don't thank me, girl. On an occasion like this you cannot wear a provincial creation.'

Nevertheless Anna kissed her cheek, relieved and certain that this was to be all. If so, then Molineux would have no wish for her, and she would be free . . .

Happily she carried the box to her chambers, scorning James's offer of assistance, and found Lady Edwin waiting for her in the sitting room.

She stood up as Anna came in, her blue eyes widening. 'What on earth?'

'A dress, from Grandmama's own maker,' said Anna, laughing as she plumped it down and slipped off the cord. 'It is such a surprise. I cannot wait to see it.'

'Let me help you.' Eagerly Lady Edwin plucked away the lid and pulled back the silver paper, only to gasp and suddenly frown as Anna radiantly held up the gown.

To Anna, who for a moment could notice nothing else, it was the most beautiful thing she had ever seen. The dress was slim and straight, falling in multiple tiny pleats from the short bodice, and fashioned of cloth-of-silver, which reflected Lady Riddell's opulent taste and yet enchanted Anna by its very unusualness. Over it floated the sheerest gauze, as fine as gossamer and spangled in tiny silver stars. Laughing, Anna spun around, holding it against her, and ran to the looking glass.

'It's beautiful!' she exclaimed. 'Oh, Aunt Beatrice, I never in my life imagined I should ever wear anything so lovely. Do you like—'

But Lady Edwin was gone, with a curt slam of the door. Anna frowned in startlement, unable at first to understand what was wrong. She knew how much Aunt Beatrice wanted the diamonds herself; surely she . . .

Anna looked back at her reflection as realization slowly dawned on her. The dress would make a striking foil for the diamonds. Of course it would. It had been designed with the necklace in mind.

Slowly, her lips pressed together, Anna laid down the dress, taking care not to crumple its folds despite the fact that Betty would have to press it. Then she went to stare blindly out the window. Why had she thought she could escape? She could never do so, for Rotham did not want her.

That evening when she came downstairs, gripped in the greatest trepidation beneath her calm exterior, Anna had the scant satisfaction of stunning every eye in the room. Molineux broke off his comment to Mr Murvey to stare at her as he never had before. Lady Edwin, herself a paler vision in blue satin, raised one hand in a resigned little salute. Rotham, standing alone by the fire, showed such open admiration and delight Anna blushed.

'Anna! By Jupiter, you're a regular out-and-outer,' cried Neddie, coming forward with a grin and thus forcing her to drop her eyes from Rotham's. Neddie circled her in so comical an imitation of an ogling town buck on the strut, she began laughing and regained her equanimity.

'Neddie, you absurd boy! Stop it at once and spare my blushes.'

His blue eyes met hers ingenuously. 'Well, you know, you're rather pretty when you crimson up.'

'Taking the petticoat line at your age?' drawled Rotham, joining them. 'My dear boy, how precocious.'

Neddie flushed to the roots of his hair, but rallied. 'It ain't as though she's some twittering little chit who hasn't the least thing to say for herself.'

'Quite true,' said Rotham, quizzing her mercilessly with his eyes.

'Carpet-knights, both of you,' she retorted, laughing, and was about to lay her hand on Rotham's arm when Molineux came up to offer his.

'I think, Cousin, that I should lead you in,' he said, his dark eyes gazing into hers with a significance that sent her heart plunging all the way to her slippers.

She sent Rotham a speaking glance, but with a light shrug he stepped back. Chagrined, Anna gave Molineux charge of escorting her to the vast hall, where the table had been moved around to allow room for two additional lengthy trestles. It was a baronial scene, with the great platters of venison, boar, roast goose, and mutton being set down and the Yule log blazing out a mighty fire. On a side table stood two enormous punch bowls in readiness for the coming contest, and on another sprawled a heap of gifts for the tenants of both Farrowsleigh and Chevely Hall, who were to be the guests tonight. The gifts for the family were collected in a more discreet corner. Anna allowed Molineux to lead her over to inspect these, her breath suddenly failing her as she spied a narrow box with her name upon it. But there was one of identical size for Lady Edwin, and Neddie, and Molineux.

Anna slowly drew in a breath. 'She means to keep us guessing to the last, doesn't she?'

Molineux nodded, a hard glint in his eye. 'Ah, here it is,' he said, pointing to a small package wrapped in gold paper. 'Percy's candy. Rotham gives him bonbons every year. It is the only sweets Dr Gibbon will permit Percy to have since his health is so uncertain.'

She made some comment, being distracted by the entrance of the tenants, looking properly awed by their surroundings as they shuffled in past a stern Dobbs in their best clothing and most serious expressions.

Neddie's spaniel galloped in by them, barking in high spirits with one silky ear turned foolishly back.

'Down, Pepper! Down at once!' said his master severely, quieting the dog and making him go lie down by the fire. Pepper obeyed, but his stumpy tail went on wagging furiously and his large brown eyes gleamed so brightly Anna was sure he would soon be into mischief.

When everyone was assembled and placed, James threw open the doors and Dobbs announced, 'The Earl and Dowager Countess of Riddell!'

Anna held her breath as they walked slowly in and made their way past all the bowing people to the family table. The countess, gowned regally in tucked silk and splendid rubies, leaned more on her cane than she did upon the arm of her son, but her face shone with a kind of grim pride as she brought him forth for his one public appearance of the year. The earl, on the other hand, looked strained with excitement as he hobbled along. He was turned out very fine in his black swallow-tailed coat and white satin knee breeches. A sapphire stud gleamed from the snowy folds of his shirt front. His gossamer hair was carefully ordered, and indeed, he acted almost normal until he suddenly broke free from his mother and ran to scatter the presents.

'Which is mine? Which is mine?'

Anna bit her lip, and murmuring started through the hall with some shaking their heads in disapproval, but Rotham strolled over to the earl with a casual air.

'Hullo, Percy, old dear,' he said, taking the earl's arm. 'Yes, your candy is in its place. Ah, not yet!' Deftly he took a gift from Percy's eager clasp and frowned at it a moment in seeming puzzlement while Molineux tensed beside Anna. The the duke shrugged and tossed the package back among the rest. 'Come along, Percy, do! You must have patience.'

The earl's handsome face puckered, but with some coaxing he was placed in his chair beside the countess, whom Molineux seated.

Her ladyship's lips tightened for a moment, then she gave the earl a nod. 'Make your speech please, Percy.'

He blinked at her somewhat blankly, his eyes traveling back to the presents.

The countess tapped his arm. 'Percy! Make your speech.'

He looked out over the faces and seemed at last to recall what was expected of him. Awkwardly he stood up and raised his hand. 'You are . . . you are all welcome to Farrowsleigh,' he chanted in a rushed singsong. 'Let us begin.'

Lady Riddell smiled, and with applause that set the earl grinning, the tenants sat down to their dinner. It was a merry, hearty meal, with many toasts drunk and good cheer increasing as the wine was poured with a free hand. When it was done, the tables were shoved aside and musicians struck up a lively reel.

Rotham laid down his napkin and beckoned a finger at a footman to help him rise from his chair.

'With your leave, my lady?' he said and sent a gay look of challenge at Molineux, who nodded.

Servants brought out the ingredients while Rotham tucked back the fine lace at his wrists.

'Come here, Edwin, and assist me,' said Molineux with a hint of a confident smile. He noticed Percy's longing glances at the presents, and his smile broadened before he returned his gaze to Neddie. 'You must learn how to mix the Farrowsleigh punch.'

Anna placed herself at Rotham's elbow, her eyes widening as she saw what he intended to mix together.

'Good heavens, sir! I hope it will not all explode,' she said, provoking him to a dry smile. 'But I cannot see how the contest is to be fairly decided since your tenants will be loyal to your bowl and ours to my cousin's.'

'Ah, sweet words of doubt,' he murmured, deftly peeling an orange. 'We shall switch the bowls about and they won't know, will they?'

Anna stepped back and watched him work, quite astonished at the liberal quantities of rum, brandy, heated wine, and gin he threw together. Molineux took exacting care with his measurements, scorning the gin completely as a gutter drink fit only for pugilists and fishwives, but the only ingredient Rotham paid especial attention to was the sugar. Then he tossed in the fruit and began to stir while Molineux was still hard at work combining his wines.

'Good 'Rack punch, sir!' said Rotham with a glint in his pale eyes. 'I beg you to take the first taste.'

Molineux frowned and shook his head curtly. 'When I am finished, curse you.'

The duke laughed and dipped himself a cup. He tossed it down, coughed with enough force to pain his ribs, and said weakly with one hand pressed to his side, 'By Jove . . . perfect!'

'Rotham!' called the countess sharply. 'Come here and talk with me if you are finished with that acid mixture.'

The duke obeyed, and, seeing that her grandmother really desired assistance with the earl, Anna sent James for the jackstraws and soon had Percy engrossed in the game.

But for her own part, Anna could not lose herself in the high spirits of the evening. The tenants, replenished by the punch, danced themselves all hollow. She watched them, she smiled, she kept her uncle occupied, but all the same she was desperately aware of the underlying suspense and the swift passing of the minutes. Lady Edwin flirted outrageously with Rotham and turned Mr Murvey quite crimson-cheeked when she allowed Neddie to lead her through a lively jig that showed far more ankle than was seemly. But beneath her gaiety the strain showed in her lovely face, and her eyes, like Percy's and Molineux's, kept going to the presents.

All too soon for Anna, the dancing ended, and it was announced that his grace's punch had won the day. Cheers went up, and Rotham smilingly raised a hand in acknowledgement. Molineux's dark eyes narrowed, but he went forward readily enough to shake Rotham's hand.

'Presents!' cried the earl, clapping his hands. 'Presents *now*! I want mine!'

'Yes, yes, of course, Uncle Percy,' said Anna soothingly, catching his hands and giving him a smile. She glanced at Lady Riddell, who nodded. Anna led the earl to the table and began picking out all of the ones with his name on it. The spaniel came up to press against her, and she bent down to pet him, watching while the earl began tearing open all his presents at once in such excitement he hardly knew what he was doing.

Molineux touched her shoulder. 'Come and sit down. He doesn't need our attention now, thank God.'

She glanced at the earl again in time to see him exclaim over the puppet she had bought him. Smiling, she let Molineux seat her beside Lady Edwin, but inside she had tensed.

The slim boxes were distributed. Standing a bit aloof from them, Rotham put up his quizzing glass. They all sat there for a moment as though no one dared look. Anna grew very conscious of the merry exclamations from the tenants as their own revelry continued at the other end of the hall.

Lady Riddell's chuckle brought up Anna's eyes. She met the countess' amused gaze and set her chin. Her fingers pulled away the ribbon.

'Oh,' said Lady Edwin, staring at a pair of particularly fine gloves.

'Grandmama, how splendid!' said Neddie, brandishing a leather dog collar. He grinned at her ladyship before calling Pepper to him and buckling on the new collar.

Holding her breath, Anna slowly opened her box, and stared in stunned and overwhelming relief at the ivory fan within. 'Oh! Thank you—' she began warmly, but just then Molineux drew out the diamonds from his box with such an expression of triumph Anna's words died in her throat.

'My lady.' He shot the countess a look and bowed deeply.

'Jupiter, Mollie,' said Neddie, troubled. 'I never thought you'd get them—'

Molineux laughed and turned to Anna. 'My dear?' And she was obliged to sit there, with head high and cheeks flaming, while he fastened the heavy necklace around her throat. As awesome and breathtaking as its beauty was, it nearly choked her. His fingers lingered a moment on the back of her neck in a small caress that stiffened her spine, then he took her hand, bidding her rise. Together they faced the rest of the company. Anna could not help but glance at Rotham, who had paled, as the tenants quieted and Molineux said, smilingly, 'Miss Templeton has done me the honor of—'

An anguished cry cut him off. Percy stood facing Neddie, his fists clenched, his eyes blazing as the young viscount taunted him by holding the box of sweets just out of reach.

'You are bad! *Bad!*' cried the earl, on the verge of tears. 'It is *my* candy!'

'Edwin!' said Molineux sharply, taking a step forward, but the boy only laughed defiantly and raised a piece to his lips.

'You must learn to share, Uncle Percy,' he said as the earl began to cry.

Anna's brows snapped together and she shoved past Molineux to slap Neddie with all her strength. The bonbon flew to the floor and rolled, to the delight of Pepper, who swallowed it with an eager bark for more. Holding his cheek with tears of pain in his blue eyes, Neddie stepped back, but Anna meant to brook no more of his nonsense. She wrested the box from his defiant hand.

'You wretched, horrid boy! How dare you seek to spoil his one pleasure? You ought to be caned, taking it from him before he could have even one piece.' Breathless, she turned to her uncle, seeking to give him the candy, but he was hysterical now and would not accept it or be soothed.

'James!' snapped Molineux in exasperation as Anna put the candy on the mantelpiece. 'Get Kelby at once.' He switched his glare to Neddie. 'Damn your eyes—'

'Good God,' said Rotham slowly, his eyes widening. He pointed. 'The dog!'

They all looked at the spaniel, who suddenly convulsed and with a heart-rending groan, began writhing about the floor.

'Pepper!' Neddie threw himself down beside the dog, vainly

trying to hold it still, tears running down his face. 'Pepper, what's wrong? Do something, Mollie!'

But in moments the spaniel was dead, twisted and stiff in the final throes of its horrible death. Anna turned her face away, unable to bear the sight of it. Lady Edwin cowered in her chair, no sound whatsoever in the great hall save for Neddie's sobs.

Then Molineux's jaw set itself and he walked up to the frowning duke, who had rested his hand on Neddie's huddled shoulder. 'Poisoned, your grace, wasn't it?' he snapped, his dark eyes hard. Rotham's fair head jerked up, and their gazes locked. 'I find it quite interesting, your grace,' said Molineux with awful clarity, 'that it was candy that *you* brought. But then, poison seems to be one of your hobbies.'

'My God,' said someone, and as Anna abruptly sank into a chair she realized she was the one who had spoken. She stared at Rotham's white face, seeking denial even as the truth of Molineux's accusation stood before them all, not to be denied. But why? *Why?*

Kelby came running in to take away the exhausted, frantic earl. Rotham's lips compressed as he watched Percy go out. Then his gray eyes flicked to Anna as he said, with a coldness that shocked her, 'And you believe this, too, Miss Templeton?'

'You need not make him a reply, Anna!' cried Lady Riddell, her eyes snapping. 'You need not.'

'Victor,' said Neddie, rising to his feet with a look of anguish. 'How could you?'

But Anna went on gazing up at the duke, horror and denial and certainty within her. It could not be true! But she had seen it happen. She must, no matter how her heart might break, no matter how he might look at her in this moment, believe it.

She gave him a slight nod. 'I do,' she said through stiff lips while the world seemed to shatter around her.

He dropped his eyes, but not before she saw the pain in them. Her heart would have sent her flying to him then, but doubt – cold and damping and dead – held her motionless.

'Dobbs!' said Molineux, lifting a hand. 'Send for the magistrate.'

But Rotham raised his head as murmurs, some heated, began to swell through the hall. 'You forget yourself, sir,' he said in glacial tones, his affectations quite gone. 'I am beyond the reach of magistrate or constable. Call on my peers, if you dare.' And with a contemptuous glance that had Molineux clenching his fists, Rotham strode out with not a single hand reaching forth to stop him.

Chapter Thirteen

Pepper was carried out in a blanket, and Beavins came to take a stricken Neddie up to bed. When all the tenants and the musicians were gone, the rest of the family continued to stand together around the countess.

'Monster!' she said at last, striking the arm of her chair. Her withered face had no color. 'I never paid much attention to you concerning him before, Oliver. I wish I had.'

Molineux took the box of candy from the mantelpiece and stared at it a long while before at last uttering an oath beneath his breath and flinging it upon the fire.

'Neddie could have died!' exclaimed Lady Edwin, huddled in her chair with her hands shredding her hankerchief. 'He could have *died*! If Anna had not . . . ' Her drenched blue eyes lifted to Anna. 'You saved him. Dear God, if not for you—'

'How damnably cool of him,' muttered Molineux, clenching a fist. 'Attempting it here in front of us. I told all of you. I said he should have been dealt with when the duchess died so tragically, but I was ignored as you said, Grandmama. Now look at what has come of it.'

'Pray, stop!' cried Anna, whirling to face him. Every word of accusation was like a piercing thorn, and she could not bear for Molineux to be so self-righteous. 'All of this is absurd! He likes Uncle Percy. What possible reason could he have to do such a thing? *If* he did so?'

'Of course he did so.' The countess jabbed her cane at the fire. 'That is plain to us all. But why?' Her lips suddenly trembled and she pressed a hand against them. '*Why*?'

'He is quite mad, of course,' said Molineux. 'What can be done about it, Murvey? How do we bring charges against a duke?'

'Dear me.' The solicitor shook his head, looking much

152

distressed. 'It is a grievous business, a most *serious* matter. I suppose the regent—'

'Anna. Beatrice. Come.' The countess stood and gripped Anna's arm hard with her thin fingers. 'I can bear no more. Come.'

Together the three of them went out, moving slowly at the countess' pace. At the first landing on the stairs, Lady Edwin left them, hastening away with her handkerchief to her face.

'The fool,' snapped Lady Riddell, continuing on up the stairs with Anna's assistance. 'She had better pray her thanks tonight that her son escaped. God knows I cannot do so.'

Anna gasped. 'But, Grandmama—'

'Well?' Lady Riddell's eyes swung around to pierce her. 'How can I be truthful and say I want Percy's life to continue in this horrible state?' Then her eyes fell, and she shuddered. 'But not that kind of death.'

Anna frowned, the sense of betrayal overwhelming her again. 'All the things Cousin Molineux said about him were true. I would not believe them. I thought it all vicious slander.' She bit her lip, her eyes filling with tears. 'Oh, Grandmama, I thought I—'

'At least your penchant for Rotham's company is over,' said the countess with a snap. 'Even I let myself be blinded . . . But I'm tired. Let us be done with the subject. He'll never hang, of course.'

'Hang?' Anna's eyes widened. She stopped short. 'Oh, no—'

'It's what he deserves.' Lady Riddell's nostrils flared. 'But it won't happen. He *is* a duke, and the peers shan't find him guilty. Probably they would think him kind for trying to put Percy out of his misery like some wretched dog.' Her voice hardened with bitterness. 'The regent – fat, pompous buffoon that he is – once had the effrontery to remark something of the sort to me, and Rotham is one of his favorites. No, he won't hang, but I shall see him driven out of England for this before I die. That I swear!'

When Anna reached her own chambers at last, the sight of them was repugnant to her. She could not simply go to bed. Her mind went over and over the evening in a relentless round, exhausting her, but she came to no resolution between the chaos of her mind and heart. Catching up a cloak, she went downstairs and let herself out on to the terrace, the cold of the night at once taking her breath.

The sound of a carriage being brought around made her leave the shelter of the terrace and go to where she could watch Rotham's departure. It was a grim scene, mostly silent as Wilkes struggled to load the portmanteaux himself while the footmen stood by, unmoving in a condemnation that needed no words. Then Rotham came out, his step weary, the caped greatcoat he wore swirling about him like a black shadow. He paused to glance about before getting into his chaise and saw her, although she withdrew at once into the shadows.

To her supreme vexation, he came over, his face unreadable in the darkness, but the purpose about him easily seen.

'Beatrice?' he called softly.

That infuriated Anna past all prudence. She stepped out from her corner of concealment and said sharply. 'This is no farewell. I came merely to be sure you were going.'

'I see. What a pity for you.' Without warning he seized her wrist and pulled her so near she could smell the starch in his linen. The very closeness of him seemed to direct her anger into an inner fire that melted the strength from her limbs and left her helpless in his grasp. His kiss did not repulse her as Molineux's had done; instead she wanted it. She wanted it so badly the longing hurt her.

For an instant they were one, joined by the flame within them. Then she came a little to herself through her swirling senses and realized her free hand was sliding up around his neck. Shocked at herself, she stiffened abruptly and slapped him.

'How dare you!' she gasped, breathless and terrified of her own weakness.

He crushed her harder against his chest when she would have struggled free. The hood of her cloak fell back, revealing the faint paleness of her face in the shadows and the muted gleam of the diamonds.

'What a damnable woman you are,' he whispered and kissed the racing pulse at her throat while with all her remaining strength she fought to remember what he was and what he had done.

'Unhand me, sir, or I shall scream!'

'I believe you would,' he murmured, as breathless as she. He released her then, save for a light but unshakable clasp of her wrist which kept her from fleeing. 'My God, I can't bear to leave you behind. Come away with me, Anna. I—'

'You are quite . . . mad,' she said, and it took all of her will to say it coolly against the desires of her heart. 'Do you forget this evening? Do you expect me to? I am not a jade for your leisure!'

'Damme, did I say you were?' he cried in exasperation, dropping his hand from her wrist. 'Anna, listen to me. I swore once that I'd never open my heart to another female again, yet what must you do but come and steal it away from the moment you—'

'I don't want to hear you.' She averted her face, her bosom heaving. 'You are clever with your pretty speeches, but what you do and what you say are not the same. How can I trust you now? And suppose I did run away with you like some abandoned wanton. Would you feed me a poison bonbon when you tired of me?'

In the awful silence that followed, she gasped, putting out an involuntary hand. 'No, I—'

'Oh, pray do not bother to scuttle for an apology you do not mean, my dear,' he drawled in a voice that cut like slivers of brittle glass. 'I am sure Mollie has thought up some wonderfully clever explanation of why I should be eager to murder my neighbors. Or perhaps I merely wish to give Neddie a head start on his inheritance?' Rotham paused. 'If I were of a murderous disposition, I assure you Molineux would have long ago been my victim. Has he, in his numerous little comments upon my personal affairs, mentioned his rather unsuccessful attempt to cuckold me? But stay, I am putting you to the blush, my most proper Miss Templeton. Well, when you are his wife, you may ask yourself now and then if your worthy husband's ambition to be Lord Riddell does not upon occasion take him a trifle . . . too far.'

'What do you mean?' she demanded, her senses reeling, but with a slight inclination of his head, Rotham turned on his heel and strode away, leaving her shivering and anguished in the darkness.

'Rotham!' she called, but he never looked back. In moments the horses were whipped up, and his carriage moved away.

Growing conscious of how cold she was, Anna ran back into

the house, still flushed from his caresses, still longing for more, still unable to trust him again. But the doubts he had planted refused to be squashed. Had he spoken truth or spite concerning Molineux and his late wife? And why did he wish her to wonder if Molineux had poisoned the candy? Anna knew her cousin capable of doing so, but it would have gained him nothing since Neddie stood between him and the earldom. Then her eyes widened as she realized how close Neddie had come to death tonight.

The servants had retired, leaving the house wrapped in silence, but it was then while she stood gripped in her own suspicions that she heard voices raised in anger coming from the library. In silence she tiptoed to the doors and cautiously eased one just slightly ajar. Peering in with her breath held, she saw Molineux and Lady Edwin glaring at one another, their voices hushed but furious.

'And I tell you it is finished, Oliver!' she was saying, her rich tones not arch and pretty now. 'You know very well that if I had had the least idea you meant him to be poisoned, I should never have—'

'It is far too late for scruples, Bea, and you know it,' snapped Molineux, pacing away from her.

'Neddie was nearly killed in his stead simply because you sought a flair for the dramatic.' Lady Edwin's eyes flashed. 'What became of your promises that the earl would die quietly, and without suffering, in his sleep? Did you suppose death by poisoning would look natural? When I bought that box of bonbons I never dreamed—'

'Will you cease enacting a Cheltenham tragedy? For God's sake, we are not finished yet.' Molineux checked his outburst and smiled in a way that chilled Anna to the core. 'In fact I am rather pleased at having pointed suspicion to Rotham.'

'You are mad!' she said, gesturing. 'Victor is a favorite of the regent's. He has *cachet* everywhere in spite of your petty slander against his wife. No one who knew her believes she was incapable of killing herself. And no one who knows Victor will believe he tried to murder Percy. Why could you not leave well enough alone, Oliver? You are too ambitious.'

'No!' With startling suddenness, he seized her arm, causing

her to cry out. '*You* are the one who is too ambitious, Bea. I have humored you thus far—'

'Blackmailed me, you mean!' she retorted, her shapely bosom heaving, only to gasp with tears of pain as he tightened his grip.

'Don't forget yourself, my lady,' he said with a sneer. 'At any time I can expose you and that insufferable brat to the countess. At any time. You know it. Just as you know I had no intention of harming St. Byre.' He drew her nearer and seized her chin. 'You doxy.'

Her blue eyes widened. 'No, Oliver! *No!*'

He drew back with an arrogant laugh. 'I have no intention of foisting myself upon you. No, indeed, not with my ice maiden still to tame—'

Trembling, Anna drew back from the door and put cold hands to her flaming cheeks, gasping with the sight of Molineux's mocking, arrogant face seared forever upon her memory. How dare he presume, how dare he take matters into his own hands! But she knew what he was now, and his callous discussion of the attempt to end Percy's life more than horrified her. Her hand stole up to her bosom, where the diamonds lay so heavily. Wed her indeed. She would lead apes in hell first, no matter what he might threaten against her father. Rotham would help her . . .

But dear God, she had refused Rotham! How had she been so stupid? So blind? Her heart had tried to tell her, but in a moment of pride she had thrown him contemptuously away. She must apologize. She must make everything right!

Dawn – gray, bleak, and wretchedly cold – saw her galloping across the upper meadows, taking fences and hedges with a reckless disregard for prudence. Her mount began to foam, and stumbled as they crested the last hill, but with a ruthless hand on the reins she steadied him and sent him on without slackening the pace. She would run him into the ground if she had to.

The duke's pennon had been lowered from the top of the house, frightening her momentarily, but a traveling chaise, laden with luggage, stood in the drive. She drew in a deep breath and let her horse slow to a weary trot, reining up as Rotham came out of the house. He carried his sleeping daughter in his arms. When he saw Anna he frowned and put Alicia into the carriage. For a moment Anna was sure he meant to ignore her, but then he walked over to her, removing his hat as he came up and grasped her stirrup. He gazed at her with a face that showed he had neither slept nor shaven. His gray eyes were bitter.

'You are not welcome on this property, Miss Templeton.'

She frowned, stretching out a hand. 'Please! I have been a goose, I know. After you left last night I overheard Molineux and my aunt talking. He—'

'Do you suppose any of that matters now?' he broke in, raising a brow.

Her frown deepened. 'Oh, pray, don't come the ugly! Of course it matters. We must find some way to prove his guilt.'

'We? Tut, my dear. I think it unlikely.' His mocking smile faded and a muted glitter showed in his eyes. 'You made your choice, did you not?'

'Rotham, please! I—'

'Yes, I fear you crammed this poor brute unnecessarily,' he added, raising his quizzing glass at her mount. 'We cannot offer you refreshment or fire. I have closed the house.'

She gestured in frustration. 'Must I grovel? I tell you I am sorry. I—'

'Are you?' He shrugged. 'You may grovel if you like, but it is not a pleasant business. I know. I thought of trying something of the sort last night. Thank God I refrained.' He shot her a harsh look as she bit her lip. 'No, my sweet. I was quite about in my head to think you would make me the happiest of men as my wife. You are no different from the rest of your sex. Good-day.'

But she would not be dismissed, no matter how much he hurt her.

'Where are you going?' she asked desperately. 'If you run away, your guilt will be sealed in the eyes of the world.'

'I have told you that I no longer care.' His eyes searched her face for a moment as though impressing every detail upon his memory. Then abruptly he shook his head and walked away.

For a moment she sat there, disbelieving. How could he be so hard, so cruel? Why could he not forgive her this one mistake? Furious tears blinded her, and she wrenched her horse around to send it galloping away with a lash of her crop. Halfway home, her horse stumbled again, this time sending her off in a rattling fall that left her winded and stunned. For a while she could only lie there, then finally she pushed herself up into a sitting position and began to weep uncontrollably. But when her tears were spent and she was left aching and exhausted and numb with cold, her heart was just as heavy as before.

She had suffered no injury from her fall. Catching her horse, who had not run at once home to his stables, she led him along until at last she found a stump and with this for a mounting block was able to climb back into the saddle. She had lost her crop, but she did not even bother to look for it. She could think only of Rotham turning away from her in that bleak way as though his very soul had been frozen in ice.

Reaching the stables at last, she dismounted, ignoring the curious looks from the stableboys, and walked into the house, only to gasp as she rounded a corner and came up face to face with Molineux.

For one hideous instant she could do nothing but stare at him, accusations welling up inside her. Then she realized she dared not speak, not when there was no one to help her against him. Her eyes fell.

His hand gently touched her face, rubbing away a smear of mud from her cheek. 'You have been out riding at this hour, in this cold? Why? Did you take a fall? Are you hurt?'

She swallowed, seeking to school her voice. 'I did fall, but I am perfectly well, thank you.'

'You're shaking with cold. Come to the fire.' Putting an arm around her shoulders while she did her best not to flinch, he led her into the morning saloon, where a comfortable fire was blazing. While she stretched out her hands to it, thinking miserably of Rotham and how she would never see his wicked smile again, Molineux said, 'You must not ride out again without my groom in attendance. I should not wish any harm to befall you.'

He feared she might run away. Scorn blazed within Anna, but all the same she knew she was trapped.

'You do not look as though you slept well. I own that does not surprise me. I fancy none of us did. Edwin suffered nightmares, I'm told. Have you breakfasted? You should eat, then go upstairs and endeavor to rest a bit before we go to Christmas chapel.'

As she turned obediently to go out, anxious to be away from

him, he snorted scornfully. 'Well! I fancy chapel is one place where Rotham shan't dare show his nose. Curse his arrogance! He should have spent the night in gaol. But we shall have our retribution, Anna, you may be sure of that.'

Her eyes met his dully. 'I wonder that you do not call him out.'

He smiled, tracing her cheek with a finger. 'Would you like that? Ah, no.' His smile broadened as her eyes fell. 'Be assured, ma'am, that I shall seek satisfaction through the law first.'

Somehow she managed to nod and leave him without telling him what a hypocrite he was. Going upstairs, she reached into her pocket for her handkerchief and only then remembered the sovereigns she had knotted inside it. She clenched them in her hand and with a set expression walked on.

When she was dressed for chapel and had choked down half a roll from her breakfast tray, Anna went to Lady Edwin's door and knocked. Going in, she found her aunt half dressed with her golden hair still down her back. The abigail was dismissed, and Anna met her aunt's eyes briefly before placing the gold coins on the dressing table.

Lady Edwin's blue eyes widened, and she looked up with a gasp.

Anna nodded. 'Yes, I have decided you are the one who has been trying to frighten me away from Farrowsleigh. But I am not able to leave, so I return your money.'

Her aunt sat very still for a moment, then shrugged. 'Very well. I suppose you overheard us in the library. We were imprudent to meet there.'

Anna stared at her. 'How could you seek to kill poor Uncle Percy? Does he cause you harm by living?'

'Yes!' Lady Edwin stood up with a curt gesture. 'The witless creature needs no title and privilege. Neddie—'

'Neddie's time will come,' said Anna angrily. 'What you and Cousin Molineux have tried to do is unconscionable.'

'Will you dare read me a homily? You, who came here to toadeat your way into her ladyship's purse?' Lady Edwin tossed her head. 'You are just as mercenary as the rest of us. Just because you have gained the diamonds and a large portion of money does not mean you may now dictate to me. And if you dare do so to Oliver, you will speedily find out how foolish you are.'

Anna compressed her lips. 'I have agreed to marry a man I despise. That is a far different thing from attempting murder, and nothing you can say will make the two comparable.'

Lady Edwin flinched. 'Very well! You are right. It is not the same. It is—' She took a hasty turn about the room, then stopped to send Anna a frightened, half-angry look. 'You are not to repeat what you heard to anyone. Do you hear? Not to anyone!'

'Yes, while another attempt is made upon Uncle Percy, I suppose,' said Anna with scorn. 'I shan't stand by and do nothing to help him.'

Lady Edwin shrugged. 'He is in no danger now. But you had best guard your tongue and so I warn you. If Oliver finds out that you know—'

'Why do you not tell him now?' asked Anna, lifting her chin while fear shot through her. How alone she was, how alone in this awful house where no one could be trusted. 'You have wanted rid of me all along.'

'Ninny!' said Lady Edwin with a little stamp of her foot. 'I am not your enemy. I have been trying to help you!'

'By frightening me in the night?' retorted Anna.

'Yes! It was all I could think of. And if you suppose I have enjoyed crawling through horrid, dirty passageways for your sake you are much mistaken.' She shuddered. 'A most loathesome business.'

'But why?' asked Anna, frowning. 'I am all at sea.'

'Because, you goose, I *know* what Oliver is better than anyone. He has his good qualities, of course, but if ever he finds your weakness that is where he grasps you, and he never lets go.'

Anna turned away, the fear clutching her again. 'My father.'

'Yes.' Lady Edwin sighed. 'I quite wasted my time in seeking to drive you away. I'm sorry.' Her blue eyes, wide and suddenly tragic, met Anna's doubtful ones. 'I wished only to help you, since I cannot help myself, but I have failed.' Gesturing resignedly, she went away to seat herself by the fire in a graceful posture of dejection.

Her anger fading, Anna followed. 'Aunt Beatrice, please. What hold has he on *you*? How can he force you to aid his wickedness?'

'If I don't obey him, he has sworn to tell . . . ' Lady Edwin shook her head. 'No, I cannot permit him to do so.'

'Is this how he forced you to buy the candy to poison—'

'Yes!' Lady Edwin averted her face.

'But what if Neddie had died in his stead?'

Lady Edwin pressed a hand to her lips. 'Don't even say it! The thought has tormented me all night. I could not sleep, nor eat. I know I shall be prostrate before the day is over. My dear Neddie . . . '

Anna put a hand on her arm. 'We can stop Molineux. You and I can go to the authorities and—'

'No!' Lady Edwin jerked away, her face white. 'He would tell!'

'But is your secret more important than Rotham's innocence?' cried Anna, clenching her fists. 'Is it more important than seeing Molineux punished?'

'Yes.' Lady Edwin raised her chin, and there was misery but no surrender in her eyes. 'More important than anything. I know you have a *tendre* for Victor. How I pity you! But he will never trust another woman again, so really you have lost very little.'

Anna bit her quivering lip, unable to retort.

'You are very young.' Lady Edwin rose gracefully to her feet, her expression set. 'I am not going to mention this to Oliver because . . . because you saved Neddie's life. Oliver hates him so, he—' She looked down, tightening her lips. 'But Oliver does care for you. I advise you to try and please him. It is the only way to make your marriage endurable. Believe me,' she said as Anna turned her head rebelliously away. 'Lord Edwin and I had little liking for each other, and I was very foolish in the first years of our union. Don't make these mistakes, Anna. Conform. You have no choice now. And in heaven's name do not let last night become an obsession with you. To put an idiot out of his misery is not so very great a crime.'

Anna stared at her with shocked eyes. 'It cannot be justified, Aunt Beatrice, and wrapping it up in clean linen does not soften the atrocity.'

'Should you attempt to be foolish, I shan't lift a finger to help you.' Lady Edwin's blue eyes met Anna's gray ones with a hard determination that sent a chill through Anna. 'I hope you understand me, for I mean what I say.'

But in defiance Anna asked, 'And if I am married?'

'*When* you are married to Oliver,' said Lady Edwin coldly, 'you shan't be able to speak out against your husband at all, and I shall be safe.'

Anna left her then, bitterly sunk with despair. But her spirit was not quelled yet. There must be some way she could escape Molineux and his relentless plans. Gathering up her skirts, Anna hastened off to her grandmother's chambers, determined to tell her all no matter what the circumstances. But she was stopped at the door by Mrs West, unsmiling for once and quite firm.

'I'm sorry, Miss Anna. Her ladyship passed a poor night and Mr Oliver has said she isn't to be fretted now. You may see her later, of course, when you all go to chapel.'

Anna turned slowly away, gripped by growing fear. She *was* trapped. It would be quite impossible to speak to Grandmama in the presence of everyone, and besides, would the countess believe her if Aunt Beatrice was so heartless as to deny everything? Anna sighed, closing her eyes against a tremor. Molineux ruled over them all, and she was not strong enough to stop him. She could not even save herself, now.

Chapter Fourteen

That Christmas Day was hardly one of peace and good will. The weather remained bitterly cold and damp, seeping into the air of the church, and by the time the banns were read at the close of the service Anna was too numbed to care when Lady Riddell shot her a look of triumph and their neighbors crowded around outside to wish them well.

There was much heated talk about the attempt on the earl's life; apparently several men had stormed Chevely Hall that morning and they found the bird flown, as they put it, and dared, the more they talked, to slur the duke's name freely and drag up every wretched rumor about him that they could remember or invent. Naturally his grace's tenants objected to this practice, and a fight broke out in the churchyard to the considerable horror of the vicar, who got pushed down in a puddle of mud in his attempt to part the combatants and came away shivering, wet, and quite livid with outrage.

'Come, Anna. This is no scene for you to witness,' said Molineux, installing her in the chaise with Lady Riddell and Lady Edwin before going over to speak sternly to the men. The fighting ceased, but whatever he had said to them sent them away surly, and Anna knew he had somehow managed to goad them into deeper suspicion against the duke. As Molineux climbed into the carriage and the coachman cracked his whip, Anna turned her face to the window, hating her cousin with all her soul. Nor could she forgive Rotham or herself for having been such a proud pair of fools.

Lady Riddell reached out and placed Anna's hand in Molineux's. Flushing, Anna looked at her and received a smiling nod.

'Well, girl,' said the countess. 'You are nothing like your mother, I'm happy to say. No,' she went on agreeably while Anna bit her lip, 'nothing like Amelia whatsoever, eloping with an unsuitable man. You are like me, practical and ambitious.

You and Oliver will make a splendid couple. I'm very pleased.'

Molineux smiled. 'It is our delight to make you happy, Grandmama.'

But Anna could not speak and did not try.

If she had thought the two weeks until her marriage would crawl by, they did not. She prayed that illness would strike her, or that Molineux would run afoul of a poacher's stray shot. For a while she sustained herself in the hope that Rotham would return with some means of clearing himself, but he did not return and the things some said about him – comparing him to another notable gentleman, who was supposed to have killed his valet over a domestic difficulty – made Anna long to scream at them all. Her desire to run away increased to almost frantic proportions as time grew shorter, but she was now convinced that Molineux lacked compunction as well as morals and she did not dare put her father in danger.

For the most part she lived in the hands of the London dress-maker and her assistants, who had been brought in at great expense to make the trousseau. It was a ridiculously short time in which to expect them to make all the clothes Molineux and Lady Riddell insisted Anna order. There was her honeymoon, for which she would need gowns of every description, and in the spring the countess intended that she be presented to the Queen. Anna let them have their way, outfitting her in any manner they pleased. She cared only that Molineux should be punished and herself freed, but Lady Riddell brushed aside all her attempts for a private interview, advising her not to be a missish bride.

Mr Murvey returned to London with a bulging portfolio of documents and papers, and the speculation went on endlessly between Lady Edwin and Molineux as to how much the countess had changed her will. Neddie, subdued since that dreadful night, kept to his own company, his eyes anguished whenever Rotham's name was mentioned. Anna tried once to tell him the duke was not guilty and was fiercely rejected. She did not seek out his company again, and Neddie began to talk of the coming term at Eton.

The dawning of her wedding day brought the brief appearance of a wintery sun and no bad weather to spoil it. Having lost all hope, Anna had desired one of the private, almost secretive weddings so currently in vogue, but Lady Riddell had her way in this as in everything else, and numerous guests began arriving early in the afternoon to assemble in the drawing room. Lady Riddell had also decreed that Anna was to be married wearing the cloth-of-silver gown and the Riddell diamonds. Betty and Mrs West helped her dress, and Lady Edwin looked in at the last moment to make sure all was perfection.

She sighed, her blue eyes wistful. 'I must say the diamonds suit you far better than they would have me. Are you ready? It is time to go downstairs.'

Anna rose from the dressing table, taking one last glance at her white face in the mirror, before turning sharply to seize her aunt's hand.

'Aunt Beatrice, *please*—'

'Bridal nerves, my dear.' Lady Edwin patted her head, not meeting her eyes. 'Come, pinch your cheeks and strive to achieve a little radiance.'

'If you were truly as concerned for me as you pretend, you would help!' cried Anna sharply.

Lady Edwin's lips tightened. 'I did not make you come to Farrowsleigh. I did not prevent you from leaving with your father.' Her blue eyes, bright with vexation, met Anna's. 'You must not start this shilly-shallying *now*.'

Anna buried her face in her hands, heedless of the staring servants. 'I cannot marry *him*,' she whispered passionately. 'I'd liefer die!'

'What a peagoose you are!' cried Lady Edwin, stamping her foot as Mrs West slipped unobtrusively from the room. 'If you enact a scene now in front of everyone, there is no saying what Oliver will do. But be assured, you shall be made the most wretched creature alive.'

'I am that already,' said Anna, turning away with her heart like cold lead within her.

'Good God, do you still pine for Victor Chevely?' Lady Edwin clutched her arm. 'I am astonished you did not run away, or would he not elope with you?'

Anna's eyes filled with tears. 'I—'

Without warning the door crashed open, startling them both.

Molineux stood there, resplendent in a blue coat, striped waistcoat, and pale breeches worn over silk stockings. His brow was thunderous as he glared at her.

Anna glared back, too desperate now for prudence. 'I know what you are, Molineux,' she said, her chin high. 'I shan't—'

'You shall do exactly as you're told.' In two strides he was before her, large and powerful and furious. His dark eyes shot to Lady Edwin, who cringed.

'It was not I!' she cried, throwing out a hand of appeal. 'I swear I have not—'

'You tried to kill Uncle Percy,' said Anna. 'That is contemptible enough, but to throw the blame upon—'

'Anna! For heaven's sake, hold your tongue!' cried Lady Edwin.

'No,' said Anna fiercely, sending her a look of scorn. 'I have held silent too long out of fear of the consequences. But I shall not be a craven creature, nor shall I go through with this odious marriage.' Her gray eyes flashed at Molineux. 'If you have so little value for life that you—'

'Enough!' he thundered. 'You gave me your word there would be no more of these scenes—'

'That was before you tried to murder a harmless old man!'

'Harmless?' Molineux snorted. 'Are you blind? The place is falling to ruin for want of a good master. What right has Percy to be earl and he without a wit in his head? I ask you, *what right*?'

'You cannot choose principles of right and wrong to suit your convenience,' she said. 'Nor can I believe you to be so anxious for Neddie to receive the title that you—'

'Neddie?' Molineux's laugh was mirthless. 'My dear green girl, he shall never come into the title.' Molineux's eyes shot to Lady Edwin, who shook her head imploringly. 'He is illegitimate.'

With an anguished cry Lady Edwin sank into a chair, her very posture an admission.

Anna stared at them both, shocked from her defiance. 'It cannot be true! Aunt Beatrice—'

But Lady Edwin's eyes, tear-filled and passionate with hate, remained upon Molineux's sneering countenance.

'You odious monster!' she cried, clenching her dainty fists. 'You cannot command my silence now, for you have broken our bargain.'

He smiled in an unpleasant way. 'You were a fool to think I would ever allow that impudent by-blow to be earl in my stead. Good God, Beatrice! No man could be that noble. But I shall have everything soon: Anna, the diamonds, and the title. And you, Beatrice, shall keep your silence or lose your son altogether.'

'Oliver!' Staring, Lady Edwin threw out her hands. 'What do you mean?'

Molineux shrugged, studying his nails. 'Oh . . . a stray shot from a poacher. Another attack by a highwayman. A fall from a horse. Boys fall into scrapes all the time. But really, I think a naval career would do him a world of good. He is at a young enough age to begin. Certainly ship's discipline will teach him to curb his saucy tongue.' Molineux shrugged. 'And perhaps someday, when and if he becomes a mature young man with good sense and an eagerness to defer himself to me, I can employ him as my steward.'

She stared at him, horror and fury wrestling upon her pretty countenance, and abruptly burst into tears.

Molineux smiled in a cold fashion. 'I thought you could be brought to agree.' His gaze shifted to Anna, who was struggling to regain her wits scattered by these attacks. 'As for you—'

'Yes, will you offer me next some new threat against my poor father?' she asked tartly. 'You may save your breath, sir.'

'Bottle your pride,' he said with equal sharpness, his dark brows snapping together. 'I am not the monster you think me, Anna. I have no intention of bringing Walter Templeton to harm. But I might be induced to drop my accusations against Rotham.'

Her breath caught, and he gave her a dry, rather malicious smile.

'Yes, I thought that would appeal to you. I could do a great deal toward clearing up Rotham's unsavory reputation.'

A little silence fell over them, broken only by the muffled sounds of Lady Edwin's weeping, as Molineux stood watching Anna. Rebellion swept her, making her long to fling the diamond necklace in his face and walk out. But she knew, as did he, that she could not refuse this chance to restore Rotham in the eyes of all men. Molineux might not be a leading arbiter of the *ton*, but if his malicious tongue could be silenced it would mean a great difference.

Part of her stood in horrified disbelief as she raised her eyes to Molineux's in surrender, but where Rotham was concerned she was past reason.

'Very well,' she said inaudibly, and Molineux gave her a curt nod.

'Let us have no more delays, if you please, or the guests will begin to sense something amiss.'

He walked out, beckoning curtly to Lady Edwin, who raised reddened, bleary eyes in accusation.

'You foolish, unnatural girl! I told you to hold your tongue. Now see where it has led us.'

But Anna merely looked at her in pitying silence as she hastened out with her handkerchief to her face. For a moment Anna stood there motionless, trying to gather her strength, then she drew on her gloves and left the room.

Neddie, looking elegant and quite manly in his coat of blue superfine and starched cravat, stood waiting for Anna at the head of the stairs. It was of course the earl's place to give her away, but since that was obviously out of the question, the task fell to Neddie as the heir. Only, he was not the heir, and no doubt as soon as the ceremony was performed Molineux would see that the bottom dropped out of Neddie's world.

Together they started slowly downstairs. Anna could hear the rustle and murmur of the guests below. She closed her eyes, sending up a prayer, but took no comfort from doing so. She would never see Rotham again, and even if she did it would be as Molineux's wife. A desperate quiver ran through her and she stopped.

'Jupiter!' said Neddie, looking at her in sudden alarm. 'Are you going to swoon?'

With all her will she rallied and lifted her head to shake it slightly. She would not go to Molineux looking coerced. She would never give him the satisfaction of *taming* her. The arrogant creature might look elsewhere for his pleasure, for she would never show him anything but cold indifference.

A faint gleam of spirit kindled in her eyes. She lifted her chin and said clearly, 'I have no intention of swooning. You may be easy.'

'You dashed well gave me a fright,' muttered Neddie and led her on.

The guests rose as the double doors of the drawing room were flung open and she and Neddie entered. Molineux and the vicar waited at the far end of the chamber, and near them sat Lady Riddell, regally garbed in puce satin and enormous pearls. Neddie blenched at being the center of so many eyes, but he stuck to his duty, while for her the walk seemed endless.

Then, at last, she stood beside Molineux, who took her cold hand in his warm one and smiled in a faint, undeniably smug way that set her blood boiling. She would not be conformable, she vowed as the ceremony began. She would not be anything he liked. But then she felt Molineux's dark eyes fall upon her as he murmured an answer to the vicar, and she knew fresh fear that undermined all her planned defiance. If she ever made him hate her . . . dear God, he would sweep her aside as ruthlessly as he did anything or anyone else who stood between him and what he wanted. That was when she thought she might indeed swoon, but somehow she stiffened her quaking knees and managed to go on standing erect.

The vicar, much puffed by the importance of the occasion and the largess he expected to receive from his patroness Lady Riddell, allowed himself to be carried away into the most elaborate of orations and quite sermonized them before an impatient snort from the countess sent him back finally to the matter at hand.

The vows were spoken – Molineux's clearly, Anna's inaudibly – and the vicar raised his head to say in portentous accents, 'If there be any man who can give just cause why this marriage should not take place, let him—'

A sudden commotion outside the room drowned out his warning. He broke off, flushing to the roots of his windswept hair, and heads turned as one of the doors was flung open with a resounding bang.

Rotham stood upon the threshold, attired in exquisite Bath

coating, a cravat of graceful fold, and pale-colored pantaloons worn with tassled Hessians. Heads craned, mouths gaped, and shocked murmurs started humming as the duke raised his quizzing glass to one eye, with the lace falling back from his wrist, to survey the company at his leisure.

'Sink me,' he drawled aloud. 'I appear to be a trifle late.'

With a muscle working in his clamped jaw, a livid Molineux gestured at James, who went for the duke, only to receive a gracious smile and the proffering of his grace's hat. Thus thwarted, the footman took the beaver, and Rotham came straight toward Anna, who was standing breathless and unconscious of all save that Rotham had come back for her. She put out a hand involuntarily as he reached them, and with a growl deep in his throat Molineux pulled her behind him.

'Damn your eyes, what are you doing here?' he demanded hoarsely, and the vicar began to sputter out a milder inquiry of the same nature.

'Oh, weren't you finished here? You must excuse the interruption, Vicar,' said Rotham in a light, seemingly careless way, drawing off his gloves. 'But I do fear the wedding is off. Mr Molineux has another matter he must attend to first, don't you, Mollie?' Smiling, the duke stepped up to Molineux and threw a glove in his face.

There were gasps, Anna's among them. Molineux stood rigidly, his dark eyes blazing.

'As you like,' he said at last through his teeth. 'Now?'

Rotham bowed. 'Name your weapon.'

'Pistols,' snapped Molineux, clamping his jaw even harder. 'By God, sir, you—'

Rotham turned away to take Anna's hand, and only then did the steel in his eyes soften. 'Are you well, Anna? Damme, I fear I simply had to come back.'

She nodded, her eyes brimming with fear for him. What if Molineux killed him? Her fingers tightened on his.

'They're going to duel?' The squire shoved back his chair in outrage. 'Someone ride for the magistrate! Demmed coxcombs—'

Rotham kissed Anna's hand with an ardor that shot a

flame to her heart. 'This shan't take long, my dear. Come, sir!'

'They're going to duel?' The squire shoved back his chair in outrage. 'Someone ride for the magistrate! Demmed coxcombs—'

Rotham kissed Anna's hand with an ardor that shot a flame to her heart. 'This shan't take long, my dear. Come, sir!'

Together they started out, but Lady Riddell rose to her feet, her withered face furious.

'I forbid this disgusting spectacle! Do you hear?' She rapped her cane upon the floor. 'Rotham, you are a madman. Get out of my house!'

He curled his lip. 'When I have killed your grandson, madam, not before.'

'By God—' Molineux took a vicious swing at him, but Rotham dodged nimbly and said with a sneer, 'Let us not descend to common brawling before the ladies, sir.' He raised his quizzing glass at Lady Edwin, who had swooned, and permitted himself a slight frown. 'Demmed unhelpful of her.'

'There will be no duel,' snapped Lady Riddell. 'You, sir, belong at the end of Tyburn's rope, and if you don't cease your ogling and leave this house at once, I shall have the dogs set on you!' She lifted a hand to beckon to Dobbs. 'Escort his grace out, and let us get on with the wedding.'

'No,' said Anna so clearly the murmurs started again. She lifted her chin to meet her grandmother's outraged glare. 'I shan't marry my cousin, ma'am. Here.' Unclasping the diamonds, she thrust them into the countess' astonished hand. 'You may keep your diamonds and your money. Thank you, but I do not require them.'

Nonplussed, the countess stared at her. 'You would give up all I offer in favor of a murderer? Have you no natural feelings?'

Anna's eyes flashed. 'Indeed I do, Grandmama! And before you are so quick to cast accusations at his grace, perhaps you had better first look to Molineux.'

'Shut up, you little jade,' he snarled, his brown eyes

172

blazing. 'You can prove nothing of what you say.'

'But I can!' cried Lady Edwin, reviving with a sudden shove against the hand holding hartshorn to her nostrils. She rose unsteadily from her chair, her blue eyes enormous in her white face, and raised a hand. 'And I shall!'

'Enough!' Lady Riddell's lips compressed to a thin line and she sent a curt glance around at the gaping company. 'If we must wash our dirty linen, let us do so in private.' She walked out of the drawing room, her back so erect with fury no one dared offer her assistance.

Molineux snorted and stalked out after her with a jerk of his head at Lady Edwin to follow. As she tottered by Anna with one hand pressed to her bosom and the spark of defiance in her eye, Neddie went to her, but she shook off his solicitous hand and bade him stay behind.

Anna took Rotham's arm and whispered worriedly, 'Rotham, the most awful thing! Neddie is not . . . well, he isn't . . . ' She colored and burst out desperately, 'Lord Edwin's! Molineux has been holding that over Aunt Beatrice's head for an age and making her the most miserable creature in the world.'

The duke had been gazing at her with considerable tenderness, but at her pronouncement his thin brows drew together and he said with a touch of impatience, ' 'Pon rep, I've never heard such fustian in my life. Neddie was no more born on the wrong side of the blanket than was I, and if he had been, Molineux would have denounced him long ago. No, no! I'll wager he's threatened Beatrice by telling her he would say such a thing to one and all.'

Anna frowned. 'But she—'

'Well! The scandal amounts to the same thing whether the tale is true or not.' Rotham's expression grew rather grim. 'I should know, my dear, since he's chosen to practice his slandering deceits upon my reputation often enough. Let us go and break straws with this blackguard. But first . . . ' Leaving the drawing room, he drew her into a secluded corner and said, 'Anna, my dearest, I can do nothing until I know I have your forgiveness. I treated you abominably, and I deserve to lose you, but—'

Shyly she put her fingers on his lips to silence him. 'Since you went away, every moment has been a walking nightmare. Not just because of Cousin Molineux but . . . ' Her eyes fell from his ardent ones, then rose again. 'I have missed you so! I was so sure I should never see you again.'

He drew her into his arms, his heart hammering beneath her cheek. 'That, my darling, you need never fear again. Once I have dealt with Mollie, you shall find me constantly in your pocket, for I mean to be a most unfashionable husband and adore you!'

'Oh!' She lifted a radiant face to his, but an instant later her expression clouded and she drew back with a tremor. 'But this duel! Cousin Molineux will kill you. Oh, you mustn't face him!'

His clasp tightened on her agitated hands. 'Anna, I had meant to kill *him*, if only to make you a widow.'

Her eyes widened. 'But . . . but Neddie told me you are a poor shot.'

'Did he really?' Rotham looked put out. 'What a devilishly unhandsome thing to say. You shouldn't let him tell you such shocking whiskers. Long as my arm, 'pon my honor.' His lips quivered, and suddenly he threw back his head in laughter. 'Can't shoot. Good Lord!' he gasped, wiping his eyes. 'A fine sort of mawworm I should be to call Mollie out if I were unable to comport myself with a pistol.' Then he sobered and raised her hand lightly to his lips. 'Trust me, Anna. I am not the fribble I appear.'

She smiled, her eyes only for him. 'I have known that for a long while.'

His eyes crinkled, and thus he entered the library with her while the others waited grimly.

'This must all amuse you greatly, sir,' said Molineux furiously, taking a step toward them. 'By God, not only do you dare try to kill my uncle, but you also interrupt my wedding, and now you have the damnable effrontery to dally with my wife!'

'I am *not* your wife,' flared Anna, her hand clenched upon Rotham's arm. 'And I thank God for it!'

'That's enough from you, you damned baggage—'

'Please, sir, your language,' said Rotham, raising a pained hand, but with a look in his eyes that boded no good for Molineux. 'Remember you are in the presence of ladies.'

'Bah!' Molineux sneered. 'We all know you killed your wife for her money, and now you would like to wed Anna for hers.' His dark eyes bored into Anna, who was shocked at his persistence with these lies. 'You are a fool, my dear. He may have a title of acknowledged importance, but despite it he's nothing but a gazetted fortune hunter and a despicable cur.'

Rotham stiffened, but Anna was quick to retort, 'I have no fortune, as his grace well knows. You, sir, are the one who wishes to marry me for money. And you, sir, are the dastardly creature who invented the fable about his grace's poor wife. We all know *that*.'

'Silence!' commanded the countess, looking completely out of temper. 'I will not have you all screaming at one another like brazen savages! Let us settle this as soon as may be.' She put a hand to her brow. 'I do not know how I shall be able to hold up my head to the county again after today's wretched display. Oliver.' She gave him a nod.

'No!' cried Lady Edwin, holding out her pretty hands. 'You must not listen to his odious lies! He—'

'Lies?' snapped Molineux with a fierce gesture. 'And what of yours, Beatrice? Madam,' he said to Lady Riddell, 'St. Byre has no claim upon the title. He is a natural child.'

For a moment they stood in stunned silence.

'Good God.' Groping for a chair, Lady Riddell sat down heavily. Her piercing eyes swung to Lady Edwin, and their gaze held no mercy. 'Beatrice,' she said in an awful voice, 'who is Neddie's father?'

Lady Edwin's eyes filled with tears, and for a moment Anna feared she meant to flee the room. But instead she faced the countess and said in a voice bitter with mortification, 'Your son Edwin, my lady. I was *never* false to him.'

Lady Riddell snorted contemptuously. 'And what of the night you never returned from the ball? The night you and Edwin had the appalling bad manners to quarrel publicly?'

Anna gasped at this unexpected attack and looked to Rotham, who squeezed her hand.

Molineux had begun to smile faintly in triumph, but Lady Edwin raised her chin.

'I spent the rest of that horrid night driving around the park in my carriage, ma'am. I . . . I wished to make Edwin sorry. And afterwards he did treat me less like a . . . a stick of furniture.' Lady Edwin's blue eyes flashed. 'You still doubt me because you always believe Oliver, but if you will trouble to think, ma'am, you will remember that Neddie was born seven months after my little escapade.' She shot a defiant glance at Molineux. 'I was already *enceinte*, and so, dearest Oliver, you may drag my name through the mud, but the facts still remain. I no longer care what scandals your wretched tongue may next invent. I no longer care! Neddie shall be earl, not you. Never you! You are the one who tried to kill Percy, thinking, I suppose, that if you slandered Neddie's parentage people would eventually hold you as the heir to the earldom.'

Molineux laughed, but there was strain now in his voice as he said, 'You have lost your wits, Beatrice.' He walked over to stand by the desk. 'Grandmama does not believe your little tale. You may as well be quiet.'

'No!' she retorted, stamping her foot. 'I shan't be quiet. I was a fool to fear you and what you might do to my son.' Drawing a deep breath, she faced Lady Riddell. 'I bought the bonbons for him to substitute for Victor's. I did not know then what he meant to do with them—' She broke off with a little cry, staring in horror at Molineux, who had taken a pistol from the desk and aimed it at her.

'You jade! Do you think you can accuse me of anything I shan't be thanked for?' His eyes, black with fury, blazed at Lady Riddell, who was staring at him, appalled. 'What right has Percy to sit here as earl and master of these acres? What right? He has no more right than the dog that died in his stead.'

'Oliver!' cried Lady Riddell.

'No!' He gestured violently with the pistol, his eyes never leaving his grandmother. 'Everything is going to ruin. The tenants are lazy oafs, and anything I try to do to stop the decay is resented by you as well as by them. I should be earl, madam! Not Percy and most certainly *not* young Edwin. I am the only one who truly cares for Farrowsleigh, and if you are honest you will admit it.'

Rotham took a step forward, but like a flash Molineux whirled to train the pistol upon him.

'You!' His dark face twisted in a sneer. 'My lord duke, who has all. What business have you to poke your nose into my affairs?'

For one dreadful moment Anna was certain he meant to shoot Rotham in cold blood. Certainly the temptation gleamed in Molineux's eyes.

Rotham raised a hand framed in fine Mechlin lace. 'You know you are finished,' he said flatly. 'Beatrice has no more need to fear you.'

'Doesn't she?' With an abrupt laugh that chilled Anna, Molineux aimed the pistol at Lady Edwin, who screamed.

'Rotham, no!' cried Anna as the duke flung himself forward to seize Molineux's wrist and drag it down.

The report was deafening. White as paper, Lady Edwin crumpled to the floor. Anna would have run to her, but the deadly struggle of the two men was going on between her and her fallen aunt. Anna stood there, her hands pressed to her mouth, her bosom heaving as she watched them pound at one another with forceful crunching blows.

Molineux's mouth was bloody from a cut lip, and for a moment Anna's heart leaped in the hope that Rotham was to vanquish him. But just then, Molineux dodged the duke's fist and retaliated with a savage blow to Rotham's half-knit ribs. With a grunt, Rotham fell unconscious to the floor, his face absolutely white. Someone was beating on the door, and there were shouts of inquiry outside. Pressing the back of one hand to his bleeding lip, Molineux paused for breath with a hunted look on his face.

'Come in! Come in!' cried Anna, finding her voice at last. 'Quickly, I beg you!'

Then she screamed as Molineux seized her by the wrist and began dragging her across the room to the French doors leading on to the terrace.

'I'll take those diamonds, Grandmama,' he snarled, bending

to snatch the necklace from Lady Riddell's lap.

But his greed was his undoing. Lady Riddell struck him across the shoulders with her cane, forcefully enough to snap it in half. 'Butcher!' she cried, her voice quivering with rage. 'Cur!'

He recoiled from the blow, dropping the necklace, and Anna boxed him soundly on the ear with her free hand. Cursing, he flung her from him and bent for the necklace, but desperately she kicked it into the fire. By now Neddie, the squire, and others had burst in, all demanding an explanation at the same time. Molineux threw open the French doors with a blast of frigid air and escaped.

'Mama!' Aghast, Neddie ran to Lady Edwin and tried awkwardly to lift her off the floor.

The men fell on Rotham with a cry of, 'Here's the scoundrel!' and dragged him upright so roughly, Anna cried out and ran to him, seeking to free him from their abuse.

'You are wrong!' she said, frantic that they should not hurt him more. 'Molineux is the one, not—'

'Neddie!' suddenly cried a rich, terrified voice, causing Anna's head to snap around. 'You odious boy, you will drop me.'

'Beatrice!' snapped Lady Riddell as Neddie stood there staggering under the burden of his mama's indignant weight. 'Do you mean to say you are not shot? I was certain Oliver did not miss.'

'No, I am perfectly well.' Lady Edwin struggled down as Neddie set her on her feet, revealing a sufficient quantity of petticoat and rounded limb to cause Squire Wetherby to crimson and Major Comstead to look quite fascinated. Then, as they stared at her, she threw her arms around her son's neck and dissolved into a flood of tears.

'Squire!' said the countess. 'Unhand his grace at once! You are guilty of the gravest impertinence and if you have added to his injuries I do not know how you shall be obliged to answer for yourself.'

'Gently,' said Anna, as the unconscious duke was laid upon the sofa. 'Oh, someone ride for a doctor at once!'

'Someone had better ride after Mollie!' said Neddie, struggling to no avail to free himself from his hysterical parent.

'By Jove!' The squire threw out his chest as the countess grimly made the facts known. 'The greatest piece of infamy I've ever seen. He shan't get far, my lady. That, I promise you.'

'No!' Unsteadily the countess pushed herself to her feet and stood grasping the back of her chair for support. Her gray eyes swung piercingly across the room, sparing no face. 'Molineux will not be hunted down.'

'But, Grandmama,' said Anna, her hand clasping Rotham's limp one. 'You cannot mean to let him go scot-free.'

'Suppose he should escape the country?' demanded the squire.

'Then let him!' said Lady Riddell fiercely. 'He is my grandson, and in spite of his wickedness, I cannot in fairness say he had no reason for his actions. Can you?' She glared at Anna, whose protests slowly died unspoken. 'His exile is sufficient punishment. I shall not seek more.'

'Dash it all, my lady!' The squire actually shook his fist at her. 'What is the use of law and order if you do not employ it?'

Her withered lips tightened. 'The only use I require at the moment, sir, is that you be good enough to rescue my diamonds from the fire. I am persuaded the cleaning bill shall be outrageous. Look at them!' One bony hand pointed indignantly at the grate. 'Black as coal. The setting is quite ruined.' She sniffed and said, 'Edwin!'

'Yes, Grandmama?' He looked up at her, still troubled of expression, while Lady Edwin clutched his arm.

Lady Riddell glared at him for a long moment while Anna held her breath and Lady Edwin looked ready to swoon again. Suppose the countess chose to believe Molineux's lies?

'If I give you the Riddell diamonds, they shall be for your bride to wear one day as the Countess of Riddell. You are not to sell them for paste copies or gamble them away. Is that clear?'

He nodded, frowning a little. 'Perfectly clear, Grandmama,' he said as Lady Edwin straightened in open relief. Then he shot a puzzled look at Anna. 'But don't you wish Anna to have them anymore?'

'I do not,' said Lady Riddell tersely, glaring at the blackened necklace, which the squire had raked out upon the hearth with the end of a poker. 'We made a bargain, and she did not keep it.'

Lady Edwin clasped her hands together, her pale, tear-stained face shining. 'Oh, at last we are rid of that horrid man!'

Lady Riddell eyed her grimly and said, 'I wonder why you never confided in me until now, Beatrice. How could you be such a widgeon?'

Lady Edwin met her gaze with simple dignity. 'Because you gave me no reason to think I should be believed.'

Rotham suddenly stirred, raising a hand to his brow and opening his eyes. They focused on Anna's concerned face, and he said weakly, 'I appear to have been trounced. How deucedly embarrassing. Is Beatrice dead?'

'Far from it.' Anna smiled, smoothing the golden hair back from his brow. 'The ball ruined the floor, but missed her altogether. And Molineux has run away so you need not duel, thank God! Are you much hurt, my love?'

For answer he caught her hand and kissed the palm, his eyes telling her all she had ever wanted to know and more. He smiled. 'There's a parson in the drawing room and a special license in my pocket.'

'Yes, oh, yes!' she cried, her gray eyes shining, and helped him to sit up. 'But can you stand through it? I am persuaded you have rebroken your poor ribs in being heroic.'

'For you, my darling, I can do anything—'

'Victor!' Neddie came rushing over, his young face puckered in concern. 'Are you all right? You look sadly out of curl, I must say. Jupiter! I wish I could have helped you draw Mollie's cork. Grandmama means to let him leave England unscathed, which is the shabbiest thing imaginable—'

'My dear boy, do pray contain yourself,' said Rotham, laying a hand upon his shoulder. 'He is quite ruined. Would you have him hanged as well and bury the Farrow name in scandal? Leave it, my boy.' Rotham frowned in some impatience. 'As a matter of fact, you may leave *us*—'

'Yes, but what's to be done with this half-finished wedding business?' demanded the squire loudly. 'Here's the poor young lady with no groom in hand now, musicians paid for, and the bridal supper untasted. Demmed waste, I say.'

Frowning, the countess looked ready to deliver a blistering set-down, but before she could do so, Rotham dropped Anna's hand with a sigh.

'My dear sir!' he said, raising his quizzing glass at the squire – only to frown as he found the glass shattered within the frame. 'Nothing is to be wasted. Kindly return to the drawing room and endeavor to regain your natural composure. I promise your presence shall be rewarded.' He waved his hand languidly to send them all out.

But the squire stood pat. 'Dashed free in the countess' house, ain't you, Duke?'

'Oh, I shortly expect to run quite tamely here.' Rotham smiled so broadly the squire grew quite flustered. 'Be so good as to ask the vicar to come to me now, will you? Thank you, sir. What a good fellow you are.'

Grasping Neddie's arm, the countess started out, too. The squire stared at Anna, who blushed, and said, 'But, Lady Riddell! Are you leaving your granddaughter here *alone* with this gentleman? I was mistaken in thinking him capable of murder – and for that, your grace, I humbly beg pardon – but damme, madam, the fellow is hardly—'

'Don't meddle, Squire,' said the countess sharply. 'I won't say it's what I planned for the chit, but she could not do better for herself.' Lady Riddell sniffed. 'A *duchess* and her the daughter of that wretched tutor. Bah!' She glanced at Anna. 'I suppose, girl, you'll be wearing Rotham's emeralds when next you come here.' The countess met the duke's twinkling gaze severely but rapped his knuckles with her fan. 'The necklace is quite passable, although not as splendid as mine. Come along, sir, and leave them.'

'Yes, do run along, Squire,' said Rotham with considerable impatience. 'Or I shall kiss the lady regardless of your presence.'

Anna choked, trying not to let a gurgle of laughter escape her as the affronted squire drew himself up and followed the countess out. But shyness overtook her the moment the door was shut.

'I wonder,' she asked, 'how soon until the vicar will come in.'

'Too soon, most likely,' said Rotham, drawing her into his arms.

'But your ribs—'

'Goose,' he said and at this word of endearment the future Duchess of Rotham tilted up her lips to his and let him sweep her away to their own private world, where nothing would ever stand between them again.

From the shadow of the dreaded guillotine to the sparkling frivolity of England's Regency heyday . . .

BURNING SECRETS

DEBORAH CHESTER

With her beloved uncle a captive of Napoleon's terrifying secret police, lovely Catherine de Bleu knew she had no choice but to comply with the Emperor's wishes. But even so she quailed at the impossible task he had set her. For her formidable mission was to voyage to England, and there to assassinate no less a person than the Prince Regent himself!

Catherine's charm and ravishing looks soon win her access to 'Prinny's' dazzling set and she comes close to carrying out her hateful orders. But she does not foresee the machinations of the unscrupulous and arrogant Sir Giles Thorne, a determined adversary who would test her mettle to the last . . .

If you love the very best in Regency romance, you will be enthralled by BURNING SECRETS, a breathtaking new novel from the creator of A LOVE SO WILD and SUMMER'S RAPTURE.

HISTORICAL ROMANCE   0 7221 2285 3   £1.95

THE TREGALLIS INHERITANCE

Mary Williams

From the spellbinding author of TRENHAWK
comes a haunting West Country romance which
tells of the young gipsy girl Mara, who has the
power to bewitch and beguile any man who
crosses her path – even Justin Tregallis, the
handsome young heir to the wealthy Penraven
estate. But is Mara really what she seems?
Beneath her flashing eyes and fiery charm lies a
heart as wild and treacherous as the windswept
moors and dark woodland that were once her
home – and a reckless spirit that could lead a man
to his doom. . . .

WEST COUNTRY ROMANCE   0 7221 91227   £1.75

He forged a glittering dynasty out of the South African wilderness

KING OF DIAMONDS

CAROLYN TERRY

There was something masculine and enticing about Matthew Harcourt-Bright, something which the society ladies of Victorian England found dangerously seductive. At sixteen, he had a countess for his mistress; at nineteen, he was poised to marry a duke's daughter.

But then there was scandal, and the doors of the great houses were slammed in his face. Vowing vengeance, he fled to the untamed hinterlands of South Africa, there to make his fortunes among the diamond fields. Still the women pursued him – Alida, the tragic Boer girl; Lady Anne, a member of the aristocracy that had once spurned him; Katherine, the scheming temptress who tried to win his heart.

Some he loved, others he exploited as ruthlessly as he did his diamond mines. But nothing mattered more to him than his desire for revenge on English society – until he met the one woman who would not be dominated by his wealth and charisma, who could finally free him from the torment that wracked his soul . . .

GENERAL FICTION   0 7221 84042   £2.50

A selection of bestsellers from SPHERE

FICTION

DELCORSO'S GALLERY	Philip Caputo	£2.25 ☐
SOPHIE	Judith Saxton	£1.95 ☐
THE BRITISH CROSS	Bill Granger	£1.95 ☐
COMPANY SECRETS	Andrew Coburn	£2.25 ☐
FALL RIVER LINE	Daoma Winston	£2.95 ☐

FILM & TV TIE-INS

THE RIVER	Steven Bauer	£1.95 ☐
WATER	Gordon McGill	£1.75 ☐
THE LEGEND OF THE DOOZER		
WHO DIDN'T	Louise Gikow	£1.50 ☐
BEST FRIENDS	Jocelyn Stevenson	£1.50 ☐
NO-ONE KNOWS WHERE GOBO GOES		
	Mark Saltzman	£1.50 ☐

NON-FICTION

INTREPID'S LAST CASE	William Stevenson	£2.25 ☐
TALKING TO MYSELF	Anna Raeburn	£1.95 ☐
AROUND THE WORLD IN 78 DAYS		
	Nicholas Coleridge	£1.95 ☐
HAVING A BABY	Danielle Steel and others	£3.95 ☐
A JOBBING ACTOR	John Le Mesurier	£1.95 ☐

All Sphere books are available at your local bookshop or newsagent, or can be ordered direct from the publisher. Just tick the titles you want and fill in the form below.

Name _____

Address _____

_____

Write to Sphere Books, Cash Sales Department, P.O. Box 11, Falmouth, Cornwall TR10 9EN

Please enclose cheque or postal order to the value of the cover price plus:

UK: 55p for the first book, 22p for the second book and 14p for each additional book ordered to a maximum charge of £1.75.

OVERSEAS: £1.00 for the first book plus 25p per copy for each additional book.

BFPO & EIRE: 55p for the first book, 22p for the second book plus 14p per copy for the next 7 books, thereafter 8p per book.

Sphere Books reserve the right to show new retail prices on covers which may differ from those previously advertised in the text or elsewhere, and to increase postal rates in accordance with the PO.